'sutomu Sato

stration Kana Ishida
stration assistants Jimmy Stone,
ısuko Suenaga
ign BEE-PEE

"Only three weeks remain until the Thesis Competition. We decided you were the only person we'd be able to add to our team at this point."

Suzune Ichihara

Magic High School's student council treasurer. More suitable to be called a "beauty" than a "pretty girl." Has a composed appearance. Her nickname is Rin, but only Mayumi calls her that.

Erika Chiba

Tatsuya's classmate. Has a bright personality; a troublemaker who gets everyone involved. Her family is large and famous for *njutsu*—a magical technique that combines swords and magic.

"Oh, found him! Heeey, Tatsuyaaa!"

"…………"

Leonhard Saijou

Nicknamed "Leo." Part of Class 1-E, like Tatsuya. His father is half-Japanese and his mother a quarter. Specializes in hardening magic.

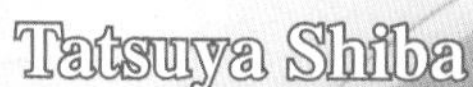

The older brother of the Shiba siblings. A student of the National Magic University Affiliated First High School. Part of Class 1-E. One of the Course 2 students, mockingly called "Weeds." Specializes in designing Casting Assistant Devices (CADs), among other things.

"I don't want them to know my strength in this situation. I'm counting on you, Miyuki."

"Roger!"

Miyuki Shiba

The younger sister of the Shiba siblings. Part of Class 1-A. An elite who entered Magic High School as the top student. A Course 1 student, called a "Bloom," whose specialty is cooling magic. Her lovable only flaw is a severe case of a brother complex.

"Creeper,
lecher,
Peeping
Tom—close
the door
already,
stupid!"

"Did we figure out where Tatsuya Shiba was going?"
Xiangshan Chen
Head of the Great Asian Allianc
Army's Special Covert Forces. A
man with a cruel personality wh
will not hesitate to make sacrific
for the success of a mission.
"Was I too forward?"
Zhou
A handsome young man who let Lu and Chen into Japan. Supplies them with housing in Yokohama Chinatown.

"Leave it to me."
Ganghu Lu
Ace magician of the Great Asian Alliance Army's Special Covert Forces, rumored to be number one at killing people in hand to hand combat. A violent man known as the Man-Eating Tiger.

The Magic Association of Japan's All-High Magic Thesis Competition

A place for high school students from around the country to present their research findings in the fields of magic science and magic engineering. It is an event given much attention because not only do the presentation team representatives get scouted by magic research institutions but some theses are also directly recorded in the Encyclopedia of Magic and go on to be used in universities and corporations. Though it is dubbed "All-High," the only schools that teach magical theory via the official education system are the nine affiliated with the National Magic University. Like the Nine School Competition, the Thesis Competition is essentially an event in which the schools compete with one another. While the former features martial battles, the latter features literary ones, and some call the events two halves of a single whole.

The greatest difference between events that thrive within nonmagic high schools, such as debate competitions and research presentations, and the All-High Magic Thesis Competition is that the Thesis Competition includes live demonstrations. A thesis presentation involves the use of magic devices and a live demonstration of the magic onstage. In order to make this happen, many highly advanced and time-consuming preparations are necessary, such as designing the magical equipment, creating spell-assistance systems and writing software to control it, and securing bodies to install it all on. In the days right before the competition, every school mobilizes in its entirety; they rally not only their tech clubs and art clubs but also their purely theoretical clubs and those with high proficiency in magic, all in order to bring success.

The competition is always held on the last Sunday in October, and the venue alternates between Kyoto and Yokohama. This is because the Magic Association of Japan's headquarters is in Kyoto, while its sub-headquarters of sorts in the Kanto area is located in Yokohama. This year, the competition will be hosted by the Yokohama International Assembly Hall.

First High chooses three students to send to the Thesis Competition with a school-wide thesis-screening assembly, after which the selected competitors work together to write up the thesis and prepare the presentation. In general, for a unified sense of direction, the team is made up of one main writer and two others to whom work can be delegated. This year's main member is Suzune Ichihara. The thesis's title is "The Technical Possibility of Gravitational Magic Program–Loaded Thermonuclear Fusion Reactors."

The Irregular at Magic High School

YOKOHAMA DISTURBANCE ARC I

6

Tsutomu Sato

Illustration Kana Ishida

NEW YORK

THE IRREGULAR AT MAGIC HIGH SCHOOL
TSUTOMU SATO

Translation by Andrew Prowse
Cover art by Kana Ishida

Edited by ASCII MEDIA WORKS
First published in Japan in 2012 by KADOKAWA CORPORATION, Tokyo.
English translation rights arranged with KADOKAWA CORPORATION, Tokyo, through Tuttle-Mori Agency, Inc., Tokyo.

Yen On
1290 Avenue of the Americas
New York, NY 10104

Visit us at yenpress.com
facebook.com/yenpress
twitter.com/yenpress
yenpress.tumblr.com
instagram.com/yenpress

First Yen On Edition: December 2017

Yen On is an imprint of Yen Press, LLC.
The Yen On name and logo are trademarks of Yen Press, LLC.

The publisher is not responsible for websites (or their content) that are not owned by the publisher.

Library of Congress Cataloging-in-Publication Data
Names: Satou, Tsutomu. | Ishida, Kana, illustrator.
Title: The irregular at Magic High School / Tsutomu Satou ; Illustrations by Kana Ishida.
Other titles: Mahōoka kōkō no rettosei. English
Description: First Yen On edition. | New York, NY : Yen On, 2016–
Identifiers: LCCN 2015042401 | ISBN 9780316348805 (v 1 : pbk.) | ISBN 9780316390293 (v. 2 : pbk.) | ISBN 9780316390309 (v. 3 : pbk.) | ISBN 9780316390316 (v. 4 : pbk.) | ISBN 9780316390323 (v. 5 : pbk.) | ISBN 9780316390330 (v. 6 : pbk.)
Subjects: | CYAC: Brothers and sisters—Fiction. | Magic—Fiction. | High schools—Fiction. | Schools—Fiction. | Japan—Fiction. | Science fiction.
Classification: LCC PZ7.1.S265 Ir 2016 | DDC [Fic]—dc23
LC record available at http://lccn.loc.gov/2015042401

ISBNs: 978-0-316-39033-0 (paperback)
978-1-9753-0082-1 (ebook)

10 9 8 7 6 5 4 3 2 1

LSC-C

Printed in the United States of America

The Irregular at Magic High School

YOKOHAMA DISTURBANCE ARC ①

An irregular older brother with a certain flaw.
An honor roll younger sister who is perfectly flawless.

When the two siblings enrolled in Magic High School,
a dramatic life unfolded—

Character

Tatsuya Shiba

Class 1-E. One of the Course 2 (irregular) students, who are mockingly called "Weeds." Sees right to the core of everything.

Miyuki Shiba

Class 1-A.
Tatsuya's younger sister; enrolled as the top student. Specializes in freezing magic. Dotes on her older brother.

Leonhard Saijou

Class 1-E.
Tatsuya's classmate.
Specializes in hardening magic.
Has a bright personality.

Erika Chiba

Class 1-E.
Tatsuya's classmate.
Specializes in *kenjutsu*.
A charming troublemaker.

Mizuki Shibata

Class 1-E.
Tatsuya's classmate.
Has pushion radiation sensitivity. Serious and a bit of an airhead.

Mikihiko Yoshida

Class 1-E. Tatsuya's classmate. From a famous family that uses ancient magic. Has known Erika since they were children.

Honoka Mitsui

Class 1-A. Miyuki's classmate. Specializes in light-wave vibration magic. Impulsive when emotional.

Shizuku Kitayama

Class 1-A. Miyuki's classmate. Specializes in vibration and acceleration magic. Doesn't show emotional ups and downs very much.

Subaru Satomi

Class 1-D. Frequently mistaken for a pretty boy. Cheerful and easy to get along with.

Shun Morisaki

Class 1-A. Miyuki's classmate. Specializes in CAD quick-draw. Takes great pride in being a Course 1 student.

Akaha Sakurakouji

Class 1-B. Friends with Subaru and Amy. Wears gothic lolita clothes and loves theme parks.

Eimi Akechi

Class 1-B. A quarter-blood. Full name is Amelia Eimi Akechi Goldie.

Azusa Nakajou

A junior and the student council secretary. Shy and has trouble expressing herself.

Mayumi Saegusa

A senior and the student council president. One of the strongest magicians ever to grace a magical high school.

Hanzou Gyoubu-Shoujou Hattori

A junior and the student council vice president. Very serious and a good student.

Suzune Ichihara

A senior and the student council accountant. Calm, collected, and book smart. Mayumi's right hand.

Koutarou Tatsumi

A senior and a member of the disciplinary committee. Has a heroic personality.

Mari Watanabe

A senior and the chairwoman of the disciplinary committee. Mayumi's good friend. Good all-around and likes a sporting fight.

Isao Sekimoto

A senior. Member of the disciplinary committee. Wasn't chosen for the Thesis Competition.

Midori Sawaki

A junior and a member of the disciplinary committee. Has a complex about his girlish name.

Kei Isori

A junior. Top grades in his class in magical theory. Engaged to Kanon Chiyoda.

Kanon Chiyoda

A junior. An energetic, vivid girl. Engaged to Kei Isori.

Katsuto Juumonji

A senior and the head of the club committee, the unified organization overseeing all club activities.

Masaki Ichijou

A freshman at Third High. Participates in the Nine School Competition. Direct heir to the Ichijou family, one of the Ten Master Clans.

Shinkurou Kichijouji

A freshman at Third High. Participates in the Nine School Competition. Also known as Cardinal George.

Midori Ichijou

Masaki's mother. Warm and good at cooking.

Takeaki Kirihara

A junior. Member of the kenjutsu club. Kanto Junior High Kenjutsu Tournament champion.

Sayaka Mibu

A junior. Member of the kendo club. Placed second in the nation at the girls' junior high kendo tournament.

Koharu Hirakawa

Senior. Engineer during the Nine School Competition. Withdrew from the Thesis Competition.

Chiaki Hirakawa

Class 1-G. Holds enmity toward Tatsuya.

Satomi Asuka

Nurse. Gentle, calm, and warm. Smile popular among male students.

Kazuo Tsuzura

Teacher. Main field is magic geometry. Manager of the Thesis Competition team.

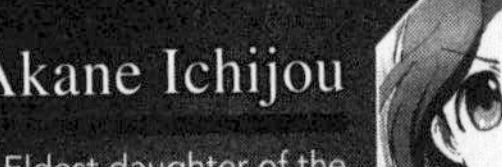

Akane Ichijou

Eldest daughter of the Ichijou. Masaki's younger sister. Mature despite being in elementary school.

Ruri Ichijou

Second daughter of the Ichijou. Masaki's younger sister. Stable and does things her own way.

Haruka Ono

A general counselor of Class 1-E.

Harunobu Kazama

Captain of the 101st Brigade of the Independent Magic Battalion. Ranked major.

Shigeru Sanada

Executive officer of the 101st Brigade of the Independent Magic Battalion. Ranked captain.

Muraji Yanagi

Executive officer of the 101st Brigade of the Independent Magic Battalion. Ranked captain.

Kousuke Yamanaka

Executive officer of the 101st Brigade of the Independent Magic Battalion. Medical major. First-rate healing magician.

Kyouko Fujibayashi

Female officer serving as Kazama's aide. Rank: Second lieutenant.

Retsu Kudou

Renowned as the strongest magician in the world. Given the honorary title of Sage.

Sayuri Shiba

Tatsuya and Miyuki's stepmother. Dislikes them.

Zhou

A handsome young man who brought Lu and Chen to Japan.

Yakumo Kokonoe

A user of an ancient magic called ninjutsu. Tatsuya's martial arts master.

Toshikazu Chiba

Erika Chiba's oldest brother. Has a career in the Ministry of Police. A playboy at first glance.

Naotsugu Chiba

Erika Chiba's second-oldest brother. Possesses full mastery of the Chiba (thousand blades) style of *kenjutsu*. Nicknamed "Kirin Child of the Chiba."

Ushiyama

Manager of Four Leaves Technology's CAD R & D Section 3. A person in whom Tatsuya places his trust.

Rin

A girl Morisaki saved. Her full name is Meiling Sun. The new leader of the Hong Kong–based international crime syndicate No-Head Dragon.

Xiangshan Chen

Leader of the Great Asian Alliance Army's Special Covert Forces. Has a heartless personality.

Ganghu Lu

The ace magician of the Great Asian Alliance Army's Special Covert Forces. Also known as the "Man-Eating Tiger."

Glossary

Course 1 student emblem

Tatsuya Shiba's CAD

Miyuki Shiba's CAD

Magic High School

Nickname for high schools affiliated with the National Magic University. There are nine schools throughout the nation. Of them, First High through Third High each adopt a system of Course 1 and Course 2 students to split up its two hundred incoming freshmen.

Blooms, Weeds

Slang terms used at First High to display the gap between Course 1 and Course 2 students. Course 1 student uniforms feature an eight-petaled emblem embroidered on the left breast, but Course 2 student uniforms do not.

CAD (Casting Assistant Device)

A device that simplifies magic casting. Magical programming is recorded within. There are many types and forms, some specialized and others multipurpose.

Four Leaves Technology (FLT)

A domestic CAD manufacturer. Originally more famous for magical-product engineering than for developing finished products, the development of the Silver model has made them much more widely known as a maker of CADs.

Taurus Silver

A genius engineer said to have advanced specialized CAD software by a decade in just a single year.

Eidos (individual information bodies)

Originally a term from Greek philosophy. In modern magic, *eidos* refers to the information bodies that accompany events. They form a so-called record out in the world, and can be considered the footprints of an object's state of being in the universe, be that active or passive. The definition of *magic* in its modern form is that of a technology that alters events by altering the information bodies composing them.

Idea (information body dimension)

Originally a term from Greek philosophy; pronounced "ee-dee-ah." In modern magic, *Idea* refers to the *platform* upon which information bodies are recorded—a spell, object, or energy's *dimension*. Magic is primarily a technology that outputs a magic program (a spell sequence) to affect the Idea (the dimension), which then rewrites the eidos (the individual bodies) recorded there.

Activation Sequence

The blueprints of magic, and the programming that constructs it. Activation sequences are stored in a compressed format in CADs. The magician sends a psionic wave into the CAD, which then expands the data and uses it to convert the activation sequence into a signal. This signal returns to the magician with the unpacked magic program.

Psions (thought particles)

Massless particles belonging to the dimension of spirit phenomena. These information particles record awareness and thought results. Eidos are considered the theoretical basis for modern magic, while activation sequences and magic programs are the technology forming its practical basis. Yet all of these are bodies of information made up of psions.

Pushions (spirit particles)

Massless particles belonging to the dimension of spirit phenomena. Their existence has been confirmed, but their true form and function have yet to be elucidated. In general, magicians are only able to sense energized pushions.

Magician

An abbreviation of *magic technician*. *Magic technician* is the term for those with the skills to use magic at a practical level.

Magic program

An information body used to temporarily alter information attached to events. Constructed from psions possessed by the magician.

Magic calculation region

A mental region that constructs magic programs. The essential core of the talent of magic. Exists within the magician's unconscious regions, and though he or she can normally consciously use the magic calculation region, they cannot perceive the processing happening within. The magic calculation region may be called a black box, even for the magician performing the task.

Magic program output process

1. Transmit an activation sequence to a CAD. This is called "reading in an activation sequence."
2. Add variables to the activation sequence and send them to the magic calculation region.
3. Construct a magic program from the activation sequence and its variables.
4. Send the constructed magic program along the "route"—the lowest part of the conscious mind to highest part of the unconscious mind—then send it out the "gate" between conscious and unconscious and output it onto the Idea.
5. The magic program outputted onto the Idea interferes with the eidos at a designated coordinate and overwrites them.

With a single-type, single-process spell, this five-stage process can be completed in under half a second. This is the bar for practical-level use with magicians.

Magic evaluation standards

The speed with which one constructs psionic information bodies is one's magical throughput, or processing speed. The scale and scope of the information bodies one can construct is one's magical capacity. The strength with which one can overwrite eidos with magic programs is one's influence. These three together are referred to as a person's magical power.

Cardinal Code hypothesis

A school of thought that claims, of the four families and eight types of magic, within which exists a natural foundation of "plus" and "minus" magic programs (sixteen in all), one can construct every possible typed spell by combining these sixteen.

Typed magic

Any magic belonging to the four families and eight types.

Exotyped magic

A term for spells that control mental phenomena rather than physical ones. Encompasses many fields, from divine magic and spirit magic—which employs spiritual presences—to mind reading, astral form separation, and consciousness control.

Ten Master Clans

The most powerful magician organization in Japan. The ten families are chosen every four years from among twenty-eight: Ichijou, Ichinokura, Isshiki, Futatsugi, Nikaidou, Nihei, Mitsuya, Mikazuki, Yotsuba, Itsuwa, Gotou, Itsumi, Mutsuzuka, Rokkaku, Rokugou, Roppongi, Saegusa, Shippou, Tanabata, Nanase, Yatsushiro, Hassaku, Hachiman, Kudou, Kuki, Kuzumi, Juumonji, and Tooyama.

Numbers

Just like the Ten Master Clans contain a number from one to ten in their surname, well-known families in the Hundred Families use numbers eleven or greater, such as Chiyoda (thousand), Isori (fifty), and Chiba (thousand). The value isn't an indicator of strength, but the fact that it is present in the surname is one measure to broadly judge the capacity of a magic family by their bloodline.

Non-numbers

Also called Extra Numbers, or simply Extras. Magician families who have been stripped of their number. Once, when magicians were weapons and experimental samples, this was a stigma between the success cases, who were given numbers, and the failure cases, who didn't display good enough results.

In the year 2095 AD, many ports had been propelled into automation to actualize twenty-four-hour operating systems, running almost entirely without human intervention. All customs clearance happened during the day, while at night, the entry, loading, shipping, and departure of vessels were fully automated, with only cursory personnel on-site for security.

The decrease in human staff led to an overhaul of every port in the country. This refurbishing more strictly cordoned off free economic zones from urban areas—a countermeasure against undocumented immigration.

Late at night, when the port facilities were running themselves, vessels were only permitted to approach those bonded areas. Vessels that needed human assistance to berth would have to wait out at sea until morning, when manned operations resumed.

It was the middle of the night right now, so loading wharfs *should* have been completely devoid of human presence.

But on this night, with the clock about to strike twelve, many were present on Yokohama's Yamashita Wharf, waiting with bated breath.

"Illegal entrants have landed via a small freighter docked to loading zone five. All personnel, immediately proceed to loading zone five."

After receiving the command over their short-distance radios, two plainclothes detectives began running, without even exchanging glances. Their expressions, however, contradicted each other.

"Sheesh. I told them it'd be over there."

"This isn't the time for complaining, Chief!"

"But, Inagaki..."

"Stop nitpicking and run!"

"I thought I was the one in charge here..."

"I'm older than you are."

"Sheesh."

After flippantly answering his subordinate, Chief Inspector Toshikazu Chiba sped up. He and the rest of security were at quay wall three right now, nearly half a mile from loading zone five. Normally, it would have taken at least two minutes to run there, but Chiba and Inspector Inagaki arrived in thirty seconds, trading banter as they went.

Normally, this wasn't a speed regular people could achieve.

And these two were no regular people—they were magicians.

"I knew we wouldn't have enough people."

"What more can we do? Only detective-magicians can deal with magical crimes."

"Even though...that's not...exactly true...huh!"

Chief Inspector Chiba spoke as he caught his breath, even as he used a surge of energy to leap high into the air. Gripped in his hand was a straight wooden sword, about one yard in total length.

Fluttering through the air like a leaf, he passed above the trespassers, who were firing recklessly in three-shot bursts. His jumping power sent him flying in a non-parabolic curve without any footholds—thanks, of course, to magic.

His bewitching aerial mobility didn't give the attackers time to line up their shots for support fire. He drove in a spiraling maneuver toward three magicians in the back line who were launching long-range attack spells. Using movement magic, Chiba was able to ignore gravity and inertia to slip by their spells. After landing, he began to trounce one after another with his sword.

On the other side of the crowd he'd jumped over, Inagaki used a pistol to gun down the shooters firing submachine guns.

Similar brawls had broken out in a few other places, but none were grave enough to require help. The two inspectors had wrapped things up, or at least close to it.

"Chief, we need to get the ship!"

"Wait—you mean me?"

"Stop complaining!"

Of the duo, the subordinate was clearly blessed with a far superior work ethic (or perhaps the superior lacked much, if any, of their own). Nevertheless, they were both at least taking things seriously enough not to sabotage the human-smuggling sting.

"Fine, fine. Inagaki, go stop that boat for me."

"...If I do it, it might end up at the bottom of the sea."

"Doesn't matter. It'll just be our manager who's liable."

"...I'm not sure why I expected you to take responsibility."

Inspector Inagaki's shoulders drooped in disappointment, but he loaded caseless rounds into his revolver with without hesitation. Then, he used his left hand to flick a switch on the grip's bottom, causing the aim-assist mechanism attached to the top of the barrel to turn on and light up.

The specialized CAD embedded in the grip of his revolver-shaped integrated armament CAD then expanded an activation sequence.

He pulled the trigger, and in that same moment, the device initiated the magic program.

A metal jacket bullet, its trajectory stabilized and penetration strengthened using a compound movement/weighting spell, traveled along the program's defined path, and pierced the small vessel's stern as it was leaving the dock.

The gunshot echoed a few times as the bubbles rising from the stern began to calm. Inagaki had done nothing more than predict where to shoot based on the ship's shape—but it had brilliantly gone right through the propeller gearbox.

"Wonderful," praised Chiba, carefree. A clasp clicked open at his hands. His weapon looked like a wooden sword, but it was actually a sword cane.

With a white, coldly glimmering blade in hand, he jumped, as if trying to replicate the scene in *Yoshitsune Jumping Over Eight Boats*.

As he landed on the vessel, he swung downwards and cleaved a metal-plated door leading to the cabin in two.

The hidden-sword technique known only to the school of Chiba, one of the Hundred Families: Zantetsu, metal cleaver.

The spell defined a sword as a singular entity instead of a mass forged from steel and iron, then moved it along a cutting path set by the magic program. The "sword" then acted like a blade of monomolecular crystal, slicing through anything in its way.

After another slash to clear an entry path, Toshikazu Chiba, eldest child of the Chiba and bearer of the family name, stepped into the ship.

"Thanks for your hard work, Chief," said Inagaki, very obviously holding back laughter.

As the sky overhead began to brighten, Chiba didn't bother to scold him for it. "Man, what a waste of energy," he muttered.

The ship he'd so valiantly cut his way into had been, amazingly enough, totally empty. It looked like the band of illegal immigrants had escaped through a hatch at the bottom of the ship only a few moments ago; water was spouting from the open portal.

The boat had already been slowly sinking, but the improvements to its ventilation courtesy of Chiba had accelerated the process. Now it was completely below the surface.

"Doesn't look like they've found the ones who escaped into the water yet," said Inagaki, casting a meaningful glance at Chiba.

"Not like we don't know exactly where they're going…" replied the young man who'd almost gone under along with the ship. His shoulders sagged as he turned his back to the rising sun and gazed westward.

Chief Inspector Chiba was looking in the direction of something not far from the wharf: a shopping district in the prefecture of Yokohama that was famous nationwide. And in the backyard of one eatery, out of view from the main roads, there was a large well.

Beside it stood a young man dressed sharply in a three-piece suit despite the early morning hour. He was in his mid-twenties. A beautiful man—not due to an effeminate appearance, though. Instead, he possessed cool, almost noble features.

The well he stared at was for disaster prevention rather than drinking, and its mouth was blocked with a pump. Without any warning, part of the crib (the cylindrical enclosure of the aboveground part of the well) under the pump crumbled. Someone had punched out a section from the inside. From the resulting hole crawled out a man soaked head to toe in water. Then another, and another. Eventually, a total of sixteen men clambered out of the well.

The final person to exit, a middle-aged man, moved to stand before the fair-faced young man, watching with a reserved smile, and held up his hand in a salute. The younger man placed his right hand on his left breast and bent slightly at the waist in return.

"First, everyone, change into clean clothes and relax," said the young man to them. "Breakfast has also been served."

"Thank you for your cooperation, Mr. Zhou," answered the middle-aged man, not sounding very grateful.

The young man maintained his smile in spite of the disrespectful tone and led the pack into the building.

One week had passed since the inauguration of National Magic University Affiliated First High School's new student council.

The students were taking their lunch break. Tatsuya had come to the school cafeteria with his friends from Class E. The previous administration using the student council room for meals had been Mayumi abusing her authority, in a way. She'd made the council room luncheon meetings customary little by little; Tatsuya hadn't wished for it. Now that a new council was in office, he had them begin using the cafeteria again.

That automatically meant that Miyuki had started using it, too. Adding their mutual friends to the group, his daily routine had included a lively lunchtime ever since the beginning of October. Still, Tatsuya, Erika, Leo, Mizuki, and Mikihiko were in a different class, separate from Miyuki, Honoka, and Shizuku, so one group always arrived first to save seats for the other. Today, Tatsuya and the rest of the Class E circle were waiting for Miyuki and the rest of their Class A friends.

"I'm sorry for making you wait."

"All finished?"

They'd waited about ten minutes. Miyuki's group had contacted Tatsuya ahead of time to let him know they'd be a while, so when Miyuki still came up to him to bow and apologize, he brushed it off with a smile. It was also a signal—making it a big deal would attract too much attention, so she should sit down.

Honoka, though, winced for some reason. "I'm sorry, Tatsuya. It's my fault we're late."

Ever since her confession that summer night they'd spent at the vacation house in Ogasawara, Honoka had a tendency to overreact to his unimportant words and expressions. Even though he realized that, though, pointing it out wouldn't do anything. If she responded positively, he could just smile—even if it was a forced grin—but when she overreacted in a negative way, he started to feel like he was bullying her, which made him uncomfortable. Unfortunately, there was no silver bullet for this problem. The only thing he could do when she misunderstood something was to clarify himself. It was a passive approach, but it was the only road open to him; he'd given up on trying everything else.

"You don't need to worry," he said. "Everything's confusing at first."

She's wincing because she thinks she offended me again, he thought. *Do I really seem that intolerant to her?* That was an unsatisfying answer, but still, he made sure to sound nonchalant as he soothed her.

"Yeah, nothing to worry about!"

"It's only been a week, after all."

Erika and Leo agreed, both showing unexpectedly (?) sincere consideration. After seeing everyone smile or say it didn't bother them, Honoka finally stopped wincing and quietly sat down.

"Tatsuya, it actually isn't Honoka's fault today," said Miyuki with a smile, backing Honoka up. "The staff room asked us to pull up records from two years ago on short notice. We left third period early, and we've been searching the database in the student council room ever since. Even Shizuku helped."

Still, Honoka was steadily shrinking back in her seat for some reason. "But…Miyuki found it right away, and I didn't know what I was doing…"

"I'm the one who took forever. If you were a turtle, I was a snail," admitted Shizuku. She clearly didn't mean anything cruel by it.

"Miyuki's been using the system since April," added Tatsuya in consolation, ignoring the innocent comment comparing Honoka to a turtle. "You just became a member, and Shizuku isn't even part of it. Miyuki has more experience than you, so it makes sense that you'd be slow at it."

As one might have gleaned, Honoka had been appointed a member of the new student council at its inauguration. The lineup now was Azusa Nakajou as president, Miyuki Shiba as vice president, Honoka Mitsui as secretary, and Kei Isori as treasurer. (In terms of actual authority, First High's treasurer was more of an auditor, and it was a tradition to choose a student in the same grade as the president.)

Originally, Azusa had actually recommended Tatsuya for the vice president seat. He'd declined, of course, but someone had opposed the idea even more strongly: Kanon, the new chairwoman of the disciplinary committee. According to her, "without Shiba, we'd get no office work done."

She'd said that in full view of both Azusa and Tatsuya, too. At the time, he almost couldn't stop his jaw from dropping. He wasn't in charge of the committee's office work—he was part of the team that did the real jobs. In fact, the "real jobs team" was the only team that made up the committee in the first place. They were supposed to be splitting up the office work. It said so right on the control transfer contract Mari had given to Kanon. Tatsuya had typed it up personally and write-protected it, so there could be no doubt.

However, Azusa had readily agreed to Kanon's insistence, and the two juniors' "misunderstanding" brought Tatsuya to his wit's end.

Regardless of his feelings on the matter, and although Azusa agreed, the new president still fought tooth and nail to get Tatsuya in the council. She didn't say it out loud, but he was pretty sure she didn't think she could control Miyuki without him there. Then again, she couldn't leave Miyuki out either.

It had literally given him a migraine.

As a result of the negotiations that he had no say in, it was decided to let Tatsuya remain with the disciplinary committee until the end of the school year, then have him transfer to the student council when the new year started.

They never did ask his opinion on it.

...I'm getting another headache just thinking about it. His own remark of Honoka recently becoming a student council member made him remember those events last week, right down to the head pounding.

Feeling someone's gaze, he looked over and saw Miyuki watching him, seeming slightly worried. Astonished at how astute his sister was, he silently indicated that nothing was wrong and started moving his chopsticks again.

"Tatsuya, are you there?"

At the sound of his sister's voice calling him, Tatsuya, who had holed himself up in the archives on the second basement floor of the library after school, pulled out of his world of letters and numerical formulas back into reality.

"I'm over here, Miyuki," he answered, looking up from his browsing terminal.

There was no wireless inside the archives. The barrier walls here attenuated most electromagnetic waves already, but they were also set up to block communications. These were intentional measures taken to prevent information leaks.

These archives stored documents and materials the school deemed unsuitable for publishing online: highly dangerous documents, depending on the intended use—like essays that departed too far from current mainstream theory and could negatively affect students. Such literature was transported from the National Magic University on physical media and placed in a closed database. As a general rule, the documents were free to use, but nobody was allowed to take them out. And, of course, they were all copy-protected, so nobody could secretly duplicate files to their own information terminal, either.

By nature, classes would almost never refer to anything in them. Using the archives suggested strange tastes—and not too many with strange tastes came here. On most days, a total of zero people used the facility. But for the past couple weeks, Tatsuya had been updating the archives' consecutive usage logs.

Despite answering Miyuki, he made no move to leave his browsing terminal. Understanding, she walked over to him. "What are you looking at?" she asked as she came, not daring to peer at his display without permission.

"Literature regarding the Emerald Tablet."

Miyuki's question was reserved as always, like Tatsuya's response was crisp as always. Others aside, he didn't really have anything to hide from his sister. Besides, she was already well aware of his research goal.

"I believe you've been researching alchemical literature a lot lately..."

However, he hadn't explained how his current research was related to that goal. Her confusion was only natural.

"Well, alchemical methodology isn't what I'm after—I'm looking for properties and the recipe of the philosopher's stone. Of course, some of the literature explains its very creation as alchemy's end goal, so..."

"You're not going to try...transmutation, are you?"

Transmutation—the changing of one substance into another—was deemed an impossible task in modern magicology. Flight magic was said to be equally impossible, but transmutation's level of impossibility was, at least theoretically, on a different level. Miyuki remembered Tatsuya agreeing and saying that the practical possibility of transmutation magic was incredibly low.

"Not that," denied Tatsuya, sure enough. He smiled. "The philosopher's stone in its strict sense—in its definition as an elixir of life—is a catalyst used in magic for transforming base metals into precious metals. Since it's a catalyst, that means the stone itself isn't an ingredient of the process but rather a tool to activate the technique."

"If 'catalyst' means what we use it to mean...then yes."

"They say the spell to convert base metals into precious metals works by having the philosopher's stone act upon the ingredients. If they could use transmutation with only a rock, without any other magical processes, then it follows that the philosopher's stone has a way to store magic programs."

"Store magic programs?" repeated Miyuki, her eyes widening in surprise.

Tatsuya looked back at her, no longer smiling. "When I was inventing flight magic, I figured out how to continuously activate gravity-controlling magic while changing the variables a little bit at a time. A lot of magicians tested the flight spell for me before it was officially commercialized, after all."

In reality, that was why Tatsuya had open-sourced the flight spell's activation sequence. The method was there, so naturally, they'd want to try it out for real. The fastest means was to have a device with its activation sequence preloaded on it. And as it happened, requests did flood in to FLT to test the flight device—not only from Japan but also from many other friendly nations, not the least of which was the USNA (the United States of North America, a federation created when the former USA absorbed Canada and Mexico). Under the pretense of trial monitoring, FLT had gotten loads of data on gravity-controlling magic from high-ranking magicians. And all of that data had made its way back to Tatsuya.

"I have a rough idea of how to use gravity-controlling magic to maintain nuclear fusion now. But if a magician has to always be there to cast the spell over and over again, there's no point. The magician would just be a part of the reactor. It would simply change their job from *weapon* to *component*."

The implementation of a thermonuclear fusion reactor using a terminate and stay resident gravity-controlling spell was one of the Three Great Practical Problems of Weighting Magic—and Tatsuya had just said that he had a rough idea of how to solve it. Even Miyuki had a hard time understanding everything Tatsuya talked about, but she perfectly understood what he wanted to say.

"Magicians need to be indispensable in its operation, but the system can't confine them. Which means I either have to stretch out the duration of the spell's persistence by a factor of days, or devise a method to temporarily store a magic program so that the magician doesn't have to be present to activate it… I'm feeling around for both, but in terms of safety, the second method would be better."

"And that's why you're researching the philosopher's stone."

Thinking normally, Tatsuya was speaking of pipe dreams; he knew that. So, when his sister nodded deeply, not doubting him in the slightest, he felt a little awkward. He abruptly changed the subject. "By the way, Miyuki, did you need something?"

The question was to cover his embarrassment, but in the end, it turned into some first-rate team play (more accurately, a nice backup).

"Oh, right! Ichihara was looking for you, Tatsuya. She says she has something to talk to you about regarding next month's Thesis Competition."

"Where is she?" That was all he needed to hear before closing his browsing terminal. He didn't berate his sister for not telling him earlier; Tatsuya had been the one making small talk, so part of the blame lay with him. No amount of blame would turn back time anyway.

"The magic geometry preparation room. She says she'll be waiting at Mr. Tsuzura's desk."

"All right, thanks. Could you return the archive key, Miyuki?"

"Yes, of course."

He stood up from his chair and handed a keycard to Miyuki. She took it from her brother's hands happily, like a puppy who was pleased someone was paying attention to her. Maybe he hadn't complained or scolded her, sure. But he still had to grin at his sister's utter lack of reservation—and objectively admit to himself that he was too soft on her.

Kazuo Tsuzura. In charge of online magic geometry classes and live instruction for Class 2-B at First Magic High School. For his main occupation, he was as a lecturer at the National Magic University, and his new appointment to First High was a temporary transfer of enrollment.

Though a young and unusually bright man who had made off with an associate professor position at Magic University, he took a very free attitude toward his research, and that had been his downfall. They'd forced him to stop by essentially telling him to come back when he had gained more experience as an educator.

But the man in question didn't mind his "demotion" one bit. In fact, he seemed happy; he could now do whatever research he liked without worry. He was a teacher of some renown, taking everything at his own pace, and was wholly indifferent to the struggle of Course 1 and Course 2 students. He'd take anyone who showed promise under his wing—albeit without considering the student's preferred pace.

He came from a main family in the Hundred Families, one of the Numbers, the first character of his surname meaning "twenty." Like Isori, he came from a long line of scientists and researchers, and was a leading national authority on the interactions of event alterations from multiple spells. The combination spells Hattori prided himself on had bloomed thanks to Tsuzura's instruction.

...That was the mental profile Tatsuya had of Mr. Tsuzura. As far as Tatsuya could judge from the data he had, he was unmistakably a weirdo. This was no mistake, either—and soon, he would get a first-hand glimpse of it.

When Tatsuya arrived, Tsuzura was the only teacher in the magic geometry prep room.

He probably makes them feel uncomfortable, Tatsuya thought. Every teacher selected for this school had superior talents. Most of them, of course, had some amount of pride in their own abilities. But compared to the genius who had obtained an associate professor position at the National Magic University in his twenties, they couldn't help but lose confidence. The more someone relied on their own gifts, the more stress it tended to create when they encountered someone with even greater gifts. Tatsuya had experienced that before as well—though in abilities outside of magic.

Setting aside whether Tatsuya's speculation was correct, the objective truth was that no other teachers were present in the room other than Tsuzura. Yet three people in total were waiting for him here: Tsuzura, Suzune, and Isori.

"You're aware of the Magic Association–sponsored Thesis Competition at the end of the month, right?" After exchanging brief greetings, Tsuzura opened with this question.

"Yes, but I don't know much about it," confirmed Tatsuya with reserve.

The man nodded once. "The Thesis Competition is boring, unlike the Nines, so it would make sense a freshman like you wouldn't know much about it. Even the number of people is different—compared to the Nine School Competition, with its big team of fifty-two people, the Thesis Competition only has three."

He couldn't help but be surprised at the teacher bluntly contrasting the numbers in front of others, but thinking about it calmly, writing a paper and presenting it didn't need much manpower. If they needed people to make little tools for the presentation, they could just round up some helpers from the school. They didn't need anyone else involved in writing the thesis itself. Too many chefs would spoil the stew. Three out of the whole school was fewer than Tatsuya had expected, but he decided it was appropriate.

"Allow me to get to the point. Shiba, would you like to participate in the Thesis Competition as part of First High's team?"

Tatsuya couldn't immediately react to that, which was to be expected; Tsuzura had given him almost no preface to soften the blow.

"...Me, sir?"

Tsuzura's question was crystal clear, but Tatsuya couldn't help but echo him.

The Magic Association of Japan–sponsored All-High Magic Thesis Competition. It was called "All-High," but the only high schools that taught magic theory as part of their official curriculum were the nine affiliated with the National Magic University. In essence, the Thesis Competition was a stage on which those nine schools would compete. If the Nine School Competition was a matching of athletic abilities, then the Thesis Competition was the other half—a combat of scholastic abilities.

"Yes, you." Tsuzura's somewhat affected polite tone was probably part of his personality. He nodded theatrically. "Originally, we planned to have Ichihara, Isori, and Hirakawa from Class 3-C take part...but Hirakawa has recently fallen ill, and last week she suddenly notified us that she intended to drop out of school. We managed to convince her not to, but she's in no condition to participate in the competition. And so, from all the people available, we decided on you."

Hirakawa from 3-C—Tatsuya remembered that name. If he recalled correctly, the engineer for Kobayakawa, who had fallen victim to sabotage during a Mirage Bat match during the Nine School Competition, was a female senior named Koharu Hirakawa.

"But why choose a freshman, sir? Doesn't the school have a screening meeting to select participants?" Tatsuya had finally remembered the application form for the Thesis Competition that had gone out over the school network at the beginning of June. At the time, he'd been in the final stages of developing the flight spell, so he had no time for anything else. And, in any case, he didn't want to stand out given his current position. He'd ignored the application straightaway and forgotten about it.

"Preparing for the presentation is group work, so you're a good fit for the job. Please ask Ichihara for the details," answered Tsuzura presumptuously before hurrying out of the room.

But Tatsuya hadn't said anything about accepting. The rumors about Tsuzura not taking a student's individual pace into consideration appeared to be far from exaggerated.

Whatever the case, Tatsuya didn't seem to have the option to refuse. Before hearing any of this, he figured the competition team simply wanted some help getting data for an experiment at most, but it seemed he had been a bit optimistic. Nevertheless, muttering to himself about it wouldn't help the situation at all, so he turned back to Suzune for an explanation.

"I was the one who recommended you. I had the other substitutes decline," said Suzune, suddenly dropping a bomb on his unstated question.

You...made them decline? he thought. "...I believe all the applicants have been toiling away, devoting no small amount of time in order to participate in the competition. I haven't even submitted an essay for selection yet. I'd think a lot of people would be unhappy with my sudden appointment." He knew he already stood out in a bad way; he really didn't want any more of this whole business of *being forced* to sow discord. "For example, how does the fourth person, after you, Isori, and Hirakawa, feel about this?"

"Sekimoto is no good. He isn't cut out for this work."

Tatsuya hadn't been giving thought to any specific person, but Suzune wasted no time saying something that almost amounted to a personal attack. He decided it would actually evolve into defamation if he ignored it, so he asked, "By Sekimoto, do you mean Isao Sekimoto—the one on the disciplinary committee?"

"Well, yes..." said Suzune—even she decided it wasn't good to state so bluntly, and she softened her tone at Tatsuya's prompting. "He and I have very different goals."

Isori continued for her: "Like Mr. Tsuzura said, three people work together on the thesis and the presentation. But if all three contribute ideas to the thesis, it won't be coherent. That means you have to get one main writer and two helpers, and they divide the labor. Ichihara is the main writer for our school this year."

Tatsuya nodded; Isori's explanation made sense in a couple of ways. They did need to divide the labor—and he understood why Suzune, with the best theory grades in the senior class, was the main.

"In other words...I suit the theme of Ichihara's thesis?" That's where the conversation was headed, but how did they come to that decision? Tatsuya had never presented a paper—*under his own name*, anyway.

"My thesis is titled 'The Technical Possibility of Gravitational Magic Program–Loaded Thermonuclear Fusion Reactors.'"

Suzune's indirect answer to his question made his eyebrows raise a little.

"Yes—my research theme is the same as yours."

The term *research theme* might have sounded like an exaggeration when applied to high school students, but she was right. One of Tatsuya's goals was a *resident* gravitational magic program–loaded thermonuclear reactor. But he'd barely ever talked about it—it was mostly all still in his head...

"...I see," he said. "You were the one monitoring us back then, weren't you?"

"'Monitor' has such a negative connotation. Please take it as 'watching in interest.'"

Not just watched—she'd probably eavesdropped, too. But he didn't say that. Back in April, in the middle of the situation with the anti-magic terrorist intervention, when he'd met up with Sayaka Mibu for the second time in the cafeteria, he'd felt someone's eyes on him but hadn't tried to figure them out. As a result, he'd tacitly consented. He had no place to complain at this point.

"There are only three weeks until the competition. We decided that the only one we could add to our team this late was someone involved with the same research theme as us."

"You...didn't think I was just making things up when I talked to Mibu?"

"I try to have a sharper eye for character than that."

She thinks pretty highly of me, he thought, giving a painful grin not only on the inside but on the outside as well. "All right. This isn't without its merits for me, so I'll assist you."

That wasn't just lip service—it really did have merits for him. He had a pure academic interest in how Suzune was trying to solve one of the Three Great Problems anyway. If he could use this as part of his own plan, then he would.

"What should I do, exactly?"

"First, I'd like to explain the Thesis Competition in broad detail. Isori, do you mind? I know none of this bears repeating for you."

"I don't mind. Go ahead, Ichihara," said Isori, bowing a little.

Suzune nodded back, then took three portable blackboards off a shelf rack on the wall and handed one to each of them. Portable blackboards were a form of electronic paper with wireless data-transmission capabilities. Thin boards, the size of large report paper, made so conference attendees could hold them in one hand and read a document during smaller meetings that didn't need big screens. They were full-color, of course, but text-only was generally shown in white, high-contrast characters on a black background; their color scheme was what had spawned the "blackboard" nickname.

Suzune set her information terminal on the portable blackboard's holder and called up the Thesis Competition handbook. "As I'm sure you know, the Thesis Competition is where high school students go to present research findings in magic science and magic engineering. Rather than simply presenting the fruits of their learning, it gives students with no chances to present at academic conferences an opportunity to show their own research to the world. Not only are the team members frequently scouted by magic research groups, but also some papers even get recorded directly to the Index and go on to be used in universities and businesses."

Tatsuya looked at the guide displayed in his hands as he listened to Suzune.

"The competition always takes place on the last Sunday of October. Its location alternates between Kyoto and Yokohama. Apparently, this is because the Magic Association of Japan's headquarters is located in Kyoto, and their eastern branch, sort of a sub-headquarters, is in

Yokohama. This year, the competition will take place at the Yokohama International Assembly Hall."

Tatsuya flipped through his mental calendar. Thankfully, he didn't have any plans for the last Sunday in October, the thirtieth.

"Participation eligibility permits those with recommendations from National Magic University–affiliated high schools as well as high school student groups that pass a preliminary essay selection. However, there have never been presenters without a recommendation. The rules say it's open to anyone, which is why it's called the 'All-High Magic Thesis Competition' but is nicknamed the 'Magic High Thesis Competition.'"

She was in the middle of her explanation, but Tatsuya found himself overcome with surprise and unable to stop himself from getting a word in. "There haven't been any groups without the recommendation?"

"...Shiba, for a normal high school student, writing a thesis and a presentation that goes a full thirty minutes is a lot harder than playing Monolith or Mirage."

"Isori is right. Even for us, under normal circumstances three people would never be finished preparing without the help of the student council and club committee."

Tatsuya was used to writing system specification documents, so he wondered about that claim, but kept his mouth shut.

"As a general rule, the theme can be whatever you want, with the obvious condition of staying within public morals. Two years ago, a student's theme was developing spells to replace weapons of mass destruction, but they sent him home in the advance screening."

"Sounds like one heck of a person..." groaned Isori next to him, eyes widening, evidently not having heard this before.

I know how he feels, thought Tatsuya. At the same time, he probably didn't have any room to be criticizing that student given how he'd *actually* developed spells of mass destruction. But then, the self-deprecation in his thoughts brought a question to mind: "...Sent home in the advance screening? That means his thesis wasn't publicized, right? If it was never publicized, how do you know about it, Ichihara?"

He asked it casually, but a somewhat awkward silence followed. Suzune made a sour face, like she'd accidentally swallowed a bug. Tatsuya was about to tell her she didn't have to answer if she didn't want to, but she sighed and spoke.

"...The thesis's author was the student president of our school three years ago."

...So even our school has crazies like that, thought Tatsuya, more impressed than disgusted by her admission. The Thesis Competition happened after the student council changed, and Suzune had been a member since the second half of her freshman year, so it wasn't strange that she knew about the incident. And by the look on her face, there were plenty more tales of that past president's deeds.

She cleared her throat. "There is precedent for it, so any presenters have to submit their final thesis drafts and presentation equipment—including spells—to the Magic Association beforehand."

Isori nodded in agreement—probably because it was the first time he'd heard of the episode.

"The deadline is next Sunday. We'll be sending it to the Magic Association's Kanto branch, but we do it through the school. But given the time Mr. Tsuzura will need to check over things, we really only have until next Wednesday to finish."

Even if they could do more work on the presentation after submitting everything, Tatsuya calculated that they didn't even have ten days left before the thesis needed to be done. *That's pretty tight*, he thought. *But why have Tsuzura look it over? There are more-veteran teachers here that have worked on whole textbooks for magic education.* He couldn't voice his doubts out loud (since doing so would have been rude to Tsuzura), so he kept them to himself.

Isori, though, keenly picked up on Tatsuya's misgivings and addressed them anyway. "Mr. Tsuzura is the one in charge of the selection process this year. There's a lot to do—not only do you have to support the preparations for the competition when it's outside your field of expertise, but you also have to set up all the magic experiments. It seems like they usually give the job to younger teachers."

"He may be young, but Mr. Tsuzura is very capable. He's taught us on a much deeper level than normal classes, so we should consider ourselves lucky."

Especially for Course 2 students without the right to receive personalized instruction from a teacher—but Tatsuya didn't say that.

They didn't seem to notice it, either—that half the entire student body was composed of students who wouldn't receive normal instruction, much less be taught "on a deeper level"—but he felt no reason to make them aware of it.

After that, Suzune listed off a few minor points and her explanation was finished.

Modern short-range public transportation was based on the idea of carpooling, having shifted from mass transport mechanisms to smaller numbers. This change had started thirty years ago and was nearly complete in metropolitan areas, having already spread to 80 percent of provincial towns and cities. In the remaining 20 percent of locations, no public transportation existed in the first place—people had their own cars.

When it came to short-distance commutes to work or school, devices to ferry many people at once, like linked trains and big buses, were now almost completely unused. It had been a long time since the days of middle and high school students using the same trains or buses to go to and from school together.

In almost all cases, Tatsuya went straight from school to the station, but occasionally he stopped by a café or a fast food place on the way. The road from the school to the station was about half a mile long, but the short route hosted many closely packed commercial establishments meant for students. There were not only eateries but also a myriad of bookstores, stationery stores, and clothing shops. Magic education–related goods were particularly abundant; the stores were patronized not just by First High students and faculty but also by a significant number of people on vacation.

The group of eight had just settled down at one particular café with a relatively orthodox appearance, one that they frequented enough to have started being treated as regulars there.

"What? Tatsuya, they picked you for the Thesis Competition?"

The group's detour today had come about when Mikihiko had asked why Tatsuya had been called to the geometry laboratory. And, unable to wait for their food orders to arrive for the reveal, Mikihiko had asked again. Feeling that the hastiness was a side of his friend he hadn't seen before, Tatsuya had gone ahead and explained the scene from earlier.

And that had been Mikihiko's reaction.

Tatsuya had already mentioned it to Miyuki and Honoka before, when he went to get them from the student council room, but the other five, including Mikihiko, widened their eyes in perfect circles of surprise.

"But don't they only pick three people from the whole school for the Thesis Competition?"

"I guess so," answered Tatsuya lightly to Mizuki's question. Their expressions were polar opposites.

"You guess…? You don't feel anything, Tatsuya?"

Mizuki was dumbfounded, and Erika looked a little amazed as she made her own comment.

Next to them, Leo grinned in amusement. "Guess this much is only natural when it comes to Tatsuya, huh?"

"Almost no freshmen have ever gotten into the Thesis Competition," Shizuku objected.

"But a few *have*, right? The faculty can't just ignore a genius who can add new spells to the Index." Leo, still smiling, objected right back.

"Don't call me a genius," warned Tatsuya, seeming genuinely bothered by it, not just embarrassed.

"You really don't like being called a genius, do you...?" asked Honoka, mystified, neither sarcastically nor meanly.

"The word is too convenient," answered not Tatsuya but Miyuki. Her brother just gave a pained smile at her response; he didn't say she was wrong.

"But it's still amazing!" insisted Mikihiko, blowing away the dark clouds that had begun to drift in, maybe worried about the dangerous mood. "*Supernature* picks up the winning thesis every year, and even the rest of the papers get into academic magazines all the time."

Supernature was the name of a scientific journal in England known as the highest authority on modern magic topics. On the other hand, it tended to be authoritarian, not too friendly for high school students to read. But Mikihiko was not the only one who read it; Tatsuya, Miyuki, and Shizuku, and the other members in the group did, too, and they knew its name and status well.

"Oh, but... There's not much time left, is there?" asked Mikihiko, now worried, a complete change from his excitement.

Tatsuya started to get suspicious at how extreme his ups and downs were today—maybe something happened with him, too. He didn't let the suspicion show, though, and nodded. "Nine full days before we have to submit it to the school."

"What?! But that's right around the corner!"

"It'll be fine. I'm just a sub, and they've been writing the paper since before summer break."

Tatsuya smiled and waved his hand to soothe Honoka, who had gone a little pale in the face. The gesture made everyone think *Oh, right* and breathe a sigh of relief.

"Still, this was very sudden," remarked Miyuki, frowning. "Was there some sort of trouble?"

"Apparently, the older sub fell ill," answered Tatsuya simply, still offering a smile. He hadn't explained this before, but he didn't need to hide it, either.

However, his simple answer wasn't enough to fully satisfy his sister. "That is quite unfortunate, but it still seems too hasty." The circumstances seemed convincing enough for her mind but not her heart. "I'm sure they chose you because you're right for the job, since you could handle being made part of the thesis team right away, but…"

But Tatsuya's substitution was already set in stone—and it was very much like Miyuki to think of a logical reason like that to convince herself otherwise. This time, it wasn't necessarily an overestimation of him, but he thought agreeing unconditionally would seem too narcissistic. "That's not it. If Ichihara's research theme was something I didn't know anything about, even I would have turned her down."

Tatsuya decided to deal with it using his "smile and partially disagree" method. That wasn't to say Miyuki was perfectly happy with this attitude, but while she was searching for words, someone else tossed a new question at him:

"Huh. What's the paper about?" asked Leo, leaning forward with curiosity.

One girl did give Leo a cold look, clearly wondering if he'd even understand if Tatsuya told him, but both the questioner and respondent ignored her completely.

"The technical problems of thermonuclear fusion reactors run by gravity-based magic programs and ways to overcome them."

"…I have no idea what that means."

Of course, the questioner could only partially reply to such an intense, straight-man response.

"…That's a pretty wild theme," groaned Mikihiko, face sullen. "Isn't that one of the Three Great Practical Problems of Weighting Magic?"

"Since they chose you, I thought for sure it would be a thesis on CAD programming," said Mizuki, expressing surprise.

"Oh, me too!"

"Kei is one of the members, too… With that theme, I think the team would be amazing enough to win the whole competition for sure."

Shizuku and Erika seemed to agree with Mizuki. His friends probably thought this theme was too much for Tatsuya—and for high school students in general.

Well, that was only natural. Implementation of a gravitational thermonuclear fusion reactor wasn't one of the Three Great Problems for nothing. Tatsuya decided to smile along with them and worm out of the conversation.

It was only Miyuki who failed to partake in the calm smiles. She created one on her face, but it didn't reach her eyes. She knew what research on a *resident* gravitational thermonuclear fusion reactor could mean—and she knew that her brother was most serious of all about it.

After splitting up with their friends at the station and returning home, the siblings found a city commuter in their parking place. They exchanged glances.

Tatsuya went up to the front door first and opened it.

Upon seeing the plain, unfamiliar pumps at the entrance, Miyuki stopped in her tracks, grimacing and sucking in her breath. Tatsuya gently put his arm around her shoulders. He stepped up onto the wooden edge of the entranceway with her, and then heard the pattering of slippers as somebody approached at a jog.

"...Welcome home. Friendly as usual, I see." The words came at them, tinged with a teasing note.

Tatsuya immediately narrowed his eyes and slightly tightened his grip on his sister's shoulders as she gave a start. "It's been a long time since you came home, Ms. Sayuri," he answered, his voice cold to match his gaze.

This time, the petite woman greeting them was the one to react. "Y-yes, well, it's rather convenient to be closer to the office."

"I get it," Tatsuya said curtly to their stepmother (though the siblings simply thought of her as their father's second wife—who hadn't come back to the house in nine months).

Despite her homecoming, she had neither a room nor place to sleep here. After marrying Tatsuya's father, they had been enjoying a married life as a couple on their own near the top of a high-rise apartment building that was a five-minute walk from Four Leaves Technology's main office. She'd never stayed here since the union, and yet she still lived here according to the resident registration—so Tatsuya's words had been pure sarcasm.

Seeing their father's second wife losing her cool from such a trivial jab actually made Miyuki settle down and regain her calm. Tatsuya's arm still around her, she turned and brought her face closer to her brother so she could snuggle up against him. The act was performed in complete disregard of others watching. Normally, even when they were by themselves, she never did anything this assertive—or immodest. She was purposely acting as though nobody was looking.

"I will prepare dinner immediately. Is there anything you would like to have, Brother?"

"I'd eat anything you make. There's no rush, so go get changed."

When her brother looked only at her to answer, without sparing so much as a glance to Sayuri, Miyuki giggled a little, superiority achieved. "I will. Please do tell me if you have any requests on what I should change into. I would wear any outfit if you wished it, Brother."

"All right, don't get carried away."

He pretended to poke her, and Miyuki drew her head back and danced up the stairs to the second floor.

"Well then," said Tatsuya to Sayuri—who was idly standing nearby—after Miyuki went out of sight, "let's hear what you have to say."

The unreserved manner of speaking made her frown a bit in displeasure, but nevertheless, she sat down across from Tatsuya in the seat he offered. "I feel bad for hurrying you, but I would like to finish while your sister is absent," she said. "It seems both of you still don't like me much."

She must have felt it was pointless to keep up appearances; as soon as she sat down, her attitude became franker. Not caring that he was looking, she leaned back on the sofa and crossed her legs. She had the spirit of a scientist, wearing no ornaments or makeup and only a pantsuit, so he had no issues with where to look—of course, she could have been wearing a tight miniskirt and he wouldn't have batted an eyelash.

"Miyuki doesn't seem to. Her father remarrying within half a year of her mother dying would leave a bad taste in anyone's mouth. She may look mature, but she's still only fifteen."

"...And what about you?"

"Such emotions mean nothing to me. That's how I'm put together."

"...Well, fine. Whether you mean that or not, I can't do anything about it. But if you're going to go that far, I'd like it if you heard *me* out. It may have been half a year for the two of you, but it was sixteen for me."

Oh, right. She dresses to make herself look young, but she's the same age as our father, thought Tatsuya, an idea sure to make an enemy out of all the women in the world.

Sayuri Shiba, formerly Sayuri Koba, had been in a romantic relationship with Tatsurou Shiba before he had married Miya Yotsuba. However, the obstinacy of the Yotsuba in their pursuit of high-quality genes had forced the initial two to separate. Tatsuya was aware of that, so he could somewhat understand wanting to complain.

But that was purely a problem between his father, his mother, and her—it was no business of the siblings. Considering their mother knew about their relationship during her lifetime, there was even less room for sympathy.

"In any case, what have you come all this way for today?"

Sayuri had unconsciously tried to postpone the subject; she

caught her breath at the question but then managed to begin speaking naturally again. "...I'll give it to you straight. I want you to help at the labs at the office again. And leave high school, if possible."

"It's not. If I'm not a student at First High while Miyuki attends, I won't be able to fulfill my duty as her Guardian."

An unreserved refusal to an unreserved demand.

"Even if you didn't continue with school, another Guardian would surely be assigned to her."

"Magicians are in short supply everywhere you look. Even the Yotsuba wouldn't be able to find a replacement Guardian so easily."

"You're saying there are no escorts as talented as you."

"When it comes to Miyuki in particular, that's correct."

This exchange was one they'd had over and over in the past.

Sayuri exhaled, giving a heavy sigh—one that didn't look entirely fake. "The company isn't flexible enough to let such talented staff goof off, you know."

"It was never my intention to goof off. I've already contributed massively to the company's profits this term. You've been flooded with flight device orders from the USNA Marine Corps, haven't you? Those alone should increase profits over last term by twenty percent."

Sayuri frowned in frustration. There was no room for objection.

Originally, FLT was known as a manufacturer of magical engineering–related tools and items, not of completed CADs. It had, without a doubt, been the success of the Silver model that caused the company to rise to fame as a CAD maker—in other words, Tatsuya's merits. The recent flight device in particular was a groundbreaking product that some analysts predicted would launch FLT as the number one manufacturer of specialized CADs in the world.

These achievements must have made Sayuri jealous—she'd first joined the company as a researcher, then was reassigned to the management division after not producing many conspicuous results.

But even without those personal feelings, she had a reason she couldn't say, "Okay, I see" and leave. "...Then could I at least get you to help analyze this sample?" she said, removing a large jewel box from her purse and opening it very carefully.

Inside was a single translucent orb with a reddish tinge.

"...That's a Relic of the Ni no Magatama family."

Among those pursuing magical research, a "Relic" referred to an "OOPart" with magical properties. Materials that couldn't be judged manmade but that also were clearly not naturally formed were called Relics. For example, antinite, which caused Cast Jamming, was classified as a Relic.

Furthermore, true Relics—the Yasakani no Magatama, to name one—would never fall into the hands of scientists.

"Where did they excavate this?"

"I don't know."

"I see. A matter of national defense, then." As a non-foreign manufacturer with top-class tech, FLT was often entrusted with military-related tasks. "You said 'analyze'—I'm not undertaking the task of *duplicating* a Ni no Magatama, I'm sure?"

Sayuri's expression stiffened.

Tatsuya heaved a sigh. "How could you be so impulsive? These things are too hard for modern technology to artificially synthesize. That's why they're called Relics."

OOPart was an abbreviation for "out-of-place artifact." In other words, they were objects created in such a way that they surpassed the technical standards of *the age from which they were excavated.* It didn't mean modern technology couldn't reproduce them. A Relic, though, *was* too difficult for modern tech to reproduce, which is why it possessed the grandiose name in the first place.

"This job came as a firm request from the National Defense Force. We can't refuse it."

He could somewhat understand the management decision. It wasn't just FLT—any businesses involved in magic essentially operated as usual until the government demanded otherwise. In other words, the magic industry *was* the defense industry.

The only ones who purchased magic engineering products, including CADs, were magicians, who could use magic at a practical level. The market for them was incredibly tiny compared to other industrial goods.

Given the rarity of magicians, the small size made sense. Experts said that, in Japan right now, the total number of magicians who were in magic-related professions or magical study came out to be about thirty thousand. Even if all of them bought a new CAD every year, the domestic CAD marketplace would only contain thirty thousand of them during the year. While some actually went longer before buying a replacement, plenty of magicians owned up to five or six. However, that didn't change the fact that the market was just too small.

Plus, because national policies promoted magic, magic-support devices needed to be made available cheaply. The retail price of CADs was kept low enough so that an average household's income could support buying their child one as a gift upon entering high school.

This scale and structure certainly wasn't an industry that could survive independently. Therefore, nations took expert assistance measures when it came to the magic industries. For example, Japan subsidized 90 percent of a CAD's purchase cost. Their storefront prices were a tenth of the business's calculated unit price. Japan also gave very generous grants to businesses' research funds under the pretense of contract research. Even the tallest giants in the industry, like Maximillian and Rosen, couldn't defy their respective governments. This was a fate shared by all players in the magic industry.

"But even the National Defense Force should know the reason behind the nickname Relic. They'd understand that if something was classified as one, it would be impossible to artificially synthesize. Why are they making such an unreasonable demand?"

Sayuri needed more than a short pause before composing an answer. "The Ni no Magatama seems to be able to store magic programs."

But her answer, spoken with hesitation, had enough power

behind it to break through Tatsuya's careful expression. "Has that been proven?" he asked, only managing to make himself sound dubious through full mobilization of every ounce of acting skill he had.

But it worked, and Sayuri failed to notice how interested he now was. "It's still supposition, but we have enough in the way of observational data for the military to act on."

Tatsuya pretended to nod gravely. "If it *is* true, they wouldn't be able to ignore it. I can understand that."

Tatsuya's goals weren't only the ones involving the ability to store magic programs. If someone were to implement and popularize a system to store them, semi-perpetual magic devices would no longer be a dream. Forces with no magicians could be equipped with magical weaponry. If the Ni no Magatama had the ability to store magic programs, and if it could be reproduced in large quantities, the military would see a proliferation of magical weaponry.

But at the same time, it was important to the point that they couldn't just accept the request and then come back with failure.

"Considering FLT's current achievements, I wouldn't think this is worth taking such a risk for," Tatsuya said.

"The dice have already been cast."

"Without any chance of victory?"

Considering their utter lack of know-how in reproducing Relics, the risks were too large.

Of course, Sayuri understood that all too well. "There is a chance. Your magic. With it, we can analyze it."

Now that she'd made her intentions clear, Tatsuya chuckled. They didn't need his intellect—they were after his unusual ability.

Just like they always were.

"Nothing is saying even my magic could duplicate it…but if you absolutely must insist, then please send the sample to R & D Section 3. I show up there frequently."

And Tatsuya didn't particularly mind it. He, too, was desperate for any clues regarding the storage of magic programs. But since his goal was that function, duplicating the physical Ni no Magatama was of secondary importance compared to the magic storage ability itself. Because of that, he wanted to avoid being manipulated by lab workers at the main office. Besides, the schedules for the main office's laboratories tended to be packed, so it'd be inconvenient one way or another.

"..."

But the proposition wasn't one Sayuri could accept. In her position, she needed to take FLT's power politics into account. She couldn't let R & D Section 3 have all the glory. Besides, as a more serious and more ridiculous reason, neither she nor her husband could let Taurus Silver—Tatsuya—have any more of an influential voice than he already had. Their main office's labs could start with Tatsuya in its deliverance of results, but he had many sympathizers in Section 3—pretty much all of them were aligned with him, in fact—so even the other researchers' achievements could end up being attributed to him (or so Sayuri suspected).

With no way to agree to Tatsuya's requests, Sayuri bit down and made a sour face, as expected.

"Or shall I hold on to it for you?"

Tatsuya meant the suggestion as a way to help Sayuri, who was paralyzed by conflict. And it was, in fact, the deciding factor in her breaking free of the standstill.

"Fine, then!"

Unfortunately, though, it didn't cause agreement but a breakdown in negotiations. Sayuri desperately wanted the main office—herself included—to be the one to achieve the Relic duplication. For her, Tatsuya mentioning that he'd hold on to the sample—in other words, do the research on its duplication personally—was preposterous. Of course, she'd come to him with an absurd proposal in the first place. Nobody had ever done this before. Right now, though, she lacked the composure to notice.

She stood up, her temper lost. "Yes, I see! It was a mistake to count on you for help!" She shoved the jewel case into her purse, quickly turned around, and rapidly headed down the hallway. Tatsuya followed at a steady distance, speaking to her in a businesslike tone as she put on her shoes at the entrance.

"You're in possession of valuables. Shall I escort you to the station?"

"I will be quite fine by myself. I'm going home by commuter anyway!"

"I see. Please be careful." Tatsuya bowed to her courteously, without showing any sign of offense at his stepmother's stinging response.

"Miyuki?"

At Tatsuya's call from the front door, Miyuki, who had changed into a one-piece camisole, timidly came down the stairs. Near her exposed arms, up her shoulders, and along the nape of her neck, was a tinge of crimson. Not, of course, from makeup, but clearly from shame at her previous behavior.

"Tatsuya, I…I'm sorry for doing something so childish."

She was using the word *childish*, but her attitude made it seem like she meant *disgraceful*. And yet, while clearly aware of that, Miyuki was still showing her skin like this. It seemed she was still subconsciously being influenced by her previous suggestiveness.

As she kept her eyes averted from him, Tatsuya stroked her cheek, then slid his fingers toward her chin. Then he used his index finger to tilt her jaw up.

Miyuki's almost bewitchingly fair skin reddened from her chest to her shoulders. Under her smooth, silky hair appeared a young and lively beauty, scarlet at the eyes.

"U-um…"

Though having taken up a posture of embarrassment at the act—it seemed like he was going to kiss her—she didn't take her gaze from his.

The fingers on her chin crawled back up her cheek. Miyuki absently closed her eyes, and…

"Nya?!"

...gave a short, muffled yelp.

"Wh-what are you doing?!"

"Scolding you," said Tatsuya, grinning at his younger sister, who stepped back and glared at him, face red. (It was a natural reaction, considering he'd suddenly grabbed her nose.)

"I swear...you're quite mean," she pouted, turning a cheek to him.

After chuckling for a moment, Tatsuya's face fell back into seriousness. "I'm going out for a bit. You make sure to lock up here."

"Tatsuya?" said Miyuki, wanting an explanation, her own face drawing back in surprise at the out-of-the-ordinary command to stay at home.

"I need to go back up a woman who doesn't have much of a danger sense."

Tatsuya took off his uniform blazer and gave it to Miyuki as she scowled with displeasure. "...How much will they force on you until they're satisfied?"

"Unfortunately, I can't pretend I didn't see this. Ms. Sayuri has a sample that could give a hint as to how to store magic programs," he explained, elucidating the real reason behind his "backup" as he took off his necktie and handed it to Miyuki.

That seemed to make sense to her, but then her frown deepened. "If that is the situation, then I suppose you must. Please be careful."

The conversation they'd had in the archives after school was fresh in her mind, too. She couldn't hinder her brother's goal out of hatred for their father's lover. Without telling him not to go or saying it was unnecessary, Miyuki took Tatsuya's blouson from the coatrack.

She put it on him, then Tatsuya removed gloves and a helmet from a storage box by the front door and put motorcycle boots on his feet. Then he gave a collected, polite bow to Miyuki seeing him off and said, "I'll be right back."

◇ ◇ ◇

As she sat inside the self-driving commuter, Sayuri felt like Earth's gravity had doubled.

To put it in clear words, what she felt was regret—she'd screwed up.

She thought she'd gotten accustomed to the negotiations that came with her move to the management division, but it hadn't taken her very long to lose her temper. She was ashamed of herself and couldn't help but feel depressed.

It was always hard for her to keep calm when talking to that boy. Her stepson.

And she knew why.

The fact that he was the son of her rival in love. His talent and achievements as a technical expert. That uncanny gaze, revealing no emotion. When he looked at her, she didn't feel human; she started to feel like a target of observation, a mere object.

But what she did not yet understand was that this feeling was a reflection of people treating him like a tool to be used.

What she did know, however, was that she had to get him to cooperate by any means in order for this project to work. Now, because of her short temper, it had gotten a lot more difficult.

As she stared out the window, she heaved a sigh. Suddenly, she perked up, noticing the strange lack of traffic on the roads. Then she realized she hadn't passed by any cars going in the other direction for a while now. This was a residential area, but it wasn't that late yet.

The irritation in her mind changed to unease. She called up traffic information from the commuter panel. The traffic control center had been reporting that cars destined for the station were being routed through a detour to avoid an accident in the area.

In any case, now that there was a reasonable explanation, Sayuri sighed in relief.

As he followed Sayuri's commuter car on his electric bike, Tatsuya also felt the traffic was too sparse. Voice information coming from his helmet's receiver was telling him the same things as her commuter panel.

But he found no part of that to be a relief. He didn't doubt the information itself saying the road was closed due to an accident. He'd watched Sanada and Fujibayashi team up to try to hack into the traffic control system once, so he knew how difficult it was to get into. Still, he wasn't optimistic enough to believe there were enough simultaneous accidents jamming the roads to block off every single car on all the roads from his house to the station.

It wouldn't be that hard to locate cars run by the traffic system. Commuters in particular, being part of the regional community-shared traffic body, always transmitted identification signals to prevent car thefts via hacking. The signals themselves weren't kept especially secret. He'd been tracing Sayuri's commuter from the moment he'd left the house.

And when his stepmother's vehicle was finally in sight, he spotted another car, not under the traffic system's control, tailing her at a close distance.

A warning blinked on the commuter panel. The message said a noncontrolled car was approaching from the rear.

Sayuri didn't think much of it. Some people still liked to drive in this day and age as a hobby. Since she'd originally been in the tech field, she knew drivers like that always wanted to modify their car to turn the traffic control system off. If she worried about every noncontrolled car that ever came near, there'd be no end to it.

For now, she sat back in her seat and silenced the harsh alarm.

Seeing the black car accelerate, Tatsuya immediately revved his motor.

His motorcycle had the advantage in acceleration. Given his distance and their relative positions, though, the black car reached Sayuri first.

No sooner had it overtaken the commuter than it cut right in front of her, causing its collision-evasion system to kick in.

The commuter rapidly ground to a halt, and so did the other car.

Two men got out and ran over.

On the road, where surveillance cameras monitored every inch, this was an incredibly reckless move. The method would make sense if they were illegal immigrants; any citizen or legal alien could be immediately identified from the camera images.

Tatsuya turned his headlights as bright as they would go and pointed them at the two men as they tried to pry open the commuter's door. He left them on as he got off his bike and ran forward.

A moment later, one of the men pulled out a handgun, while the other came at Tatsuya with his fist. On his fingers were brass rings, shining dully in Tatsuya's motorcycle headlights.

Grating psionic noise was coming off the men.

Cast Jamming. Magic-obstructing waves created by antinite. One attacker to disable magicians, and one to finish them with a gun. It was an effective textbook tactic for dealing with a small number of magicians—but only if they were run-of-the-mill examples.

The gun's muzzle pointed at Tatsuya. Right at his heart. The aim was precise enough that he wouldn't fully dodge it even if he immediately tried to get out of the way, and he could feel a clear murderous impulse behind it.

But the man was never able to pull the trigger.

Tatsuya's finger had initiated his own CAD before the other man's could move.

The handgun broke into pieces and scattered across the road.

One of the men, or perhaps both, shouted something. Their tones were agitated, and given the distance he couldn't make out exactly what they said. His ears did pick up the words *Cast Jamming*, though; the attackers were probably surprised theirs hadn't worked. Or maybe they were screaming about why the gun fell apart despite the magic obstruction.

Their argument wasn't Tatsuya's concern either way. It didn't matter that they were preoccupied with *unnecessary things*. He wouldn't change his plan of attack. He pulled his CAD trigger again.

The man who had been holding the gun gave a scream and fell sideways onto the road, gripping his thigh and writhing.

A moment later, the bruiser clutched his shoulder and staggered. Groaning wordlessly, he broke out into a sweat and fell to his knees, then passed out and toppled forward. His mind couldn't stand the total destruction of skin, muscle, veins, nerves, and bones that had occurred inside his wound, which looked like it was made by a super-thin needle.

Localized disassembly of a human body via the dismantling spell Mist Dispersion.

What part of the body, when stabbed correctly, would inflict physical pain that exceeded a person's mental tolerance? What part of the body, when shot correctly, could obstruct the mind's control of one's limbs? Tatsuya had a thorough knowledge of such matters, having used his own body and those of others for it.

He walked around the two fallen men and approached the black automobile. He kept his CAD leveled at the car, not attacking right away. If he carelessly damaged a hydrogen fuel car with compressed gas cylinders, he could cause a sizable explosion. The cars were normally fitted with safety mechanisms to hedge against such danger, but terrorist bombers used cars with those safeties removed. That was the way of the real world.

If Miyuki were present, he wouldn't have needed to worry about combustion, but unfortunately, she was minding the house. To the right of the road was a somewhat large river, and to the left was a line of houses. Given the possible damage to the residences and the roads, he decided he couldn't use such an aggressive method.

But that decision, to put it into harsh terms, was a kind of carelessness on his part.

Suddenly, he felt a killing intent aimed at him from above and to the right.

Partially out of reflex, he moved to dodge. Not a moment of delay or pause.

But even he couldn't avoid an assassin's bullet flying at a supersonic speed.

A burning pain shot through his chest.

The bullet pierced his left breast…

…and the impact sent his body careening.

The sniper had been incredibly precise. He'd just barely managed to avoid his vitals getting hit, but his lung had been shot clean through. The sound of the bullet came a moment later—it must have been pretty far away. Nevertheless, if not for Tatsuya taking evasive action, the bullet would have gotten him in the heart.

"Brilliant" was an understatement when it came to this sniper.

Tatsuya used the momentum of his fall to roll behind Sayuri's commuter. The bullet wound had already healed. Normally, even fatal wounds would disappear in an instant thanks to his magic.

But that didn't mean he felt no pain. He broke out into a cold sweat, feeling the intense aftershock of his pierced breast and penetrated back.

Right now, though, he didn't have time to spare for his phantom pain. He estimated the enemy's position again. Based on the direction and angle of the bullet, and the location of obstructing buildings, the sniper was somewhere in the cluster of commercial buildings across the river.

They were currently about a thousand yards away. Given the ease with which they hit a person at this distance and the small size of the hole in his back, the sniper was using pointed, full metal jacket rounds. The commuter's frame was made of synthetic resins, so to such a weapon, it would be best to consider it not much of an obstacle, either.

And to make things worse, the sniper wasn't using magic. If they had, he would have pinpointed them no matter what type of spell they used. But if the sniper wasn't using anything but pure shooting skill, then the distance made them hard to spot, even given Tatsuya's ability to perceive information bodies.

The two bodies lying on the road began to float up. The black car's door opened, and the bodies were violently sucked inside.

Tatsuya didn't try to stop it. Disabling the movement spell acting on the two men would have been easy, but eliminating the sniper threat came first.

He searched for the information bodies of the bullet that pierced him. Bringing his ability to analyze them to full operation, he began to read out the information inherent to the bullet.

The bodily fluids clinging to it.

His flesh's resistance.

The wind.

Gravity.

Gas pressure in the chamber.

All the changes added to the bullet flowed into Tatsuya's mind as compressed information. From them, he sorted through the original shooting position data and singled it out.

The process moved from the bullet to its trajectory, and from there to the sniper, going back through information, through the world's memories, through time.

From the present to the past.

And…

…from the past to the present.

With the sniper's location at the time they fired the bullet as a foundation, Tatsuya followed the memories of state changes written into the Idea—the information bodies of the world itself, recorded as information within all things.

It led him to the sniper's current position.

Found you.

His mind's eye fixed its sight on the sniper's eidos—the units of information that distinguished the sniper from other events and entities within the world's information.

He could tell the sniper was aiming at him again. The second shot hadn't come yet because it was taking time to switch from anti-personnel piercing rounds for penetrating bulletproof armor to anti-object high-speed piercing rounds for penetrating an enemy behind an obstacle.

Tatsuya could see all of that—he had all the sniper's physical information. Good fortune was the only thing he could call this as he pulled the trigger on his spell, which dismantled the sniper's entire body.

About ten minutes after the black driverless car escaped, Tatsuya decided the danger had passed and stood up from behind the car.

He peered inside to see Sayuri unconscious. This didn't concern him whatsoever—he had been fairly confident he knew her condition from seeing how the commuter never started up again. The airbags from above, below, the left, and the right had buried her in the seat like a package filled with cushioning. The system to secure passengers from accidents had been fully functional. She wouldn't have even been shocked too much. The mental strain had probably been what had caused her to faint.

Sayuri was counted as part of the Yotsuba, albeit at the family's very fringes, so she was supposed to have at least some tolerance to violence.

You'd think she was just an average *civilian*, Tatsuya thought.

After stowing the airbags, which had been developed to be reusable, he restarted the car in complete self-driving mode.

As the commuter began to slowly drive away, Tatsuya followed after it on his bike.

By the time they got to the station, Sayuri had regained consciousness. A bit pale in the face, sure, but she still had her composure. Of course, Tatsuya didn't know what she'd been like right after waking up, since he'd been on his bike. After escorting her to the cabinet platform, she shoved the box with the Ni no Magatama into his hands. It seemed to Tatsuya to express how she felt—stubbornly and desperately trying to act tough.

Once he'd seen her off, he returned home and immediately headed for the telephone. He hadn't used a mobile phone at the station because it could have been tapped, of course.

"...Don't worry about the road cameras. We're already handling them."

"Thank you very much, Major."

He had called the secret line to the Independent Magic Battalion's headquarters.

Tatsuya needed to conceal his two positions—as a combat personnel belonging to the Yotsuba of the Ten Master Clans, and as a special duty officer of the Independent Magic Battalion. His top priority was stopping the road cameras from identifying him with their image data.

Tatsuya straightened and saluted Kazama on the monitor.

"Still, they were quite tenacious. You may not have been in an urban center, but firing a rifle in the city?"

"I won't deny that I miscalculated, sir, but his skill was incredible."

"You said he wasn't using magic, right?"

"He wasn't, sir. I have no doubt."

Using a bullet-guiding spell always created a reaction in the form of an event alteration. Using a super-sense spell always carried psionic waves to the identified target. If he'd used magic, there was no possible way for Tatsuya not to notice.

Kazama knew of his perception as well as the next guy. *"Hmm... Is it possible to snipe someone at night from one thousand yards away with only an optical scope?"*

He looked down, possibly staring at a map of the sniping area. Tatsuya was no amateur when it came to sniping, but in terms of *gun-based* sniping, Kazama was far more knowledgeable. Tatsuya couldn't guess what he was wondering about, but he clearly noticed something just by listening to the story.

"...Only so many groups in the world can get their hands on such a skilled sniper. This may actually give us an easy clue as to who they are."

"I'll leave it to you, sir."

The best defense was a good offense. If you disabled the enemy before coming under attack, you could keep your own attack hidden. For Tatsuya, now that they'd crossed blades, peaceful resolution—such as not going after the enemy as long as they didn't attack anymore—was an impossibility.

"Hmm? Wait a moment... I just got a report. Looks like we found the car."

The license plate on the black self-driving car had been hidden, but not well enough to fool the crime-prevention road cameras laid out on the streets. Since they knew exactly when and where the car had been, it was easy to pinpoint.

"Once we've looked into this, I believe we'll deal with them—I'm sure you don't mind, right?" Kazama said, looking for confirmation.

"My apologies for the extra work, sir," said Tatsuya easily.

Personally chasing someone he'd let escape was a meaningless fixation, and one to which Tatsuya had no connection.

Dinner was quite a bit later than usual thanks to the unexpected street brawl, but Miyuki never even raised an eyebrow as she briskly set Tatsuya's meal in front of him, wearing her busy, frilly, pink apron.

"Your apron..." he muttered aloud.

"Did you notice?" Miyuki smiled as she turned.

Miyuki frequently wore simple, mature designs. He didn't know whether to call this "girlish," but the apron was fanciful and cute, and one Tatsuya had never seen before. "Did you buy that earlier?" he asked.

Right before splitting up at the station the day before, Mizuki and Erika had dragged Miyuki into a variety shop for teens. Tatsuya had waited outside on a bench, but they'd left the store more quickly

than expected. When asked what they'd bought, Erika kept saying it was a secret, so he'd never gotten an answer.

"Mizuki needed a replacement, so I bought one, too... Does it look strange?" asked his sister, a little uneasy, perhaps because it was so different from what she usually wore.

He could have just muttered a simple "yes," but instead he looked closely at her attire again.

The apron's length was about the same as a dress's, like it was a two-in-one "apron dress." A mini apron dress, at that. The frills, which looped around the shoulders and crossed in the back, along with the wide ribbon tied behind her waist into a bow, were cute, and her bare thighs peeking out from the hem were captivating.

Not something she could show other people, I think.

"No, it suits you very well. Enough to want to put it in my very own glass case and secretly adore it."

When he put those feelings into words, they turned into a somewhat strange expression.

"Tatsuya...that seems quite abnormal."

Her words alone might have been spoken with a sigh, but her expression made it very obvious she was trying to hide her embarrassment.

Tatsuya didn't get involved with that, instead smiling and picking up his chopsticks.

After dinner was over, the siblings moved from the dining room to the living room. Tatsuya sat down on the two-person sofa as Miyuki placed a cup of coffee in front of him, then set down her own and sat next to him.

"By the way, what did that person want?" asked Miyuki, leaving a little space between them, legs together and hands on her lap, looking at Tatsuya obliquely, unable to entirely conceal her curiosity. "You mentioned she had a sample with the ability to store magic programs."

"Well, I have to do some research to find out if that's actually true." He knew the question would be coming, and he had an answer prepared. "As always, she asked me to help." Not that he'd prepared a reasonable-sounding lie or anything, though. "But this job seems interesting."

"Will you accept it?" Miyuki was simply keeping the conversation going—she knew just from what she'd heard that her brother couldn't possibly turn the job down.

"Things being what they are, I can't pretend not to know. She gave me the sample, after all." He looked at the end of the table where Sayuri's big jewel case was sitting.

Afraid of more attackers coming to rob her, she'd forced Tatsuya to take it. She'd also pledged to leave things to R & D Section 3, so Tatsuya had no qualms with the situation.

"Is this the sample? The one that might be able to store magic programs?"

"Yeah." As Miyuki silently asked what on earth it was, Tatsuya opened the box. "A Relic of the Ni no Magatama family," he explained to Miyuki as she looked inside.

Miyuki covered her mouth with her hands and looked at Tatsuya, eyes wide. "Why would that person give you something like this?"

"It's a military request. They wanted her to copy it."

"But that isn't reasonable..." Miyuki understood, though not as much as Tatsuya, what Relics were and how absurd an experiment to copy one would be.

"I'm sure the military understands that, too. They must think it's still a challenge worth taking on."

A magic program interfered with eidos (the bodies of information attached to events), temporarily rewrote those bodies, and carried out an alteration of that event in line with what was written in the magic program—that was how magic worked. For example, a sphere with a red surface would have the information "reflects mainly red light" and "shaped like a sphere" attached to it. If you used a magic program that said "reflects mainly blue light" to overwrite that information, the sphere would change color to blue. By overwriting the natural information with a magic program, the program's information would temporarily become an event expression, aka "incident information." The effect would last until the magic program disappeared and the original information took root again.

Though magic programs had the most important role in magic execution, simply storing a magic program didn't amount to magic, as this example showed. But if you were in a state where your *own* eidos were overwritten and you could store the magic program you used to overwrite them, you could extend the duration of the applied spell's effects. If you could store a magic program as "incident information bodies" to replace the eidos originally held by an object, it was possible.

In other words, objects that could store magic programs could become objects to store magical effects.

Theoretically speaking, storing a spell that rewrote temperature meant that it was possible to maintain highs of hundreds of degrees or lows of negative tens of degrees without providing any energy. And if a magic program that overwrote movement speed could be stored, there was potential to create a pseudo-perpetual motion device.

"Just saving magic programs isn't a substitute for magicians, but the ability to save magic programs is essential to mechanically executing magic. I'm not interested in whether the Ni no Magatama can be copied, but if it really can store magic programs, I very much want to uncover the system behind it."

"I know you can do it, Tatsuya."

At some point, Miyuki had gotten right up next to Tatsuya on the sofa. As she encouraged him with her soft voice, her face dangerously close, she softly rested her head on his shoulder.

Miyuki had two policies—to personally do as many chores as she could, and to never leave Tatsuya's care to machines. She wasn't obsessive enough to do the dishes by hand, though. She was still a student, and her list of things to do piled as high as a mountain. She had to pick and choose.

After leaving all the bowls and dishes to their HAR (home automation robot), Miyuki went to her desk.

Magic high schools still required the study of topics other than magic. They did not require exams on them; instead, they placed more emphasis on daily homework. Right now, she was working on her math homework. She found math difficult compared to other topics.

For some time, she'd been staring at a problem she just couldn't solve, so she looked away from her display for the moment.

With the processing that powers modern computers with advanced interactive interfaces, one would never need to solve numerical calculations or anything unless you were someone quite deep in the field of mathematics. Still, mathematical thinking sometimes helped with putting together new spells, which is why her brother told her to take it seriously.

Miyuki gave a languid sigh. At times like these, she started to get jealous of her omnipotent brother. *Maybe I'll ask him to help…* she thought lazily, before quickly shaking her head so hard it almost made noise.

Tatsuya would have gotten right to work on analyzing the Relic. She was already a bind on Tatsuya's freedom—she couldn't trouble him any more than that. The only reason he'd entered First High was because she had. At least, that's what Miyuki figured.

It was true that you needed a magic high school diploma to advance to the National Magic University, but as with everything, there were exceptions. For example, those who accomplished academic significant deeds, like discovering a Cardinal Code, could gain entry regardless of whether they had a diploma or not. If he wanted, Tatsuya could be accepted right now, and Miyuki had no doubt he'd breeze through the entrance exams.

Miyuki knew he could only achieve his goal at a higher-level research institution like the university, and she understood this high school life was only a diversion for him. The reason he had to do it anyway was because he was Miyuki's Guardian.

For the Yotsuba, Guardians were tasked with the protection of specific individuals, even at the cost of their own lives. A tragedy had once befallen a girl of direct descent, so they had chosen "combat slaves" to protect the Yotsuba bloodline.

On the surface, they were the same as bodyguards. However, given that bodyguards were temporary, Guardians were clearly a different concept. The Yotsuba didn't decide someone was going to be a Guardian at birth, but once they chose one, the assignment never ended. Normal bodyguards who worked on a twenty-four seven system were no different, but Guardians had no right to quit the job. They could leave if the one they protected dismissed them, but until now, Guardians had all been Guardians for life.

Tatsuya could move with some freedom because he could carry out his guard duties even from a distance, as physical distance didn't influence magic. They didn't have telepathy linking them or anything like that, but Tatsuya was constantly using part of the unconscious region of his brain to observe her, with his sight that could perceive eidos. Well, it was less observation and more that he had a spell cast on her.

But even Tatsuya couldn't use magic while asleep. The distance between them didn't matter, but he still had to match her pace of daily life. Miyuki could match her own life cycle to Tatsuya's during days off and extended breaks, but on school days, Tatsuya had to match Miyuki—in other words, match the school system's cycle. Plus, even though physical distance didn't affect magic, it was still easier to deal with various threats if nearby.

Still, this was all a result of Miyuki not releasing Tatsuya from his Guardian duty. If she did, she'd be assigned another Guardian, probably female and the same age. Because no matter how short the supply of magicians was, Miyuki was the strongest contender for succeeding as head of the Yotsuba.

Of course, Miyuki hadn't wanted Tatsuya's guardianship because of selfishness alone. The mission of a Guardian was of the utmost priority in the Yotsuba family. As long as he was assigned to her, they wouldn't make him do other, more tedious things. They'd never make him play the bad-guy role, either. Nobody could criticize him strongly, whether it was their father or their father's second wife.

They couldn't force him to help them.

That was part of why she wanted him to go to the same high school as her—but she knew her dependence on her brother, her not being able to leave his side, was at the root of it.

She let out another sigh. She couldn't have her way with her own heart, nor could she get any further with this homework.

Thirty minutes later, she decided that, well, she didn't have to ask him for *all* the answers. She could just show him the ones she already had.

The next day, after school.

In order to get everything for the presentation together, Tatsuya went to the library. He really would have rather been focusing on his analysis of the sample (the Ni no Magatama Relic), but he couldn't neglect (to help with) the Thesis Competition preparations.

Libraries these days were almost entirely digitized, with paper books making up only a slim fraction of available data. If he could view that data online, he wouldn't have had to walk all the way here, but the stuff Tatsuya and the rest of the team needed was strictly controlled, inaccessible from outside.

And it was when he ventured into the reading room, looking for an open booth, that he stumbled across someone he knew coming out of one of the private rooms.

"Oh, hello, Tatsuya."

"Saegusa, getting some autumn reading done?"

He'd last seen Mayumi about a week ago, so it didn't warrant a typical "Hello, it's been a while." Instead, he replied with a harmless greeting.

At least, he thought it was harmless. Mayumi pouted a little, unhappy. "You know, Tatsuya…I'm a senior, in case you've forgotten."

"Yes, I know that..." said Tatsuya, understandably confused at her saying something so obvious, as though it were incredibly important.

"High school seniors have university entrance exams, remember? I wonder why you didn't consider that I might have been studying... Do I look that carefree?"

Mayumi's explanation only made Tatsuya more bewildered. "...You mean, you haven't been recommended yet?"

She had excellent grades, the position of student president, and she was even famous as a magical sporting athlete with numerous championship trophies. If that wasn't enough for a recommendation, what was?

But her answer was already ahead—and to the side—of Tatsuya's thoughts. "Huh? Tatsuya, you didn't know? I refused recommendations. It's an unwritten rule at First High that anyone with student council experience turns them down."

"...That's the first I've heard of it."

"Only ten people per magic high school can get recommended for Magic University, after all! We have more people taking the exam than other schools, so we want to use those ten spots effectively."

"So borderline students can get preferential recommendations?"

"You're exaggerating a little, but...basically, yes."

"That's, uh..."

It made some sense, but he still felt like something was wrong with that. Mayumi didn't look like she had any doubts, though, so he stopped himself from pointing it out.

Tatsuya's stammering made Mayumi look at him askance, but her interest quickly flew in a different direction. "What are you here for, Tatsuya?"

It upset him that she made it sound like him being here was a surprise—he was a regular at the library, and certainly used it more frequently than she did—but he didn't need to hide anything. "I'm here to get some things together for the Thesis Competition."

"Oh, that's right. Rin wanted you to help, didn't she?"

...*Help. Right...* From someone else's perspective, maybe it looked like that. Though it was a team competition just like Monolith Code, where individuals shined, one couldn't see each member's contribution to the thesis. It wouldn't be strange to think of everyone besides the main presenter as a mere assistant.

"...Oops, we'll just get in the way out here, so let's go inside," said Mayumi, gesturing to the small room she had just come from. "You were going to use it anyway, right?"

Holding the room like that was bad manners, but it wasn't like there was a line outside the door. Tatsuya nodded without reservation.

Three people in the viewing room would have made it hard to move around in, but even two made it feel pretty cramped. Mayumi was small for a girl, but ever since last autumn, Tatsuya's build had surpassed that of an average grown male. He wasn't huge or anything, but his shoulders were wide enough to take up a fair bit of space when he sat. With him sitting in front of the terminal and Mayumi on a spare stool, their shoulders were pressing against one another.

All alone with a beautiful girl in a cramped room.

But even this situation would neither excite Tatsuya nor give him the jitters. Mayumi knew that from past experience. And as for considering herself a beautiful girl... Well, it was an objective fact, so she could leave that aside, too.

As Tatsuya used the terminal with practiced hands, not bothered at all that their shoulders were touching, Mayumi, feeling no irritation, disappointment, or paradoxical caution, resumed their conversation from before.

"I'm sure it was sudden for you, but I hope you do your best."

"...It was certainly sudden." The abrupt conversation without any prelude threw him off a little, but he managed to link it with the previous interrupted conversation and avoid asking *what* was sudden. "It isn't something for you to worry about, though, is it, Mayumi?" he asked in reply, sounding pretty unconcerned, his eyes still glued to the monitor.

"Well, no. But for Rin, the theme this year goes beyond winning or losing in the competition."

"Which reminds me—they didn't ask you to be their substitute?"

"I wouldn't be able to handle the topic. And I'm not very good at using magic continuously for complicated processes."

Tatsuya felt like his question and her answer didn't link up all the way, but Suzune had a thorough understanding of Mayumi's strengths and weaknesses, so he decided to interpret that as Suzune having eliminated her from the list of candidates beforehand.

"Rin's helped me out with a lot in the past, so it's too bad I can't help her in a time like this…"

It was hard to tell from her tone whether she was talking to herself or to him, and, not seeing any way to respond to her fading words, he ended up silently typing on the terminal, continuing to pull the data he needed.

"That's why I want you to do your best here, Tatsuya. I think you'd be able to help her."

"Does Ichihara have some kind of special attachment to the theme this year?" asked Tatsuya, less out of curiosity and more because that sounded stronger than mere encouragement.

"In a way, it's the first step toward Rin realizing her dream."

That answer didn't tell him anything concrete, but he didn't plan on asking any more about it. He felt Suzune's dreams didn't have much to do with him, anyway.

But contrary to his plans, Mayumi didn't stop talking. "To elevate magicians in society. And not through political pressure, but through economic necessity. By making magic an irreplaceable factor in economic activity, magicians can truly be released from their fate of being born as weapons. A gravity-controlling, magic program–type thermonuclear fusion reactor would be a strong way to do it…is what Rin is always saying. Writing this thesis is the first real step."

Tatsuya turned to her suddenly and stared at her, his eyes wide.

Mayumi winced. "Huh? What?"

"I'm surprised. Ichihara's thinking the very same thing…"

"Huh? As you?" she asked, voice high and eyes wide.

He nodded, expression still shaken.

In truth, the idea of elevating magicians in society by having them supply economic benefits wasn't originally Suzune's or Tatsuya's idea. Though it had few supporters, the idea had first been proposed over twenty years ago. But there weren't even any signs of it happening yet. Even now, the primary *use* of magicians was for military goals. World affairs were in a lull right now, so cases of magicians being used as weapons had decreased.

Still, some said the development of magicians—not of magic—was, to this day, 90 percent for the pursuit of military objectives. And with things as they were now, it was bound to stay that way. Most magic they could put to use for people's livelihood could be replaced with machines. Whether that be controlling temperature or accelerating objects—though you wouldn't get as dramatic an effect as with magic, if something was necessary enough to social activity, you could more stably supply that with nonmagic technology.

There was no need to substitute it with magic.

There was no need to replace highly advanced automatic devices with magicians.

There was no need for magic technology to control or program those devices.

As long as magic wasn't actualizing a technology that current science was unable to reproduce, the liberation of magicians through economic benefit was no more than an idealistic daydream.

On the other hand, a thermonuclear fusion reactor that ran off a gravity-controlling magic program wasn't original to them, either. Research on nuclear fusion reactors had come to its limit fifty years ago, but now the research was on whether magic could realize it or not.

Unfortunately, that research was on the decline right now.

Maintaining a continuous nuclear fusion reaction with gravity-controlling magic was deemed so difficult a technique that it was counted among the Three Great Practical Problems of Weighting Magic—and the solar energy cycle was, at the moment, providing more than enough energy to *advanced nations.*

You could barely find anyone, at least now at the end of the twenty-first century, who discussed the connection between the elevation of magicians in society and the possibility of gravity-based thermonuclear fusion.

"I had no idea someone else with such an obscure idea was so close to me this entire time," said Tatsuya, more out of actual admiration than surprise.

For some reason, Mayumi narrowed her eyes at him. "...Yeah, well, I'm glad the two of you are getting along." Her tone of voice sounded cranky, too, not just her look.

"Well, I don't think the issue has to do with us getting along... especially since our methodologies seem to be completely different."

What is she sulking about? he thought, his reply a little defensive.

"But it's the same concept, isn't it? Tatsuya, is Rin the kind of woman you're into?"

"What?"

"Shoulder to shoulder with such a beautiful girl, and you didn't even think of doing anything. Well, I'm sorry for having such a childish body."

What in the hell is she talking about? was Tatsuya's undeniable impression.

First of all, just because people had the same research theme, they were more likely to end up as rivals than partners. And Mayumi was simply short—she didn't have a childish body. Even he thought of her as having a mature, provocative figure.

There were so many misunderstandings he needed to clear up that he couldn't even figure out where to start.

"…I'm not an exhibitionist. I wouldn't make a move on a woman in front of surveillance cameras."

Tatsuya must have been pretty baffled himself, because the first response he could think of was not a very appropriate one.

"Huh…?" His reply seemed suggestive but was actually just not well thought-out. Mayumi began to fidget, and her eyes started to wander. "Umm, then, what if there were no cameras or people? Like, if we had a hotel room to ourselves?"

"If you were making advances on me, I would accept without hesitation."

With a clatter, the red-faced Mayumi and her stool both ran into the wall; it seemed like she was trying to get as far away from him in the cramped room as she could. That was when Tatsuya finally realized he had misspoken.

Repeatedly saying the first thing that came to mind had created a misunderstanding he could have avoided.

But he felt that making any more excuses would be digging a deeper grave. Deciding it was fortunate the conversation had ended, he looked away from her and focused on his data collection.

And yet Mayumi, who *appeared* to have sensed danger, didn't try to leave the viewing room.

Three nights after submitting the thesis to the school, as Tatsuya was processing some data on his personal workstation, he noticed their home server was under attack.

The attack was coming from multiple avenues simultaneously, meaning this was no amateur hacker. This was the work of a professional data thief. That meant they hadn't coincidentally found his address—they'd aimed specifically for his house's global address.

No matter how many times he fought it off, the attacks kept coming. They were being incredibly stubborn. *I'll have to change the address again*, said Tatsuya to himself, sighing and booting up his tracer program.

The next day, during lunch break, Tatsuya was visiting the counseling room.

He was speaking to Haruka.

And, of course, talking about puberty problems wasn't on his agenda.

"...However, they cut the connection in the middle. I wasn't able to find the attacker."

Haruka didn't bother to hide her displeasure—or even pretend she felt differently—which wasn't an expression very fitting of a counselor at all. But considering Tatsuya hadn't come for counseling, and given their past experiences, nobody could unconditionally blame her.

"...And? Just so you know, I can't do network tracing."

Tatsuya almost laughed at the woman's sullen voice, but he didn't want her getting any angrier, so he didn't let this show. "I know your field of expertise, ma'am. I don't want to trouble you with that much."

"Then what is it?" Caution crept into Haruka's face. She'd learned to immediately be on her guard whenever Tatsuya said something that sounded reasonable—because there was always another side to it.

"I was wondering if you could tell me what you knew about groups that have been dabbling in secret information trafficking regarding magic lately."

Seeing Tatsuya give her a forced, calming smile, the woman scowled. "...You know what *confidentiality* means, don't you, Shiba?"

"Of course."

"..." Haruka's lips formed the beginnings of a word.

She probably wanted to say, "Are you kidding me?" he thought. He'd have been thinking the same thing. He still didn't feel bad about it, though.

"...Since the end of last month to the beginning of this month, there have been numerous illegal immigration incidents in Yokohama and Yokosuka," began Haruka, her voice sounding like one big sigh.

It wasn't easy to cut off connections after already going along with one of his generous offers. It was an elementary method to build up information connections for those in the intelligence field. And to have it directed back to her... Haruka must have been regretting this bitterly.

"The prefectural police and the bay police are working together, but they haven't found anything significant. At about the same time, manufacturers providing parts to Maximillian and Rosen have been meeting with a series of burglaries."

Maximillian and Rosen were two of the top CAD makers in the world. In other words, they were targeting businesses related to magic device production.

"Do you mean to say it's related, ma'am?"

"Given who we're talking about, it's nothing certain. Shiba, I think you should bring your thesis on physical media instead of putting it online."

That last piece of advice was the only time her voice wasn't tinged with carelessness. When Tatsuya tried to confirm her true intentions again, Haruka smoothly averted her eyes and looked at her desk.

The move implied she couldn't say any more.

And Tatsuya knew by now when to withdraw.

After school, in the disciplinary committee room, Tatsuya was talking to Isori about the hacking attempt last night.

"...Did they do any damage?" asked Isori, leaning in worriedly.

"No, that much is fine," replied Tatsuya with a wry shake of his head, putting his hands out in front of him. Isori would quickly change into a tall, androgynous, pretty girl, just with a swapped school uniform, so pressing closer to him like this, even if it had no meaning in terms of physical distance, didn't make him very comfortable. Of course, he couldn't let those feelings show, so he had to be careful not to lean back unnaturally. "More importantly, was your house all right, Isori?"

Isori gave him a blank look for a moment, then frowned and lowered his voice. "Do you mean the hacker was after…?" he whispered, his voice sounding oddly provocative.

I heard he worries about not having many guy friends, but I guess they don't hate him—they just want to keep their distance… thought Tatsuya, though he said something else. "I looked at the commands they were using. They seemed to be after documents related to magical theory. Considering the timing, I can't deny possibility of a connection to the competition."

Actually, given the timing, there was one other factor that was highly probable, but he couldn't be that honest about it. Besides, you could never be too careful.

Isori's frown deepened, and he started to think about whether he'd seen any signs like that. "Not at the moment, anyway… Maybe you should tell Ichihara about it, too."

"You're right," he agreed immediately, having already planned on doing so.

Then, a cheerful voice broke in: "Kei, here I am~," it said in a way that might have a music note dancing at the end. Without waiting for a response, the person sat right down next to Isori, took his arm, and started acting playfully. It was, of course, Kanon.

"Tatsuya, I haven't seen you in a while."

That was Mari, who had come in beside Kanon. Her words nearly had a sigh attached because of Kanon's behavior.

It was tricky for Tatsuya to say whether a dozen or so days was a "while" or not, but considering they'd seen each other every school day up until last month, maybe it was bound to feel like a long time. "Yes, it has," he replied, standing up and offering his seat to Mari.

"Oh, why thanks," said Mari with a grin, not trying to compromise, before sitting down.

A handsome woman as usual, he thought, answering, "You're welcome" and bringing another chair next to her for himself.

"So, Tatsuya, how has Kanon been doing?"

A sudden, unexpected question. Well, maybe it was natural for the previous chairwoman to think about how the current one was doing, but he was pretty sure that wasn't why she'd called him and Isori here.

"Mari?!"

But looking at Kanon's panic, he began to understand why she'd asked. *Such a charming junior-senior relationship, isn't it?* "I don't patrol with her anymore, so I don't know about that part of it," said Tatsuya, deciding to learn from their relationship, charming as it was. "She keeps things very tidy and orderly. She's especially good at getting rid of things. Though sometimes she gets a little too into it," he explained in a monotonous, deadpan voice.

Mari and Kanon both fidgeted uncomfortably. Mari knew she was never any good at keeping things clean, and Kanon had made a few mistakes now, throwing out things they actually needed and confusing whoever happened to be looking for them.

In that way, Tatsuya hadn't just been speaking about Kanon. Mari understood it as sarcasm, but Isori wasn't her, and didn't seem to understand that. Isori turned to Kanon and warned her, though only his words were strict (?), while his tone was soft. "...Shiba says things like that, but you have to do a little more paperwork by yourself, too, okay? Relying on me is one thing, but when I'm not around, you make him do a lot of it, don't you?"

Kanon answered, "...But I'm bad at it. I think we just need the right people doing the right jobs."

Her current sulking and fawning created a large gap between this and her usual imposing figure—the one that came out when Isori wasn't around. Tatsuya and Mari saw that and grinned drily.

"...Well, let's leave that discussion for another time," said Tatsuya, who figured that was enough, prompting Mari to move on to the main subject.

"Yes, let's. I actually wanted to talk about Thesis Competition security."

"Security? Is the disciplinary committee going to be handling it?"

"Yeah."

"Security" done by students at an event held outside school sounded odd to Tatsuya, but he was the only one who seemed put off by it. They probably did this every year.

"But not security for the venue itself. The Magic Association is assigning professionals for that." Mari didn't want to leave any misunderstandings up in the air, either, so she began explaining before Tatsuya asked. "What I wanted to talk about was personal security for the team members, and guards for the presentation materials and devices. The competition uses valuable material that only the people related to the university are privy to, after all. It's pretty well-known among outsiders, too, so the competition members sometimes end up being targets of industry and university spies."

It was such a timely topic that Tatsuya was a little startled. He knew this was possible, but honestly, he couldn't keep himself from feeling surprised. "…Like trying to hack into their home servers?"

"Well, it is just a high school event… I call them spies, but I mean, I don't think any small-timers could do something crazy, like infiltrate a network just to get a little bit of extra pocket change. At least, I've never heard of it…"

That would make sense, thought Tatsuya, mulling it over. In the modern world, simple unlawful access to a network was a serious crime. The theft of information in a network was given a heavier punishment than robbery. And the falsification of data was on the same level as attempted murder. Coupled with the strengthening in network security, cyber crimes weren't worth it as a business for full-time criminals.

Which meant the attack last night must have been…

As Tatsuya's thoughts were elsewhere, Mari approached the core of the subject. "What we need to watch out for are purse snatchers or people walking away with our things. Four years ago, one of the presenters on their way to the venue was attacked and injured. After that, the schools started assigning escorts to the participating members starting a few weeks before the competition."

Thankfully, he snapped out of it before missing anything he'd need to ask her to repeat.

"That goes for us, too, of course. Escorts are selected from the disciplinary committee and club committee executives, but we honor each member's personal wishes on who is actually guarding whom."

"I'll be the one to guard Kei!" interrupted Kanon, as though it were obvious.

Definitely charming, thought Tatsuya, but this time he managed not to let a dry chuckle escape.

"...Well, Isori has no complaints, so that's decided. You'll have an aide, too, of course...but, Kanon, don't kick them away like some kind of horse, all right?"

"That was mean! I wouldn't do that. I'm not a little kid."

Seeing her cheeks puff out didn't lend much credence to her claim that she wasn't a little kid, but the other three non-kids politely ignored it.

"We'll have Hattori and Kirihara guarding Ichihara."

"The club committee chairman will be her personal guard?" asked Tatsuya flatly.

"He's no match for Ichihara," replied Mari with a mean grin. "Anyway...the issue is what to do about you," she said, still grinning.

"I don't need one," he replied instantly.

Mari nodded, not trying to get him to reconsider. "Any guards we give you would just be warm-up catchers. And they'd probably just get in the way. I'll tell Hattori what we decided."

Tatsuya crooked his head to the side, belatedly noticing something. "By the way, why are you the one doing this, Watanabe?"

To supplement the part he purposely didn't say, he was asking why Kanon, current chairwoman, wasn't doing this, and why Mari, previous chairwoman and now retired, was bending over backward to coordinate the disciplinary committee and club committee.

"No real reason, to be honest..." she stammered.

Tatsuya arched an eyebrow slightly. *Overprotective, I see.*

Mari got the message and looked away awkwardly.

First High's school store had a selection that far surpassed the average high school shop.

One could say the same for all nine of the magic high schools, but they had been compelled to expand by necessity so that students could easily acquire hands-on magic teaching materials difficult to find in regular stores.

It didn't change that they were still school stores, however, and some things simply couldn't be found there. When that happened, one needed to go out to buy them.

And while this, too, was a commonality among the nine schools, shopping districts that could only be called "castle towns" formed around the magic high schools, so students could buy nearly anything they needed that the school's selection lacked—equipment, consumables, books, miscellaneous goods. That First High's shopping district was especially well-stocked has already been touched upon.

The recording film for the 3-D projectors they were using for the Thesis Competition happened to be out of stock in the school store, so Tatsuya and Isori had come to a stationery store near the station to purchase some. With the day to submit their draft to the school coming up tomorrow, they couldn't wait for the school store to restock.

"I didn't mean to trouble the two of you with something a freshman could do by himself..."

They had already exhausted over half the journey there, but Tatsuya said this anyway for two reasons: one out of sincere apology for bothering his upperclassmen, and two, the stronger reason, out of being fed up with Kanon clinging to Isori without a care for who saw.

The grass was always greener on the other side, and it seemed the reverse was also true. Or maybe everyone else just sort of understood. Kanon was the only one flirting; Isori, for his part, made it look like she was being a little unmanageable, so at least he wasn't beyond help.

Incidentally, Miyuki had remained at school. Kanon had a justifiable reason for coming—since she was Isori's escort—but Miyuki couldn't neglect her student council duties just because Tatsuya was stepping out for a bit. And she knew Kanon was going with them, so she was probably typing away in irritation right now.

"No, I'd feel bad leaving everything to you, Shiba. I want to check the samples anyway."

And the preestablished harmony was that the generally earnest Isori would reply that way.

Tatsuya wasn't about to send them away at this point anyway. It had almost been a complaint, so he didn't get into an argument with them. Things stopped with him shutting out a creepy, suppressed, mezzo-soprano giggle from his sense of hearing. Once he decided to ignore it, he wouldn't worry about it anymore. That was something he was glad he was able to do.

After another five minutes with their current pace, which kept slowing down, the three of them arrived at their destination. And there, too, Tatsuya finished his purchase right away, told Isori he would wait outside, and left the store.

As he finally got some alone time and was just feeling refreshed, he noticed a pair of eyes watching him. He didn't remember anyone tailing them. Even with the annoying, stereotypical (?) high school lovers' talk, he hadn't stopped paying attention to his surroundings.

Still, though, it was such an easy-to-detect stare that *anyone* would notice it, not just Tatsuya.

This store was on the shortest route to the station from school, basically right in front of the station. If you stuck around there, you could easily catch students on their way home. The person had probably been hiding out and waiting for him. They were physically hidden, but given how much hostility he still felt on him, the person clearly didn't have anything friendly or peaceable in mind. But they were being too artless and crude about it compared to, for example, the sniper who had shot Tatsuya the other day, for him to actually be on his guard against them.

Just as he was wondering what he should do, Isori and Kanon exited the store, having finished their shopping.

"Sorry for making you… What's the matter?" asked Isori immediately.

Tatsuya was astonished at his classmate's sensitivity; his own face was not that easy to read at the moment. To prove it, Kanon muttered "hmm?" in confusion.

Isori specialized in stationary magic like delayed activation spells and conditional-activation spells, but his power of observation was something else—maybe he was actually better suited to perception magic than functional magic.

"Nothing. I think we're being watched, that's all. I was just…" He didn't feel any real need to hide it, so he told Isori the truth. Unfortunately, he couldn't get to the end of his answer.

"What? Is it a spy?!"

Right before Tatsuya could finish and say, "wondering if I should do something," Kanon interrupted.

Loudly.

She'd basically just shouted to the scoundrel to run away, and as expected, he felt the gaze secretly watching him leave and the person's presence grow distant.

But Mari hadn't named Kanon her successor for nothing. She quickly asked, "Where?," watched where Tatsuya looked, and took off at a run without hesitation.

"Kanon, magic—"

"I know! Trust me, Kei!"

He'd probably tried to remind her *because* he didn't trust her, but Isori, who missed his chance to follow, and Tatsuya, who now had to temporarily serve as Kanon's substitute, could only watch her go.

Kanon was both a top-class magician of her generation and a sprinter in the track and field club. She obviously didn't have the leg power to compete evenly with top non-magician athletes, but an average high schooler, even a male one, wouldn't get the better of her very easily.

As she dashed, her skirt flapping in the wind, she soon caught sight of a small figure running away. And *she* was wearing the same uniform as Kanon.

Though it caught her by surprise, it was Kanon's motto not to worry about things and just do them. She had absolutely no proof this girl had been the one watching Tatsuya, but that didn't slow her pursuit. Kanon *felt* that it was her. She accelerated, trusting her gut.

She quickly closed the distance, and when she was just ten yards away, the girl looked back over her shoulder.

It was her actual face—no mask or sunglasses.

Kanon stared hard at the girl's head, burning her briefly visible profile into her memory.

Her limiting her focus on a single point, however, hadn't been anything the girl had plotted—just a coincidental gift. But regardless of her intent, it did create a hole in Kanon's alertness.

Kanon noticed the small capsule the girl had dropped behind her only after she had turned back away from her—and the fact that the capsule fell between them.

Crap, thought Kanon. She reflexively stopped and shut her eyes. She tried to cover her face with her arms, but unfortunately, she wasn't fast enough.

A brilliant light shone in through her upraised arms and stung her eyes through her eyelids. Several pedestrians who had been watching the chase scene in interest shrieked.

Leaving her left eye closed (the one she couldn't cover), she looked with her right, which had avoided harm.

The girl had gotten onto a motor scooter to flee.

Kanon's right hand flung over to her left arm. The bracelet that hung low on her wrist absorbed psionic particles, and it quickly expanded an activation sequence in accordance with the number Kanon typed in.

But before she could read it, it was destroyed by a psionic bullet that had gone around her body from behind.

"What are you doing?!"

"Kanon, don't!"

It happened at exactly the same time. It overlapped between them as she turned back around and Isori yelled, running over.

Tatsuya was standing still behind Isori, his handgun-shaped CAD raised. Isori came beside her as she stood frozen in surprise at her fiancé's reprimand. He was using his CAD as he ran, and had finished constructing a magic program. He aimed at the scooter, which had already taken off, and activated an emission-type spell called Road Extension.

The tires of the scooter, which had just begun to get away, began to spin fruitlessly.

No matter how much its motor spun, it didn't go forward. The road went on in a straight line, but she couldn't escape it. A labyrinth made of a single path.

The secret was to control the distribution of electrons between the tires' points of contact and the road to bias the Coulomb force toward repulsion, bringing their coefficient of friction close to zero. In words, that was all the spell did, but it was actually a dreadfully technical spell that required a complex magic program.

Thanks to a spell that amplified the compositely emitted gyroscopic force, the scooter couldn't fall to the side, either. Its tiny initial acceleration was eaten up by the electrostatic repulsion, bringing the girl's scooter to a standstill.

She could no longer get away.

Isori, Kanon, and even Tatsuya thought so. It was reasonable thinking, a natural judgment. Common sense dictated she couldn't get out of this situation.

But there was something they didn't know.

This girl was a complete amateur when it came to fighting.

And the more an amateur gets cornered, the more nonsensical their actions become. Desperation attempts, one might call them—but that desperation leads to escaping seemingly inescapable situations surprisingly often.

The girl pushed a button covered with plastic to the side of her left handlebar. Normal scooters didn't have a button there. To begin with, the covered button looked like it was used for an emergency bell. It was meant to be used a single time, and the button did, in fact, trigger a "disposable" gimmick that certainly seemed to be a onetime thing.

The back of the seat suddenly exploded.

Its cover flew off, and a double rocket engine within began spitting out flames.

The scooter immediately shot forward as though it was hit by something. The girl riding it was flung back, but she kept her hands tightly on the handles.

Tatsuya watched, speechless, as the girl and the scooter quickly grew smaller and smaller.

She hadn't let go of the handlebars because she was wearing gloves for that very purpose. *At least she thought that part through*, he thought.

But cramming a liquid-fuel rocket under the seat wasn't exactly what he'd call *sane*. Given the amount of fuel, estimated from the combustion duration, if worse came to worst and the scooter fell down and created sparks, she'd die in the explosion—and so would people walking nearby.

The fact that it even drove straight and stayed upright after being ignited by a rocket was a miracle. Normally, the sudden burst of acceleration would force person's hands off the handlebars and they would be thrown off. If Isori hadn't coincidentally applied that spell to amplify gyroscopic force, if the front wheel's coefficient of friction hadn't already been infinitely close to zero, that's exactly what would have happened.

If Kanon's spell had been the one to stop her instead of Isori's, the scooter surely would have toppled over and caused a horrible tragedy.

"What is that girl thinking…?"

"I guess this means we were all lucky…"

Tatsuya seemed to think the same thing as his two upperclassmen.

After abandoning the modded scooter, the girl rolled into a boxy automobile prepared by a collaborator, her shoulders heaving.

Right behind her were spouting flames. She hadn't imagined they'd be this terrifying. Hallucinations of her skirt, the back of her blazer, her hair, all burning, attacked her endlessly.

The station wagon's driver remained silent. He had no comforting words to give her.

That was reasonable; they weren't friends, just allies.

The girl hugged her shoulders. It was the only way she was able to endure. One girl, cowering motionlessly in a seat in a station wagon darkened by smoked glass.

Eventually, as her terror waned, the regret slowly rose, torturing her mind. She had reflexively fled when she was being chased, but now that she could think about it calmly, she didn't have to.

All she was doing was watching.

Her guilt was taking away her ability to think straight, and she knew that. The very fact that she felt guilt caused her an unbearable anger.

She knew she wasn't cut out for this sort of thing. Others knew her as an indoor type, and she'd never felt the need to change that. Because her dear older sister was the same way.

She looked up to her sister's talents in academics, but she wasn't as talented. Instead, she figured she would try to be an engineer and put her hobby of tinkering with machines to good use.

Then why am I going along with all these shady people? she asked herself.

The answer came back instantly, from inside her own mind.

She couldn't forgive him.

She didn't care about being rewarded for succeeding.

All she wanted was to see him mortified.

Suddenly, she chuckled. She just realized she'd gotten the better of him. There was no time to look out her rearview mirror, but surely he was watching in blank amazement as she made her clean getaway…

Her laugh was dark, masochistic, and tinged with madness. The more she laughed, the more it broke her.

Nobody in the station wagon, however, stopped her.

Inside an old building on the edge of Tokyo and Ikebukuro. From the outside, it looked like a general store management office. But in one room were tons of old computer monitors, tightly packed, with men staring fixedly at them, wearing whatever they pleased.

One of them, a middle-aged man, made a bitter face as he watched them—a screen monitoring the station wagon, showing a girl laughing maniacally inside.

"That girl—is this going to be all right?"

The man wasn't worried about her body or mind. The girl had bungled this; they were only worried someone might track them down because of it.

"That car's members were chosen by the great Zhou. No matter what happens, I don't believe anyone will learn of our presence here."

"The upstart mediator..." the man replied bitterly, imagining the person who had prepared this hideout for them. "How far can we really trust him?"

—He didn't like it, but trusting him was all they could do. That was unmistakably what was running through the man's mind.

"What about the Relic?" he said, suddenly changing the subject to get rid of the gloomy mood.

One of his subordinates at another monitor turned around and stood up. "There's no trace of anyone taking it out of Four Leaves Technology, but its current location is unknown."

"Hmph... Four Leaves, eh? Such an annoying name. No relation to *the* Yotsuba, right?"

"*Shì*. We investigated them but found no evidence of a connection. Besides, magic-related businesses in this country frequently use 'four leaves' and 'eight leaves' in their names."

"Blasted confusing," spat the man in distaste, animosity, and irritation. Even so, a tiny bit of awe came through.

Hachou, or "eight leaves," was favored as a name carrying two magical meanings: the four families and eight types of modern magic, and the Garbhadhatu Mandala, with the eight Buddhas at its center. However, *shiyou*, or "four leaves," was used in a more secular way. The name *Yotsuba* of the Ten Master Clans was a sort of taboo among those who had anything to do with magic. If a Japanese business had a name containing some reference to "four leaves," spy groups and criminal organizations would be wary of any possible connection to the Yotsuba family and hesitate significantly more before meddling. Taking the Yotsuba not saying anything on the topic as a good thing, many businesses used names meaning "four leaves" in an attempt to "borrow the influence of the tiger."

It was mere child's play, but its effectiveness couldn't be understated. They themselves were spending a lot of time and effort to be careful of the Yotsuba right now. The thought gave the man even more reason to look bitter.

"...Keep watching Sayuri Shiba. Did you learn anything from going to her house the other night?"

A different subordinate answered him this time. "It seems a pair of siblings, children of her husband's former wife, live there."

"Was she trying to curry favor with her stepson and stepdaughter?" he asked, his face implying that was absurd. He asked another question, this one businesslike. "What do we have on those two?"

"Both are freshmen enrolled at the National Magic University Affiliated First High School."

But that reply seemed to interest him. "Their names?"

"The older brother is Tatsuya Shiba, and the younger sister is Miyuki Shiba."

"Tatsuya Shiba?" The name sounded familiar to him. He called the man watching the monitor on the station wagon.

"He is the revenge target of our on-site collaborators."

"I see. A Magic University–affiliated high school... This might work out well for us." The man let a chuckle slip, then looked like he was thinking for a couple of seconds, staring into empty air. Abruptly, he gave a new order: "Add activity targets to National Magic University Affiliated First High School. Get people from other jobs if you need to. And bolster our support of the girl. *Teach her* that the most effective way to get her revenge is to leak confidential information. And *give the girl a weapon as well.*"

After this string of orders, he finally turned to a young man with a large build. "Superior Lieutenant Lu."

"*Shì.*"

"Take on-site command. If you find any stray dogs sniffing around, get rid of them," he commanded before leaving the room.

Today was the day to submit the thesis, the presentation draft, and the presentation data to the school—but neither Suzune, Isori, nor Tatsuya liked procrastinating, so they'd already loaded the memory media for the submission the night before.

The reason they were still all here during lunch break was to go over things one last time. Not the contents, but just double-checking all the submission standards. After they split up and checked separate parts, Suzune would follow Haruka's advice and give it to Tsuzura personally.

Once Isori finished doing his part of the work, he said, "I wonder if Ms. Ono said not to send it online because of what happened yesterday."

"That could be," acknowledged Tatsuya—who had already finished his work (he had the least, since he was a freshman)—quietly, so as not to disturb Suzune.

"After all, the easiest way to sneak into the school network is from inside the school."

"Though it still wouldn't be easy," pointed out Tatsuya.

Isori shrugged as—with a few old-fashioned clacking keystrokes to the sound of the classic, mechanical keyboard Suzune used—she turned around.

"Was it really a student from here?" said Suzune, adding to the conversation as she finished her check and collected the submission.

"All we can say is *probably*," said Tatsuya.

"You could get a school uniform if you really tried, I suppose," added Isori.

Suzune thought for a moment. "...You and Chiyoda can look at the student register, right?"

With Isori a student council member and Kanon the disciplinary committee chairwoman, both had the authority to view the student record database. The school blocked any intrusive information that had to do with student privacy, of course, but they could still check portraits and full-body shots.

"Kanon is the only one who saw her face..." said Isori. "All she got was a glimpse, so she couldn't make a composite photograph. There are almost three hundred female students here... If we can't narrow that down to a certain extent, we can't figure out who it was."

Isori wasn't speaking of possibilities. Kanon had actually tried this morning before eventually throwing in the towel.

"Besides, essentially all she did yesterday was run away because we chased her," explained Tatsuya. "Even if we knew who she was, all we could do is keep an eye on her. And even that might make trouble."

Suzune and Isori both knew that. The student hadn't done anything wrong—though using a flash bang to get away wasn't completely without its issues—so if they started watching her, they could end up being the stalkers.

At this stage, all they could do was take a passive, cautious position.

Once he returned to the classroom, Tatsuya found Erika in his seat.

She was the first one to notice him. "Oh, you're early today," she said, standing up right away. Staying there would have been a shameless act, so a moment after he sat down, she sat on the edge of his desk instead.

He wasn't sure if it was a plus or a minus.

Still, as Erika said, there was a little bit of time left in today's break. Instead of going onto his terminal right away, he turned to Mizuki, specifically because she seemed anxious, and asked, "What were you talking about?"

Erika, however, was the one to answer him. "She says she feels someone watching."

"Watching?" he repeated to Mizuki.

Mizuki nodded hesitantly. "Ever since this morning, I've been feeling unpleasant, like someone is watching me. Something strange, gazing at me from the shadows..."

"Like a stalker or something?" he guessed, that being the most natural example.

"What? Nobody would ever stalk me," said Mizuki, shaking her head as though the notion were nonsense. "It wasn't looking at me in particular—it was more like it had this big net ready..."

Her choice of words was vague. Was it the anxiety getting to her? Either way, Tatsuya could decipher exactly what she hadn't said: "The eyes were targeting not a single student, but more than one, or maybe teachers, or some kind of object in the school?"

"Y-yes...it might...just be my imagination, though." The lack of confidence in her attitude was partly due to her personality, but she also had no proof, so there was nothing that could be done about that.

"No, I don't think it was your imagination, Shibata," said Mikihiko as he walked over, filled with enough confidence to make up for Mizuki's lack. "The spirits in the school have been noisy since this morning. Someone's performing an onmyoudou ritual."

Since Erika was sitting on Tatsuya's desk, Leo had been sitting facing forward instead of backward like he usually was, but he turned around at Mikihiko's words. "You talking about spiritual beings? Like *shikigami*?"

Mikihiko nodded. "I can't quite get a read on it, since it's different from the techniques we use. But there's definitely a caster somewhere searching for something."

"But that's not unusual, is it?" asked Erika.

She had a point, too. This was only a high school, but it had access terminals to Magic University, numerous precious books and documents, and many talented magicians teaching classes. They were constantly targeted by people after magic technology.

"Usually, once they get stopped by the defensive spell along the outer walls, they don't try to poke their noses in for the rest of the day," said Mikihiko, refuting her claim gently, which made his voice sound more confident. "But today they seem to be trying again and again, no matter how many times the barrier blocks them. Someone probing us isn't unusual, but I know I haven't seen anything this persistent since I started school."

"...Mikihiko, you said it was a different technique than yours, right?" said Tatsuya.

"Yes, why?" he asked, face tensing, a serious concern in his voice.

"Do you mean it wasn't a Shinto technique? Or a different kind from Japan's old magic?"

Presented again with such casual words on such a heavy topic, Mikihiko's face tightened. "...I don't think it's a Japanese technique."

"Huh?" prodded Leo, eyes wide. "Does that mean it's a foreign spy or something?"

"I guess so, huh?" added Erika nonchalantly. Their words contrasted, but it didn't seem like there was much difference in what they were thinking.

"They're being rather bold," muttered Tatsuya.

"They're doing all they want. What are our police for, anyway?" This time, Erika went after the police. But the way she said this made it seem she was less angry over public authority negligence and more irritated at a relative's lack of difference.

Meanwhile, Tatsuya and Mikihiko both thought, *Huh?*

◇ ◇ ◇

At around the same time, Chief Inspector Chiba from the Kanagawa Police—more accurately, temporarily assigned to the Kanagawa Police by the Ministry of Police—would have sneezed up a storm, except for the fact that it would have been cliché.

"...What's wrong, Chief? You're getting all googly-eyed."

Inspector Inagaki, who was poking around the areas near the Yokohama Wharf where the illegal entry occurred, eyed his superior's actions dubiously.

"Err, I just felt a chill all of a sudden..."

"Are you all right? Don't start feigning an illness. We're too busy for that."

"Err, feign an illness? That's, uh..." There was a hint of criticism in Chiba's voice as well, but Inagaki had been kidding and wasn't at all bothered. "...Inagaki, I think you need to pay more attention to the whole 'rank' thing."

Inagaki gave him a cold look. The words *You're one to talk* were written all over his face, but he eventually said, "Anyway, are we finished asking questions? I don't think walking around is going to get us any more witnesses."

He was right. They'd been investigating the area for days, but they hadn't gotten any proof at all regarding the illegal entrants. Chiba gave a cynical smile to his more-partner-than-subordinate. "They're here," he said. "They just don't want to talk."

"Chief, you don't mean...?" The man's lack of concern smelled like fire to Inagaki, who narrowed his eyes sharply.

"Hey, now. You're scaring me."

"You're the scary one, Chief. What are you going to do?"

"Don't worry, no unlawful investigation here. But you know what they say—you have to set a thief to catch a thief. I was just thinking of asking around the thieves' den."

After hearing Chiba's plan, Inagaki's face soured. "...Backstage deals are unlawful investigations, too, you know."

"I think we can allow it here. We don't have the luxury of saying things like that anymore."

"Well...I guess so." Inagaki nodded bitterly.

Without giving more time to argue, Chiba got into their undercover police car that they had suitably left in a paid parking zone. After seeing his partner get into the passenger's seat, he started off toward a high-class residential area that housed a large concentration of foreigners.

◇ ◇ ◇

The undercover patrol car with Chief Inspector Chiba and Inspector Inagaki in it eventually arrived at a café parking lot in the middle of Yokohama's Yamate Bluff. After Chiba stopped the engine, Inagaki gave him a bitter look.

"Chief...breaks are good every once in a while, but weren't we going to this 'den of thieves' you mentioned?" said the subordinate, looking at Chiba as if to wonder why he was suddenly slacking off.

Chiba looked back and pretended to be offended. "This *is* the thieves' den."

"What?"

But his superior left the car. Inagaki went after him, walking up as Chiba locked the door with a remote control, and looked toward the café again.

It appeared to be a calm place, completely normal. It had a cabin-like design, and its windows had double slatted shutters—but they were all open. Nothing about it seemed "secret" in the slightest.

"Well, calling the bartender a *thief* would be rude," said Chiba. "The bartender here has an amazing information network—and no criminal record, either."

"...You mean they're a big-shot? One we can't get anything on?"

"Less a big-shot and more an *artisan*." Chief Inspector Chiba gave a slight shrug and opened the door, on which the words *Roter Wald* were written.

It was already past lunchtime on a weekday, but the place was in a popular sightseeing spot, so there were quite a few patrons.

It wasn't lively, however.

Whether it was because of the store's atmosphere or the bartender's personality, the patrons were all drinking from their cups quietly. The average age of the people there was high. Perhaps the idea of lots of tourists was a misconception—maybe the establishment had a lot of regulars.

Chiba sat down on the second bar seat from the end (Inagaki took the first), waited for the bartender to turn to them, then ordered two coffee blends.

The bartender here had the spirit of a craftsman. He'd never cut corners on visible jobs or invisible ones, and Chiba knew that well. He also knew he couldn't make any conversation until the coffee came out. As he waited idly, he casually looked around the store.

Next to them on the bar was a half-empty coffee cup. The bartender hadn't taken it back yet, so the person whose drink it was must have only been away temporarily. *Such great coffee, letting it go to waste if it gets cold*, Chiba thought idly. But the person sitting two seats over was only gone for a few moments, and soon came back while the chief was watching the cup.

The one who sat down was a young woman the about same age as him.

He turned back and sized her up out of the corner of his eye. At a glance, she wasn't what many would call a "beauty." Her clothing was average—a blouse and a skirt. But looking closer revealed good-looking features and a nice figure. It felt to Chiba that she was purposely wearing makeup that made her look plain.

After observing her that much, Chiba silently returned his gaze forward.

He mustn't be scolded as incompetent.

The simple fact that he was trying not to stand out meant he couldn't do any police questioning, either. And he realized what he was trying to do basically amounted to hitting on her.

Inagaki gave him a dubious, painful stare. The bartender, as silent as his sullen exterior would imply, poured their coffee without a word.

Chiba simply waited for his drink to come out.

Suddenly, he heard a low giggle. Moving only his eyes, he looked to see, as he had expected, that the woman was looking down, her shoulders moving.

"...I'm sorry. I thought you'd talk to me at some point, but you just kept staring right in front of you. Are you bad with women, noble son of the Chiba?"

Chief Inspector Chiba was dumbfounded. But not because he was surprised she'd guessed his identity right.

It wasn't a secret he was the eldest child of the Chiba clan. But neither had he been aggressively putting his face in public. His younger brother was more recognizable, wasn't he? The only ones who could tell that he was Toshikazu Chiba by looking at him were criminals, those in the police force, or people in very specific circles.

Namely those who lived in the world of combat magic.

"And you are...?"

"Pleased to meet you, Chief Toshikazu Chiba. My name is Kyouko Fujibayashi."

This time, Chiba was dumbfounded out of pure surprise.

Daughter of the Fujibayashi family, distinguished for its old magic...and the granddaughter of Retsu Kudou, elder in Japan's magic world. And here she was, giving him a worry-free smile.

Their group of eight hadn't stepped out of the school gate together in a while.

"Tatsuya, are you done with your Thesis-Comp preparations?"

Though it had been a while for all eight of them, Honoka left school with Miyuki every day because of student council work—meaning she took this route home with Tatsuya every day as well. But for some reason, this was the first thing she asked today.

"For now, I guess," he said. "The small things are still left, like rehearsals, making the models for the presentation, tuning spells for the demonstration—things like that."

"Sounds like a lot of work…" said Erika. "Oh, Mizuki, I heard you guys are helping make the models." Erika was neither a member of the student council nor in a position on the club committee, but she seemed oddly informed. She peered at Mizuki, who had her hair in a ponytail today.

"Oh, yes, the juniors are," said Mizuki. "I'm not doing anything, though…"

"We left all the model-making to Isori, so naturally the juniors would be the center of it," added Tatsuya.

"Huh…? Then what are you doing, Tatsuya?" asked Leo, a question that could be considered part of the natural flow of the conversation.

"I'm adjusting the demonstration spells."

"…I feel like that's backward," said Shizuku, saying what was on everyone's mind.

"Really?" asked Tatsuya, tilting his head in confusion. "When it comes to making things, I think Isori is several levels better than me."

"Well…Kei does seem more like an 'alchemist' than a 'mage,'" agreed Erika with a wry grin. "Maybe he's the right person for the job."

"Alchemist? Like in RPGs?" asked Shizuku, puzzled.

"What would that make Tatsuya?" pondered Mizuki, her comment suddenly…

"A mad scientist, of course!" (Erika) "Those aren't in RPGs." (Shizuku) "Then maybe a hermit sage far away in the mountains that teaches you secret moves." (Erika) "He'd be a pretty good physical fighter for a sage." (Leo) "Maybe an evil magician secretly plotting to take over the world?" (Erika) "Why not just call him a demon king, then?" (Mikihiko) "Nah, he'd be like the last boss after you beat the demon king. The one who comes out and says he was totally the mastermind behind everything." (Leo) "Why isn't anyone suggesting he'd be a hero type?" (Honoka) "It's fine, Honoka. I wouldn't make a good disciple of justice." (Tatsuya) "Might makes right, Tatsuya." (Miyuki) "Wow. Straight from the mouth of the demon king's little sister." (Erika)

...leading to a lively conversation.

Even as they walked down the road making noise and having fun like other students did, Tatsuya never forgot to keep an eye out. When they came to the entrance to the road leading to the café they frequented, he turned around, careful not to look at the one he sensed tailing them.

"Want to stop by for a bit?" suggested Tatsuya, deciding to wait their shadow out with a detour.

"I'm in!"

"You'll probably be busy again tomorrow, after all."

"Yeah, let's go get tea for a little while."

Erika, Leo, and Mikihiko all agreed, each seeming a little *too* assertive—but the three of them probably had their own things to think about. Without mentioning how unnatural it was, Tatsuya opened the door to Café Einebrise.

Unfortunately, their usual two side-by-side tables with four seats each weren't open, so the eight of them split up between the bar and the closest table. At the bar were Tatsuya, Miyuki, Honoka, and Mizuki. (In order of seating, it was Mizuki, Miyuki, Tatsuya, Honoka.) At the table were Erika and Shizuku near the bar, and Leo and Mikihiko facing them.

...From an outsider's point of view, it would have looked like

Tatsuya was being waited on by several beautiful girls in some kind of jealousy-inducing harem.

"Hey, welcome. You sure are a go-getter, aren't you, Tatsuya?"

Actually, not only outsiders; even the manager, who knew enough about their relationships, still came at him with sarcasm from over the bar.

"I'm sure you'd be a *go-getter*, too, if you shaved your beard," countered Tatsuya, purposely using the dead (?) term back at him.

"He's right," followed up Mizuki in her usual breezy (?) lack of reserve. "The beard isn't doing you any favors. It makes you look old."

"O-old…? No mercy today, Mizuki?" groaned the manager, stroking his gray beard—not a messy one, for he took good care of it. It was gray, but it didn't age the man as much as she said. In fact, he looked young. He could have been thirty, or even a little younger.

Gray hair, both on the head and face, was a genetic predisposition. The manager was one-quarter North German. (The shop's name meant "gentle breeze" in German, too, and it had been Leo feeling an affinity for it that led to everyone else frequenting it.)

Still, the only characteristic his ethnicity gave him was his hair color; his eyes were dark, and his visage was slender and Asian. He was a man of delicate, handsome features yet seemed to have some kind of complex about his face. He always kept his mustache and beard neat in an attempt to look manly—and it worked.

The group's consensus was that the beard didn't suit him, but the taste of his coffee made up for that and more. All eight of them naturally ordered it.

"Wow, you're going to be in the Magic Thesis Competition?" said the manager as he boiled water in the coffeemaker siphon and after hearing why he hadn't seen them in a while. "And you're only a freshman. That's amazing, isn't it?"

That wasn't entirely flattery. The manager had no talent for magic himself, but he did run a shop on the way to a magic high school, so he knew quite a bit about the world magicians lived in. Even Tatsuya often heard recent news from him that he hadn't known about during the spare moments in which they had conversations.

"This year it's Yokohama's turn to host, right? My family lives there. Is it at the international assembly hall like it usually is? That's right next to my old house."

The manager continued to talk, even while pouring their coffee, which had accumulated in the flask.

"Where in Yokohama is it?" asked Mizuki as she took a tray of four coffees from the manager, having stood up to carry it to the table in the waitress's stead.

"It's a café named Roter Wald, midway across Yamate Bluff."

"Your parents run a café, too?"

"Yeah. If you have time, give them a visit. Taste my father's coffee and decide which one of ours is better. And don't hold back—let me know!"

"Nice try, Mr. Salesman," broke in Shizuku, who was bringing the tray back for Mizuki, causing laughs on both sides of the bar.

When Tatsuya was down to a third of his coffee, Erika downed the rest of her drink, returned the cup quietly to the coaster, and smoothly rose. When she did things like that, it couldn't hide her upbringing.

"Erika?" asked Mizuki, looking up.

"I'm going to pick some flowers," she replied, casually striding farther into the store.

"Oh," said Leo a moment later, putting a hand on his pocket and getting up. "Sorry, got a call." He walked out front.

Tatsuya moved his eyes away from Leo's surprisingly polite act and looked at Mikihiko. He had a notebook (a small sketchbook, actually) open in his hands. "...Mikihiko, what are you doing?"

"Oh, well, I figured I should take a few notes so I don't forget..." he said, not stopping his calligraphy pen to talk.

"Don't go overboard; they'll find us out," said Tatsuya, narrowing his eyes at him. "Keep it simple." He looked behind Mikihiko—not at his hands—then brought his cup to his lips, back to the bar, like nothing was wrong.

"Hey, mister, you want to have a little fun with me?"

Few people used this side street, but the sun hadn't even set yet. When the man heard that, he nearly dropped his take-out drink. He turned around to see a girl in a ponytail, one whom he wouldn't have hesitated or been underhanded to describe as pretty, at the entrance to the little road. The alley led to the back door of the café he'd been watching, and she stood within it, her hands behind her back and a smile on her face.

But as soon as he saw her, he grew impatient for a different reason. "What are you saying?" he said. "You should treat yourself better than that."

"Huh? All I said was 'a little fun.' I wonder what you thought I meant..." The girl quirked her head to the side, her smile guilt-free.

He knew it—she was with the man he'd been tracking. "It's not nice to tease adults. Go back home, will you? And don't take any detours." He couldn't stop from mentally breaking out in a cold sweat, but he put his professional face on and continued to play the adult walking away after a child's prank upset him. "It'll get dark soon. There's no guarantee you won't be attacked by someone if you stay in a deserted road like this," he finished, turning his back to the girl.

But he couldn't take the next step.

"...Attacked—like by this guy, maybe?"

When he turned around, he found a well-built boy who had left the café, pounding his black glove–covered fists together, grinning.

"When you say 'attacked,' I assume you meant magically."

Sensing danger behind the amused response, the man turned around again. The girl was in a combat stance now, holding a retractable police baton. Casually, she thrust out that hand.

In that moment, he felt an irresistible pressure coming from her. The kind where if he lost concentration even for a second, his knees would shake and he'd collapse…and he knew what this pressure was called.

The will to fight.

Not the will to *kill* someone, though—pure waves of simple fighting spirit.

"Scary… You're really something when it comes to this stuff," said the voice from behind him. He couldn't be sure, since he couldn't look over his shoulder, but he knew the boy there was baring his teeth and grinning.

"Help me, somebody! I'm being robbed!" shouted the man, deciding that if he wasn't going to be able to flee, it didn't matter how his backup plan made him look.

He was just as confident in his own strength. No matter how dexterous they might have been, he wouldn't go down without a fight against a couple of fifteen- or sixteen-year-olds. Unfortunately, his current mission was the sort where he had to avoid any risks; having them turn hostile was bad for the plan.

"Whoa. No shame…"

"No, no. He was really quick to make that choice. I think that's good, don't you?"

The girl and the boy seemed subdued by his chosen method. Still, the girl kept her baton up, and the boy straightened and held up his fists.

…And nobody came to answer his cry for help.

"Oh, forgot to say…" said the boy. "It's no use calling for help. Nobody's gonna get close right now."

"They *can't* get close," said the girl. "We put up a barrier using our awareness as the pivot—and you can't get out of it without knocking us out, either."

The man realized he hadn't seen any other pedestrians for some time.

And he was made to realize another fact:

Only one option remained.

Belatedly, he tossed his drink cup aside and assumed an upright posture. Leaving his thin jacket on, he brought his arms up high, as if to guard his head—then wheeled around to Leo, bending his left arm out to a right angle and bringing it down to his stomach.

"Huh… The Hitman style from boxing, eh? Thought you'd at least have a weapon."

"Just because he didn't take one out doesn't mean he doesn't have one, stupid," advised Erika, not wasting a moment, causing the man to tsk.

But he didn't show any more impatience. He didn't have time.

The middle-aged man who had given the pitiful shriek was now fighting intensely, and he quickly closed in on Leo. From his low position, the man bent his arm and flicked it at Leo like a whip. Bullet-like punches flew at the boy; the smooth, continuous string of attacks spoke volumes—this man was a wolf, not a sheep.

But neither Leo nor Erika felt surprise. Erika had gained powerful insight through training, and Leo had the instincts he'd been born with. They'd already figured out the man was really a wolf—or rather, a highly trained hunting dog.

What was really admirable was his speed. His power. And above all, how he displayed swiftness beyond physical boundaries yet showed no magical aftereffects whatsoever.

He threw dozens of punches in less than ten seconds, rattling the two guarding arms without giving time for counterattack.

And when they finally broke through Leo's guard, one punch hit him in the face.

With a *pop* like a balloon, Leo careened backward.

Not sparing the time to watch his achievement, the man pivoted on his heel. By the time he'd turned around, he'd already hurled a throwing dagger at Erika, using the force of his spin.

There was a dry, metallic *clack*.

Erika had knocked the dagger away with her baton. As her weapon moved from inside to outside, it created a hole in her defense. The man immediately reached out for a left straight at her face…

…before dodging the baton as it flew back faster than his fist. He pulled back, but not his fist—instead, he pulled his whole body back in a leap. But a moment later…

"Gah!"

…he took a shoulder tackle counterattack to the back and crashed face-first into the road.

"…Wow, that stings. This guy's no ordinary human. Didn't feel like a machine, either, so…chemical enhancement?" muttered Leo, who had performed the tackle from behind, rubbing his punched jaw and looking to the road with a merciless stare.

"…Yeah, well, you're weird, too. That punch hit you square in the face, didn't it?" answered Erika, more cautious about the man groaning and trying to get himself off the ground then her ally, Leo.

"Well, about a quarter of that is because I'm a magician with roots in a research lab. Not gonna lie and say my genes are a hundred percent natural," said Leo with a painful grin to Erika's sharp gaze, cruelly kicking the crawling man in the gut.

"Gurgh!"

"Behave. We're not gonna take your life. We just want to know why you've been tailing us," said Leo as he lifted one leg from the road. Erika, in the corner of his eye, looked exasperated at the somewhat indecent violence.

But the question had been clear. "…Wait… All right, I surrender… I'm not…your en'my an'way… Stomping at me for this…'s a little much…"

"Yeah, right. If you'd punched someone else, they'd have died, you know."

"That goes…for you, too…" As the man coughed between words, he got up. "If my body wasn't enhanced, that kick would have crushed an organ or two."

The man's talking became more fluid, as though the pain had waned, though he was still sitting on the road.

"If I didn't think you were enhanced, I wouldn't have done it." Leo's words weren't repentant in the slightest. "And if you're not our enemy, then give us the short version. We can't exactly leave the barrier up forever."

"Fine. I'd rather not draw attention, either." The man heaved a resigned sigh.

"Then why not introduce yourself first? I'm sure you know our names already."

"Jirou Marshal." The man didn't give Leo a yes or no, instead replying with a name that could have been real or fake. "I can't go into too much detail about who I am, but I'm not with any government agency, domestic or foreign. And, as I already stated, I'm not an enemy of yours."

"Which means you're an unlawful agent."

Once again, the man didn't say yes or no to Erika's conclusion.

"...And?" prompted Leo, rankled. "You won't give us the truth if we asked who you are and where you're from anyway, so tell us what you're after, and what the situation is."

"My job is to keep watch over magic high school students to make sure cutting-edge magic technology isn't stolen by the East, and if any high tech that could be a military threat to the East *is* leaked, to deal with it," explained the man who called himself Jirou in a businesslike tone.

The *East* was a term used two World Wars ago, and Leo and Erika knew that USNA intelligence and military operatives alike used it often, even today. But that didn't prove right away that this man was related to the USNA. He could have been purposely using local terms to mislead them about his origin.

"I bet your employer, at least, isn't related to Japan. Otherwise, why on earth would you be going through all this?" demanded Leo.

The man shook his head and sighed. "I knew Japan's peacetime complacency was fixed, but to hear even *teenagers* asking that..." he said. "The world's military balance isn't just a problem of one country. If Japan's practical technology finds itself in the East, it could damage the West's advantage. Both the Federal Soviet Republics, which has placed importance on improving magic programs themselves, and the Great Asian Alliance, which is diverting its resources toward reviving magic of previous generations over modern magic development, are very quickly starting to use Japan's electronics-based magic engineering technology for military applications. It's not just Japan, though—the USNA and various western European nations are both experiencing an increase in spies targeting magic engineering tech. Your school is one of the East's targets, too."

"Peacetime complacency? How many decades ago is this? We know there're voyeurs hanging around. We didn't let our guard down. We noticed you tailing us, didn't we?" spat Erika, unappreciative of the man's superior tone.

"I'm not a spy—I'm here to stop them," the man said. "I'm not your enemy, and we have no conflict of interest between us." He stood up from the road and made a show of dusting himself off.

He bent down to neaten the hems of his pant legs so politely it seemed sarcastic (and it probably was about 30 percent sarcastic) and then straightened back up—with a small pistol, small enough to hide in his palm, in his hand, its muzzle pointed directly at Erika.

"!"

"What is *this*?!" shouted Leo.

"I didn't use this before, but it's proof I'm not an enemy."

"...No, you just *couldn't* use it. It would have left too much evidence," retorted Erika.

The man grinned. "That, too. Anyway, I believe I've said what I needed to. I'd like to clear out of here, so could you tell your friend to undo the barrier?"

His words and attitude were light, but his stance had no openings. Erika and Leo didn't have a death wish—this wasn't an adventure they wanted to go on.

Modern magic had acquired speed rivaling firearms through the advancement of CADs. That, however, didn't mean they were faster. Not even necessarily *as* fast. A gun only needed a trigger to fire a bullet and bore out a person's flesh; modern magic needed a process—reading in an activation sequence and constructing a magic program. Magic had a higher degree of freedom than guns, superior power, and the ability to create a field to block bullets; it could make up for the speed gap to a certain extent. That was all. If a single shot could take a life, or put them out of combat, that "extent" in the speed gap was a decisive factor in determining victory. This was one of those times.

While Erika and Leo stood silently, Mikihiko, who must have been watching them with a spell, released the barrier he'd put up.

"...Then allow me to take my leave," the man said. "Oh, right, one more thing: some advice. Tell your friends to look after themselves. And not to relax even when they're at school." Finishing, the man brought a small canister out of his jacket.

He pushed a button on the lid, then tossed it right in the middle of the triangle the three of them made.

Erika and Leo both jumped back.

With a soft burst, a thick, white mist exploded around them. They closed their eyes, but, realizing that the mist didn't seem to be poison, opened them again.

But by that time, there wasn't a trace of the man who called himself Jirou Marshal.

In café Roter Wald in Yamate, Yokohama, Chief Inspector Chiba and Fujibayashi were enjoying light conversation. Having taken a liking to him, though he didn't know why, Fujibayashi was talking to him incessantly, so Chiba hadn't even broached the topic of what he'd actually come here for with the bartender. She was a skilled talker, and Chiba was enjoying the conversation as much as she seemed to be. Of course, his partner Inagaki didn't share this opinion.

Chiba had nearly forgotten about his original goal behind coming here, when an effervescent tone rang in Fujibayashi's hands. It wasn't loud enough to bother the other patrons, but Chiba could still hear it from the next seat over.

Fujibayashi took her information terminal from her purse and glanced at the message. A moment later, she returned it and gave Chiba a pleasant smile. Whenever she made an expression like that, it showed how pretty she was.

Despite his age, Chiba's heartbeat increased.

"I'm sorry, Chief. I need to step away for a moment."

Fujibayashi hadn't looked at him suggestively or made any meaningful gestures—but Chiba still realized, without a reason, that the message had to do with her *job.*

"...Yes, please do."

She rose, bowed to him, handed a credit card to the bartender, and headed out to her electric coupe in the parking lot.

After climbing into the driver's seat, Fujibayashi reached out and switched her control panel screen to information terminal mode.

Self-driving cars that used a palm-rest controller had no steering wheel. The controller served as an accelerator, a brake, a gearshift, and a steering wheel all in one, so that was only natural. The palm-rest type of controller was meant to bring out a more instinctual way of driving, but as a side effect of the vision-blocking steering wheel being absent, the entire dashboard in front of the driver ended up being one big control panel (a multipurpose display with both a console and an instrument panel). Depending on how you customized it, you could bring functionality and ease of use rivaling that of a home-use terminal into the car with you.

And as for Fujibayashi's car, it had gone a step further—several steps, in fact, having all the functions of an actual information terminal in it. Enough to let the small coupe have processing power on the level of a battle command vehicle. Its communication functions were made to match, with high-sensitivity and high-output items on board. Add Fujibayashi's own magic expertise to the mix and the car could exhibit enough electronic warfare capabilities to be called, without exaggeration, an electronic warfare vehicle.

"Tatsuya's friends are quite the handful, too."

That wasn't her unconsciously talking to herself—those words were purposeful so that she could align a spell. Using the connection called Tatsuya as a guidepost, she overlaid the Idea information network with her electronic one.

"Mikihiko Yoshida. Former wonder child of the Yoshida… The child seems to be an adult now, but it would be nice if he paid a little more attention to the fact that he's in a city."

Names symbolized entities. Speaking names was a means of identifying them. With the name of someone familiar—that is, to whom one's mental distance is short—as a reference point, she began to align her focus on the target using magic by saying aloud a proper noun, as well as the target's actions and status.

"But even old magic gets recorded by the surveillance systems."

Compared to modern magic, old magic—especially spirit magic, or magic of the type called SB magic—was said to be difficult for roadside surveillance cameras to capture. However, that wasn't due to how hard it was to capture the magic itself but the difficulty in identifying who used it. The usage was always recorded, and Fujibayashi had been given the very urgent mission of falsifying those records.

Hushing up unlawful magic usage wasn't her job, but she knew they didn't want any unnecessary attention paid to Tatsuya or those around him. The more people related to him, the higher the possibility of them alerting her actual prey and causing them to stay away. In other words, Kazama and the others were using Tatsuya as bait…

…but that's not enough to bother you, right?

That was all she said to herself before activating the rare skill possessed by the Electron Sorceress.

Jirou Marshal, unlawful operative from a certain country, utilized his enhanced leg strength to run about one train station away, then came to a halt. He'd been going as fast as a racehorse, so fast he ran the risk of standing out. But he hadn't stopped just now because he'd decided he'd reached safety.

Just the opposite, in fact.

His running speed wasn't something a normal human could match, no matter how much training they did. Yet something had been sticking right on his tail the whole time. He hadn't seen what—or who—it was yet. Still, Jirou Marshal had no doubt that the "thing" following him was a person.

He knew without checking that it wasn't the pair from earlier. He wasn't senile; he would notice if the people he'd directly confronted had come after him. And being a solo operative, as usual, he didn't have a team with him. If they'd dispatched him some unplanned backup, their first priority would be to notify him so that there wouldn't be any friendly fire incidents. But he hadn't received any such communications since starting his current job.

...Where?

Marshal looked down slightly and focused his senses, listening. He knew from experience that when people sensed the presence of another person, it was more than likely due to the solidity of sound. The one tailing—no, chasing—him would never show him or herself visibly. He decided the person must be hiding somewhere he couldn't see, watching.

But his prediction was wrong.

Suddenly, he felt a presence that made him shudder, and looked up.

In front of him stood a man, *not making a sound.*

In hindsight, he'd blocked off the sounds coming from ahead of

him. Something other than his five senses had alerted his body to the danger.

The man was Asian, with a toned figure. He wore gray exercise pants and a gray jacket, with a blackish tracksuit underneath, all quite plain. His face wasn't especially handsome but not especially ugly, either. Without a doubt, he looked like a person you could find anywhere—but he caused Marshal to feel like he was staring down a wild beast that devoured humans.

Marshal knew the man's face. "The Man-Eating Tiger..."

Not that he'd met the man in the past. This was the first time he'd seen him in real life.

"Ganghu Lu..."

The one whose name he'd just unconsciously muttered was someone at the top of the "Take Caution Around These People" file he'd been given at the beginning of the operation. Rumored to be the leader in the Great Asian Alliance when it came to killing in hand-to-hand combat, the ace of the GAA Army's Special Covert Forces...

By the time he recognized that, there was already a gun in Marshal's right hand, pointed at Ganghu Lu. His body, which had gone through countless hours of repetition training, had selected an action quicker and more precisely than he could think about it.

However, his finger couldn't pull the trigger.

Before he could squeeze it, Ganghu Lu's fingers were stuck in Marshal's neck.

The man's thumb penetrated his throat, and the gun fell from his hands.

Marshal watched the scene in a daze. When had his neck been pierced? No, before that—when did he get in this close? He hadn't seen any of Ganghu Lu's movements.

Before the pain, which had been overwritten with surprise, reached Marshal's brain...

...his mind was painted over in eternal darkness.

* * *

Ganghu Lu slid his right hand out of the throat it was buried in.

His fingers were stained red, and yet there was surprisingly little blood loss.

Using his clean left hand, he removed a folded piece of paper from his inside pocket and neatly wiped down his right hand. After absorbing Marshal's blood into the paper, Ganghu Lu threw it onto the corpse. As it fell, it unfolded into the size of a handkerchief, then stuck to Marshal's body.

Then, the bloodstained paper erupted with a flame redder than fresh blood. The flame spurted to life in the middle of the paper, then became a ring and expanded.

Inside the ring was nothing. No cinders, none of the corpse's clothing the paper had covered; none of the flesh, nor its bones. As the paper burned away, the flame began to spread over the dead man.

Then, the ring of fire *began to devour the corpse*.

Ganghu Lu watched as the flames eventually vanished and the corpse disappeared, then turned on his heel.

Not a single person was anywhere nearby. No voices, no footsteps, nothing to indicate the presence of a human anywhere.

The only witnesses were the thoroughly destroyed roadside cameras.

In the cafeteria, where they had all met up, Miyuki was surprised by Erika's sour expression.

"Erika, is what happened yesterday still bothering you?"

Right up until they'd parted at the station, Erika had been severely frustrated at how they'd been outsmarted at the very end by what appeared to be an unlawful operative from the USNA intelligence department. She didn't speak of it, but her attitude made it evident. For someone who usually hid her true feelings behind a mischievous smile, her demeanor had been very frank, but seeing it prolonged into the next day was even more unusual.

Erika's answer was half yes, half no. "Oh, him getting away with it isn't bothering me."

Her using the expression "getting away with it" made it obvious that she wasn't being honest about how she actually felt, but as she implied, that didn't seem to be the only thing.

"What he said bothers me..." she admitted. "We can't be safe even if we're in school? Are the students in danger...?"

It didn't seem like Mikihiko, Honoka, and Shizuku understood, having been removed from what happened in April, but Tatsuya and Miyuki guessed right away what was nagging at Erika.

During that incident, Sayaka had been used by a foreign operative wearing the mask of a terrorist. She still hadn't completely gotten over that yet.

"Well, I want to pass on a repeat of something with such a bad aftertaste as much as you do," offered Tatsuya, who knew and understood, in consideration for Erika's feelings. "But they haven't done anything yet, so we can't just search for them and catch them, right?"

"I guess that's true, but..."

The peevishness in her voice was an expression that she wasn't fully convinced. *But it looks like I got her to quit the detective act*, thought Tatsuya. All things considered, Erika wouldn't likely be described as softhearted, but it was a different story when her close friends were involved, even if they weren't necessarily directly affected.

"But if we're always on the back foot, that puts us at a disadvantage, doesn't it? Things will work out one way or another if they come in and start punching people, but if it's a thief or a burglar..."

"We can't let that be the only thing that bothers us..."

After Leo and Mikihiko expressed their qualms in sequence, Tatsuya smiled and shook his head. "Nobody walks around with data on their terminal, so there won't be any physical theft. Besides, it's strange to worry about bag snatchers in school, isn't it? I mean, I can't say the odds of hidden photography are zero, but that applies to everything, not just the competition. If someone wants to steal data inside school, the fastest way would be to fish around in directories with low security. I personally try not to be that dumb. Maybe you're just letting the shady words of a suspicious person confuse you."

"I guess...but I don't think that guy was the same one who was using that spell to search us yesterday. We need to be careful of that, so I think we should stay vigilant."

"I know that."

Despite having voiced an objection to Tatsuya's explanation earlier, Mikihiko seemed convinced for the time being.

As for Erika and Leo, they appeared to still have something to say but were unable to find the words to argue.

◇◇◇

Unlike the Nine School Competition, where the representative team had fifty-two members, the Thesis Competition had only three. The numbers were so different that even comparing them seemed meaningless.

Nevertheless, the Thesis Competition was regarded as equally important.

One reason was because it was a real arena for all nine magic high schools to vie for supremacy. The schools that didn't do well in the Nines would be especially excited at the prospect of a revenge match.

One other reason could be that the Thesis Competition directly involved far more than just the three students chosen for the team.

The biggest difference among the All-High Magic Thesis Competition and the speech contests and research conferences familiar to non-magic high schools was that the Thesis Competition included a demonstration of the findings during the presentation.

Thesis presentations would include live demonstrations of magic, using magical equipment, on the stage. They would be models meant only for that presentation, but paper models wouldn't mean anything. Competitors either worked magic in real life, or simulated doing it—that was the contest's defining feature.

It was common to see students designing magical equipment and producing systems to assist spell casting, the creation of control software, as well as bodies to load that software into it. Then targets (if those were required) were manufactured, testers and support personnel found, and even people to erect shields to handle event safety: When the competition rolled around, not only the tech and art clubs but also the purely theoretical clubs and anyone with high grades and practical skills would be mobilized, all to push for their school's success at the actual event. Incidentally, a greater number of people were involved with the presentation than the Nine School Competition.

With the event taking place the Sunday after next, work was

proceeding not only after school but also during allotted hours in the school day, under the pretense of self-production and self-practice. The whole building was abuzz—no, a-*clatter*—with the clanging of machine tools and the rattling of magic usage. Prototypes and instruments crowded together across the campus, and some girls had volunteered to organize a drink-and-snack delivery team for the students hard at work. The group even had to use a 3H, a Humanoid Home Helper, owned by the robot research club.

"Oh, found him!"

In the middle of the tumult was the one Erika was searching for.

"Heeey, Tatsuyaaa!"

As she waved her hand and shouted, Leo turned his whole body to the side to pretend he didn't notice. Mikihiko kept behind her at a tricky distance of two meters, also looking away. Both of them were pretending they didn't know her.

"Erika, we can't get in his way…"

Mizuki, who wasn't as shameless as Leo, couldn't help but tug on her friend's sleeve, even knowing it wouldn't do anything—and it didn't.

When Erika walked up, unruffled, Tatsuya, who had paused in his work, just gave a pained smile, like he didn't have any other choice. However, there were others in the middle of an experiment who scowled at her, of course.

"Chiba…could you, like, read the situation here?"

One of those scowling was Kirihara, present on guard duty.

"Huh? Saya, you're watching, too?"

But Erika answered—or rather, one-sidedly talked to—Sayaka, who was standing next to him.

"Look, you…" said Kirihara, exhausted.

"Eri…" Sayaka smiled painfully. Still, Kirihara didn't fly into a rage—maybe that meant he'd started to grow up.

But Tatsuya, seeing not just Kirihara but also his other upperclassmen at the end of their patience, beat him to the punch. "You don't look like you're here to watch, Erika. Need something?"

"They wanted Mizuki's help with something, so I was going with her."

Erika looked willful and selfish, but she wasn't stupid. Sensing by his tone of voice that he was warning her, she answered simply, without wasting any breath.

I see, thought Tatsuya, turning his attention to Mizuki, who was busy bowing to her seniors in the art club.

"Erika, come over here."

Seeing a chance—though it was odd to call it such—Miyuki reached out from the side and brought Erika inside the ring of onlookers. Sayaka, too, left Kirihara and went next to Erika as the operation test of the magic equipment, forced to take a temporary break, resumed at Isori's signal.

"What are they testing over there? It looks like a giant light bulb."

Supported by a pedestal and four arms was a clear sphere 120 centimeters across. She was right: At a glance, it looked like an oversize light bulb. Of course, by this time, light bulbs had all but disappeared from the average household, so Mizuki gave her a confused look when she heard the word, tilting her head to the side.

"It's the cold plasma generation device for the presentation."

Miyuki knew what a light bulb was, but she wholly ignored the joking part and answered Erika's question.

"Cold…" repeated Mikihiko. "Would you be talking about cold fusion?" Like Leo, Mikihiko had been maintaining his stance as a complete stranger, before those words surprised him and he forgot what he had been doing before. (Also, Mikihiko had never gotten away from using formal speech when talking to her.)

Erika, too, seemed to have gone through her science knowledge, and a moment later a question mark popped up over her head. "Thermonuclear fusion is a reactive type, and apparently you don't necessarily need super-high temperatures for it."

"…"

"…I'm sorry, Yoshida. I don't understand much about it myself.

You should ask my brother about it later," added Miyuki, seeing Mikihiko give a blank look.

He simply shook his head in response.

Erika was speaking in hushed tones with Sayaka and throwing meaningful glances Mikihiko's way, but Miyuki smiled (with her lips only, not her eyes) and quickly put a word in. Leo had been watching the test device silently from the beginning, eyes sparkling with curiosity.

Now that they had an unintended silence, Isori signaled to Suzune. Suzune then poured psions into the big desktop CAD Tatsuya was monitoring. A much more advanced spell-support mechanism than the small CADs they carried on their person began to run, and a complex magic program consisting of many layers of processes activated.

Hydrogen under high pressure turned into plasma, and the detached electrons collided with the luminescent glass to give off light. This phenomenon was more simply performed by running high voltage through certain gases, but what they had was a high-level spell that split off those electrons without supplying any energy, then defied electromagnetic attraction to move only the electrons to the outer parts; controlling the spell required a sustained event-altering force.

"So it *is* a light bulb."

Fortunately, Erika's rude murmur was drowned out by cheers of "We did it!" and "The first step worked!" from nearby people. Even looking at others, Leo clenched his fists in front of him, Mikihiko folded his arms and nodded, and Sayaka jumped and clapped her hands. (The exception was Miyuki, who merely smiled quietly as though success had been predetermined.)

The glass vessel maintained luminescence for ten seconds. As the light faded, excitement waned. This was because they'd created only *one* of the big props; there were plenty yet to assemble. The helpers who were gathered around the test began going back to their respective stations. As they did, Erika noticed Sayaka staring at one of them.

"Saya, what's the matter?"

"That girl..."

What she got in response wasn't an answer but her talking to herself.

"Wait, what's wrong?"

"Hey, Mibu?!"

Sayaka suddenly started running, and Erika and Kirihara got off the marks after her. A moment later, Leo followed. Miyuki watched them, eyes wide, then realized Sayaka was chasing a female student with pigtails.

"Wait right there!"

Hearing a halting voice right behind her, maybe figuring she couldn't compete in speed, the female student stopped in the grassy courtyard.

She turned around. "What is it?" she asked, voice hard. Impudent, depending on how you heard it.

"Are you a freshman?"

The First High uniform didn't differ among grade levels. Sayaka's question was based on her features and constitution.

"...Yes. You're Mibu, a junior, right?"

"Yes. Sayaka Mibu, from Class 2-E. Course 2, just like you."

The only difference in uniforms was the presence of the emblem. It distinguished between Course 1 and Course 2 students.

"...I'm Chiaki Hirakawa, from Class 1-G," the girl said reluctantly.

Sayaka heard footsteps stopping behind her—Erika and the others had caught up. They had probably heard her introduction just now. In fact, Kirihara muttered "Hirakawa?" back to himself. Sayaka hadn't heard the surname before, but he must have.

Of course, the reason Sayaka couldn't let this freshman go wasn't because of her first *or* last name; it wouldn't have mattered if she'd heard it before or not. She didn't have time to be worrying about things like that.

"Hirakawa, the device in your hands... That's a wireless password breaker, isn't it?"

Chiaki Hirakawa's face paled. She quickly hid the portable terminal behind her.

"Hiding it won't help. I've used the same device before."

The girl's eyes widened.

A password breaker was a piece of password-stealing malware made into hardware form. Contrary to its name, it didn't stop at password authentication—the device could automatically disable all sorts of authentication systems and steal information files. It could only be used for criminal purposes. Which meant if Sayaka had used it before, then...

"...That's right. I was a spy's pawn, too, once." Sayaka's face twisted into a pained expression, but she kept her eyes on Chiaki as she spoke. "Let me warn you. Cut ties with them now. The longer you go along with them, the harder it will be for you afterward."

"...What do you care how hard it is for me?" she asserted brusquely, turning her back to them. An unapproachable refusal.

But that was far from enough to make Sayaka flinch. "There's no way I can leave you be!" she yelled, voice firm and eyes firmer, at the now-aggressive girl. "It's been six whole months, and sometimes I still start shaking and can't stop. Sometimes I accidentally bite my lips so hard they bleed, or make a fist so hard my nails cut into my skin." She was actually shaking as she spoke. "I don't know who you're going along with right now, but I can say this for sure: They don't have your interests in mind. Not one bit. They're just using you as a disposable tool!"

There was a truth to Sayaka's words. This was no debate in theoretical ethics—this was real life.

But the hatred lurking in Chiaki's heart was deeper rooted than Sayaka thought. "I know that!" she shouted defiantly, turning a hateful glare on Sayaka, who caught her breath. "Of course mafias and terrorists wouldn't care about the people they use. You joined up with them without even knowing that? Excuse me for sounding rude, but how old are you?"

Her dry, ridiculing words told Sayaka that this freshman wasn't like her. Sayaka had a goal she strove for—but she didn't know how to achieve it, and that's how they got her.

The girl was right. Sayaka had been a helpless child. She wasn't about to deny that. But the girl before her still didn't seem any more adult than her.

She wanted something so badly that she was willing to cooperate with criminals to get it. But what would she do when she did? Go back to her high school life like nothing happened? Or would she remain a member of the criminal organization? Sayaka felt like she was purposely ignoring what would happen in her own future.

It seemed to Sayaka like she was just stubbornly refusing everything others said.

"Abandoning yourself won't get you anything, and won't leave anything behind!"

Still, Sayaka couldn't help but say something. She was sure, from experience, that sometimes you needed to force someone to stop even if they didn't want to.

"You wouldn't understand. I'm not helping them because I want something."

But what she got in return was, naturally, another firm rejection. Sayaka dimly knew the girl wouldn't respond to their attempts to persuade her. She'd been the same way. Persuasion could come later. If they let her get away now, she'd never come back to this side. That considered, Sayaka made up her mind—she might have to get a little rough.

"Kirihara?"

"Got it."

Kirihara immediately understood Sayaka's signal. Unfortunately, neither of them had a weapon, but neither seemed worried. This freshman had no understanding of martial arts or hand-to-hand fighting. Both of them had eyes enough to see that. It would be easy for the two of them, together, to capture her.

Objectively speaking, Sayaka's and Kirihara's judgment was correct.

That is, had their opponent not been carrying a weapon.

Somebody much worse than terrorists or the mafia was using Chiaki.

The moment Sayaka and Kirihara stepped forward, Chiaki threw a small capsule at them.

"Get down!" shouted Erika, the first one to notice it.

The two of them reflexively covered their eyes with their arms.

A brilliant flash made it through their arms, penetrated their eyelids, and burned into their eyes. If anyone there had retained their eyesight during the flash, they would have noticed that Chiaki's eyelids were painted black. Masquerading as mascara and eye shadow, the shielding paint protected her from flash bangs.

Chiaki pointed her right hand at Sayaka. Spring-loaded darts shot out of her sleeve.

Erika, who had successfully blocked the flash by crouching and covering her eyes, knocked the long, spindly darts away with a tree branch as she stood up.

As the darts split apart, a thin, purplish mist began to spread from them. Erika instantly discarded her weapon, shoved Sayaka out of the way, and covered her own mouth with her blazer sleeve.

Kirihara, who hadn't completely recovered from the flash bang, took in a gulp of the smoke, now dispersed enough to be transparent. Suddenly, he swayed, then dropped to his knees.

Nerve gas?! Erika though to herself in frustration, not opening her mouth. The girl was more meticulous than they'd thought. Since they couldn't carry CADs in school, she couldn't use Acceleration magic very well. They had a numbers advantage, but the handicap given by a weapon was just that large. And if they didn't know what kind of weapons she had up her sleeve, they really couldn't act carelessly…

…but one man present wasn't bound by this logic. Leo had dropped down onto the grass (having taken Erika's warning literally), but just now began dashing savagely toward her.

Chiaki shrieked at his intensity. She hurriedly aimed her right hand at him. Either there was more than one gun for the trick darts, or she had a different projectile hidden in there.

Whatever it was, nobody ever saw it.

Because Leo had suddenly vanished from Chiaki's sight.

She paused, petrified, and a moment later took a severe impact to the waist, pushing her over while leaving no way to resist. She hit the back of her head, and passed out.

"…Did I overdo it?" asked Leo over his shoulder, having tackled Chiaki with both hands.

"Maybe…" said Erika. "Anyway, would you get up already? It basically looks like you're trying to rape her."

"You…! That's not what this is!"

"Yeah, yeah, I know, I know."

Erika looked down with a tired face, though her eyes were the definition of serious. They weren't watching Chiaki, who remained on the ground, but Leo as he stood up. She looked like a professional gambler sizing up a thoroughbred at a derby.

Kanon, having heard the commotion (as the disciplinary committee chairwoman) and run to the nurse's office, where she saw the unconscious freshman on the bed and the junior couple getting treatment, sighed.

After hearing what had happened from Sayaka, she sighed again. "You overdid it…"

Kirihara and Sayaka must have felt as if Kanon, normally a train on a rampage, telling *them* they overdid it, was undeserved. Still, their opponent had hit her head, and was still unconscious from it, so they couldn't find the words to object.

"Anyway, what the heck did she do? From what you told me, she was just in possession of an illegal electronic device. But she didn't actually use it illegally or break any school rules with it."

There was no way to object to that indication, either. Not for Sayaka, who was always earnest and serious, or for Kirihara, who didn't exactly have a silver tongue.

That, though, wasn't enough to make *everyone* present apologetic. "I think possessing an illegal hacking tool is grounds for catching her," challenged Erika.

Kanon leveled a sharp stare at her. "...The problem is that they went too far. Crime and punishment have to be balanced."

"Hey, I mean, I didn't try to catch her because I wanted to punish her. We were just trying to rescue a school friend from the hands of dirty adults."

"Do you always knock people out to rescue them? She hit her head hard."

"What were we supposed to do? She brought out hidden weapons and everything. I don't see why I have to get hurt just because I want to save someone."

Kanon and Erika glared at each other.

Sayaka started to panic a little at the volatile mood, but the nurse here, who was in a position to scold both of them right off, wasn't trying to mediate, so she couldn't find the right moment to say something.

"Anyway, Chairwoman Chiyoda, we'll leave the rest to you." The one to speak was Leo, who had been standing to the side. "Let's go," he said to Erika, gesturing with his head that they should leave the room.

"Wait, what's your problem?" said Erika angrily, changing her target to Leo.

But this time, it didn't evolve into a stare down.

Leo gave only a momentarily exasperated glance at her, then turned around. "The rest is the disciplinary committee's job. I don't know about you, but I'm good just knowing none of this bothered Tatsuya, Mizuki, or Mikihiko." Then he started to walk away.

"Would you wait?!"

Erika chased after Leo, also leaving the nurse's office.

As the voices of the noisy freshmen (with at least one of them being very annoyed) disappeared down the hall, Kanon regained some of her calm.

She looked at the freshman lying on the bed again. Her face spurred Kanon's memory, but there was no way for her to be sure, since the girl was unconscious. Instead, she turned to look at the nurse.

"Anyway, give me your honest thoughts—how is she?"

The nurse, Satomi Asuka, answered her with a placid smile. "There's nothing to worry about. I didn't find anything wrong with her brain or bones. She should wake up soon enough."

Asuka had a specialized healing-type ability that allowed her to visually detect biological emissions and identify abnormal spots on the body. The ability let her deliver more precise diagnoses just by looking than most precise examination instruments in hospitals. If she said the girl was all right, it meant they could rest easy.

"Then, I'm sorry to bother you, but could you contact me when she does?"

"Sure. Oh, but if she runs away, don't complain to me, okay? I don't have any combat abilities whatsoever," answered Asuka, smiling pleasantly.

Kanon grinned and nodded. "You would never let a patient out of your sight, Ms. Asuka."

Then, she escorted Sayaka and Kirihara, whose treatments were complete, out of the nurse's office.

◇ ◇ ◇

Kanon was the disciplinary committee chairwoman, but right now, she was also Isori's bodyguard.

The bodyguard system for the Thesis Competition assigned multiple bodyguards to a single target. There was one other junior bodyguard for Isori, but Kanon wasn't about to foist this duty onto somebody else.

That was why she'd returned to the schoolyard, where the experiments were being conducted, without waiting for the freshman, who she had to question, to wake up.

And once again, that galling underclassman of hers—basically Erika—had caused some trouble. For whatever reason, one of the male students was watching her with a dangerous expression. Erika was ignoring it, looking away and almost whistling in feigned ignorance.

Feeling a headache coming on but unable to pretend she didn't see, Kanon grabbed the nearest disciplinary committee member and asked him. "Wait, Shiba, what the heck's going on over there?"

Tatsuya *was* a member of the committee Kanon led, but more importantly, right now, he was one of the representative members for the Thesis Competition and involved with the experiments' progress.

Currently, he was one of those being guarded, and for a bodyguard, even if she wasn't assigned to him, addressing him while he was busy typing away on a keyboard would have been out of the question. Kanon didn't seem to be conscious of that, though.

Sure enough, Miyuki raised her crescent eyebrows behind him, but Tatsuya didn't seem particularly offended. He stopped scrolling down the screen and turned. "It appears Sekimoto isn't fond of Erika and Leo loitering around."

After looking at the situation again, he was right—Sekimoto, not Erika, was the one gathering annoyed stares. Kanon sighed and went over to the arguing pair.

"...Sekimoto, could you tell me what the problem is?"

There was no term limitation for disciplinary officers. As long as a member didn't voluntarily quit, they'd be part of the committee until they graduated. Mari and Tatsumi had resigned when the student council changed, but Sekimoto was still a registered member. He was the only senior currently in the committee.

"Chiyoda... Well, it's nothing important. I was just being cautious—they weren't picked by the disciplinary or club committee for this, so I don't want their loitering to cause a problem for you."

Though it wasn't in Kanon's character to do so, she wanted to put her hands over her face. Her unmistakable thoughts right now involved why her senior wanted to make trouble on purpose.

"...For the sake of next year and the year after that, there's no reason to stop freshmen from watching the experiments," she said. "If they're getting in the way of our bodyguard duties, the bodyguards will handle it. You weren't nominated for the job this year, so would you be so kind as to leave this to us?"

Sekimoto narrowed his eyes, but Kanon turned to Erika without giving him time to object. "And could the two of you go home for the day, too? What happened before could be viewed as four-on-one violence, depending on how you look at it."

Kanon was trying to save the situation while things were still hazy. Erika smiled coldly at her. She knew this was only a makeshift way of doing things, but seeing Erika smile like that made the blood go to her head. Still, if she exploded here, it would only make the situation worse.

As Kanon gritted her teeth, Erika casually turned her back. "I'm gonna get going. Tatsuya, Miyuki, see you tomorrow."

"...Yeah, I'm getting out of here, too. Later, Tatsuya."

After the two freshmen readily withdrew, Kanon sighed in relief.

Just then, her terminal vibrated, notifying her that she had a message. After checking it, she wandered away from Sekimoto, who still seemed to have something to say, and back to the nurse's office she'd just come from.

"Oh, Kanon, wait!"

Isori, who had been focused on monitoring the data coming from the measurement instruments with his terminal, quickly rushed up behind her. He was abandoning his post in the middle of the experiment, but nobody found fault with him.

Sekimoto gave an interested stare at Isori's display, which he hadn't closed—before a hand reached out from beside it and shut the terminal off.

"Ichihara."

"I'd thought you had no interest in practical themes like this."

Sekimoto turned away, his expression sullen. Suzune answered with a poker face that gave nothing away.

"...I still think that we should be more focused on improving foundational theory and spells themselves, like with Cardinal Codes, but it's not like I have no interest in applications."

"I don't recall making light of foundational theory. We actually need more scrupulous inspection of foundational theory than research of theory for the sake of theory so we can mitigate the risks that come from practical implementation."

"Inspection and research are different. Research is creation. Just inspecting things won't get us anywhere."

"There is no value in theory that isn't useful. Theory exists so it can be made into something practical."

"It may not seem useful now, but research into foundational theory will bear more fruit in the future."

"Bearing more fruit in the future isn't grounds to reject the small advancements being made right now. The future is built on top of the present."

Both seniors argued calmly—but also stubbornly. As Tatsuya watched surreptitiously from across his monitor, he became convinced.

She'd already explained once that Sekimoto's rank in the Thesis Competition's selection committee hadn't been fourth, but second, right after Suzune. Still, Suzune's almost hostile rejection of when she'd told him that had left an impression.

At the time, Tatsuya had been a bit mystified as to why Suzune seemed to be so stubbornly against Sekimoto being part of the team, but now he knew such an attitude was only natural when their fundamental viewpoints differed so much. And as far as Tatsuya could see, Sekimoto felt the competition more strongly. Tatsuya got the impression that he still felt like the other boy was more fit for the team.

At times, too much pride led to a loss of the restraints normally provided by reason. Sugarcoating her arguments probably wouldn't make Sekimoto back down. As far as he could tell, it was hard to think this would be the end. Sekimoto'd take more direct action next time—that was for certain. Whether that action would be legal and peaceful he had no proof of.

—I just hope this doesn't turn into trouble—

With a powerful hunch that that wish wouldn't be granted, Tatsuya still couldn't help but wish it anyway.

Leo left the school gates and silently followed Erika.

Even so, for him, it didn't feel like they were going home from school together. For all intents and purposes, there was only one road from the gates to the station. He simply didn't have any urgent matters that would have made him pass her by. And Leo thought it was the same for Erika, too.

They were just walking in the same direction, and their paces just happened to be the same, too.

"Leo?"

So when she suddenly called his name, he stopped out of surprise.

Erika had stopped, too. "Do you have time today?"

He didn't immediately understand the question, so he stood there dumbly for a moment. Erika spun around. Her skirt fluttered into the air, but Leo's eyes were glued to hers.

Those eyes without a speck of softness.

Those eyes without a hint of mischief.

Her eyes were painted with a steel-blue vigor, looking like they could slash into him at any moment.

"Do you?" she asked again, short.

That broke the curse on Leo. "…I don't have anything going on, really."

"Then come with me."

She spun on her heel again and started walking away at a brisk pace. Leo followed at the same speed, still silent. Visually, it was the same as before.

But the nuance had changed completely.

Upon Kanon waiting for Isori and entering the nurse's office, Asuka, the one who had sent the text, greeted them with a placid voice. Still, considering she was physically holding down a struggling Chiaki, the term *placid* went out the window.

"Ms. Asuka…what happened to not having 'any combat abilities whatsoever'?"

This was not the first time she'd asked that question even though she knew the answer.

"Please, this is *nursing*, not *combat*."

"…" "…"

Kanon was not the only one to stare at her unintentionally, and she also wasn't the only one to purposely not point that out.

"Umm…" she began. "I'd like to hear what she has to say, so would you relea—err, have her sit down, please?"

"Sure." Asuka's smile deepened as if to praise her tact in quickly rewording her request. She sat Chiaki up.

Kanon felt a slight chill at what could have happened had she said what she originally intended.

As if to sweep that away, she shifted her gaze to Chiaki, now upright, shaking her head a bit.

"Were you okay *the day before yesterday*?" asked Kanon.

Chiaki blinked her eyes wide open before hastily looking down to hide her face. She must have only now realized the one chasing her near the station had been Kanon.

"First then, now today..." she continued. "You sure are reckless. If you'd made one little mistake, you would have ended up badly hurt." There was no sense of interrogation in her voice. In fact, it sounded gentle. "But it's escalated too far for me to stay quiet and watch. You haven't done anything yet—which is exactly why I have to stop you."

This was Kanon overextending herself. Now that she'd been named disciplinary committee chairwoman, a sense of duty to rehabilitate underclassmen had blossomed. If she hadn't been given that position, then considering her natural hasty temperament, she would have forgotten about any sense of obligation rather quickly.

"You said earlier to Mibu that you weren't doing this because you wanted something. Why were you thinking about stealing data?"

But despite this newfound commitment straining Kanon to the limit, it appeared to resonate with the person it was directed toward.

"...Stealing data wasn't my goal. My goal was to overwrite the magic equipment program for the presentation and make it unusable. That's why I borrowed the password breaker."

"You wanted to make our school's presentation fail?"

Underneath her controlled, considerate expression, she seethed for a split second. Of all the things, she was trying to ruin Isori's big moment (by Kanon's subjective viewpoint). She was being truly tolerant today.

"That isn't it! I didn't want them to fail or anything!"

But Chiaki's response wasn't quite what Kanon had expected. Kanon had been tightening her shoulders so she wouldn't explode, but this felt like a letdown. The surprising words and Chiaki's attitude seemed honest. Kanon, at least, felt Chiaki was telling the truth.

"...I hate to say it, but that man would easily recover from that," said Chiaki. "He has enough skill. But if the program broke right before the event, he'd *have* to start panicking, even if just a little. He might even have to pull a few all-nighters in a row, and then get sick, hopefully. I just wanted to make him sweat!"

"You're doing all this to annoy him...? Thankfully, this didn't turn into anything major, but depending on how it went, you could have been expelled from school, you know."

"I wouldn't mind that! As long as I can scare and frustrate him! I can't forgive him for only ever getting the good deals...!"

On the bed, Chiaki began to sob.

Kanon, face perplexed, turned to Isori. He'd been listening to them from a few steps away. He nodded to Kanon and sat down on a stool next to the bed.

"Chiaki Hirakawa..." he said. "You're Koharu Hirakawa's younger sister, right?"

Chiaki's shoulders, which had been caved in and trembling with sobs, now gave a different kind of jolt. Isori, who had been on the Nine School Competition's technical staff, of course knew Koharu Hirakawa, who had also been part of the engineering team. "You think it's Shiba's fault your sister ended up like that, don't you?"

Isori had been present during the incident that had eventually caused her to quit school, so he'd immediately figured out who *that man* and *him* referred to.

"...Isn't it?"

What came softly out of Chiaki's mouth was an execration.

"He could have prevented Kobayakawa's accident, but he didn't. He didn't try to save her, so my sister felt like it was her fault..."

Isori gently placed a hand on Chiaki's shoulder, but she smacked it away. He looked at his hand, then spoke again, his voice tinged with bitterness. "If Shiba is at fault for that accident, then so am I," he said. "I didn't notice the trap. That goes for all the other people on the technical staff, too. Shiba isn't the only one responsible."

This wasn't simply a way to defend Tatsuya. The senior Kobayakawa still hadn't recovered her magical capabilities after the falling accident during the Mirage Bat match in the Nines. As one of the staff members present at the time, Isori felt regret and responsibility.

"Please, don't make me laugh."

But Chiaki, her face still down, ridiculed his feelings. Kanon, angry, stood up, but Isori held her back with his hand.

"My sister didn't know, either," said Chiaki. "There's no way you could have, Isori. But he could have noticed it. *That person* said so, too. But he didn't do anything because it didn't have anything to do with his sister!"

This time, Kanon looked at Isori with a worried expression. Isori was making the same face. Neither of them could understand Chiaki's words, her attitude. It almost sounded like she was praising Tatsuya. They even thought they could see a yearning in her. They were so confused by it that the term *that person* slipped right on by them.

"He can do anything, but he never acts first... I'm sure he's doing it to make fun of people he thinks are incompetent."

Isori answered Kanon's look with a silent shake of his head. Isori sort of knew how Chiaki felt. When people were betrayed by something they believed in, they would feel even deeper hatred toward the enemies they'd already been fighting. Even if that belief was entirely based on a one-sided *faith*.

"He can use magic just fine," said Chiaki, "but he was lazy on purpose to be put in Course 2. And now, I'm sure he's trampling all over everyone's pride, Course 1 and Course 2, and gloating about it!"

"Okay, okay, that's enough."

As Kanon and Isori stood speechless before Chiaki's hateful, irrelevant condemnation, the nurse interrupted her speech in a voice lacking any semblance of tension. "Doctor's orders. Chiyoda, could you continue this tomorrow?"

"Ms. Asuka..."

"I'll give her to a University-affiliated hospital to keep overnight," she said. "I'll contact her parents, so the two of you should go back to your preparations. There's not much daylight left, right?"

Kanon seemed to want to argue with Asuka's request, but Isori stopped her, and they both left the nurse's office behind them.

Erika sat next to Leo in a two-person car.

Alone with a girl in his grade in a tiny vehicle. Even Leo, who put food before fairness and fights before flowers, couldn't help but feel a little conscious about it.

He knew it was just Erika, but it was still a little uncomfortable. Maybe if it had been someone else, it would have been less so.

Objectively speaking, Erika was a rare beauty. Whether because of her looks or her fondness for martial arts, even her casual posture, with her elbow on the window frame as she stared outside, she seemed attractive. Plus, he thought he caught a whiff of something sweet. Unable to candidly look at her, given that he was sitting next to her, but unable to ignore her outright, his eyes ended up drawn in for glance after glance. Leo had quickly begun to regret taking her up on her invitation without asking where they were going first.

The silence was amplifying his discomfort, but fortunately it didn't last for very long.

"...Don't you think it's too simple?"

"What is?" he said to the sudden question, secretly relieved he managed to answer in a normal voice.

"Yesterday, we get a warning about unknown foreign spies infiltrating, and today we find a student with a tool that spies use," said Erika. "And the whole thing was so shabbily put together, like they *wanted* us to find her."

"Shabby... I mean, I feel like it was pretty troublesome."

"Stupid. Catching her was the only hard part. She was walking around with a hacking tool in broad daylight. Can you believe how careless that was?"

"Amateurs, right?" decided Leo.

"Yeah…" she answered vaguely, nodding. She didn't seem convinced.

"What's wrong?" Erika was being unusually inarticulate, and Leo realized she felt something that couldn't be settled with a joke or levity.

"It isn't over…" she stated. "She might have been sent to feel things out."

"As a decoy to make us let our guards down while the real ones are somewhere else?"

Right now, her silence meant yes.

"…And you wanted me to play detective with you to smoke them out?"

"Hah, no," denied Erika.

Leo felt more relieved than angry. It seemed like this alone time in the narrow space was making his mind malfunction.

"I don't expect you to do any brain work."

"Say that again!" Of course, he still couldn't let *that* abuse go.

"You and I aren't cut out for brain work, right? We can just leave that stuff to Tatsuya."

But after she turned the same abuse upon herself, he found it hard to argue.

"We have a more fitting role than doing something that doesn't suit us," she said.

This immediately clued him in on what she was thinking. Their thought patterns really were similar—though both of them would have vehemently denied it. "Bodyguards, then."

—The enemy was after things related to the Thesis Competition. They didn't have to go through the effort of smoking them out—they'd come voluntarily once the competition got closer.

"We'd be doing less defending and more counterattacking, though."

—They just had to lie in wait for them.

"Whoooo, you're a scary woman… You want to use Tatsuya as bait?"

—If nothing else happened, then great.

"Tatsuya wouldn't die even if you killed him."

—And if they did attempt something, Tatsuya wouldn't go down without a fight.

"Ha-ha, you're right."

—All they needed to do was concentrate all their efforts on squashing the spies' necks.

Leo and Erika had reached an agreement—not a verbal one but one on a second sound channel.

A low menacing laugh echoed through the small interior.

If Tatsuya had heard their exchange, he might have announced he was breaking off relations with them. Fortunately (?), he wasn't here.

However, the laugh ended suddenly. "But there's something we still need in order to do this," said Erika, her expression turning hard.

"What's that?" Leo asked honestly, surmising it was something serious.

"Leo, you have first-class potential as a foot soldier. In battles using pistols or knives, I think you could outclass Hattori and Kirihara."

The sudden, unexpected high praise, rather than making him happy or suspicious, confounded him.

"In terms of potential, Miki's pretty up there, too. But you're probably better than him in visible battles."

But it only took a few seconds for his brain to restart. "…And? Potential—that means you've got a problem with my current abilities, right?"

Despite Leo's sharp counter, Erika nodded, not particularly surprised. "I said there's something we still need, right? You don't have a finisher."

"A finisher?"

"A finishing move, a killing move. Whatever you want to call it. A skill that will always bring down an opponent. Something to make the opponent feel really threatened. Something that just having would put you at an advantage, even if you didn't use it. You don't have one of those."

"...And you do?"

"Yes. I need my personal broom for it, but with it, I have a secret sword technique that could crush an opponent with certainty."

"Huh..."

"You don't have a skill that will kill an opponent for sure, right? Depending on how you tuned and used that Mini-Communicator Tatsuya made, it could be a pretty lethal weapon, but it doesn't have the sharpness to be a real finisher."

The cabinet moved to a low-speed lane. They were approaching their destination.

"...I guess I don't have any skills that assume I'm trying to kill someone."

During the April incident, Leo had been put in the rear guard, and hadn't actually fought any Blanche members. Unlike Kirihara and Erika, he had no real experience with violence of the sort that could rend flesh and break bones.

"Are you prepared to learn one?"

Erika's gaze pierced through Leo's eyes.

"Are you prepared to bloody your hands? Because that's probably the sort of enemy we're up against. And maybe it doesn't have to be us to do the job. Maybe our teachers, or our upperclassmen, or even Tatsuya would do it for us. But if you want to get involved for real, instead of just watching from the sidelines, I think you're going to need the resolve to kill or be killed."

"That's a dumb question." Leo's eyes never once looked away from Erika's as he answered, simply and clearly.

The cabinet decelerated, slid into the station platform, and stopped. Erika opened the door and stepped down onto the platform. Leo exited after her, then smelled salt water in the air. He knew they were somewhere quite close to the ocean, near the border of the Kanagawa prefecture, before looking at the name of the station.

Erika stopped and turned around.

"Then I'll teach you one."

Backlit by the sunlight over her shoulders, she spoke.

"The secret sword technique, *Usuba Kagerou*, the Antlion. A perfect skill for you."

◇ ◇ ◇

The sun had long ago set, and the road home to the station was lit by street lights.

Today, instead of Leo and Erika, Kanon and Isori were with the group.

"...I see. So that was her motive." Tatsuya nodded, looking convinced after Kanon fairly reluctantly told him what she knew about what was going on.

"But why?!" Honoka fumed. "She's just hating you because of a misunderstanding!"

"Or maybe she's venting," said Shizuku next to her, puzzled, clearly having trouble understanding. None of this was convincing to either of them.

"She probably couldn't help but vent..."

"I'm sure she loves her older sister... That doesn't mean we can approve of what Hirakawa was trying to do, but I think I can understand her feelings a little."

In contrast, Mikihiko and Mizuki gave words mixed with sympathy. Tatsuya was deeply interested in the brilliant difference in impressions between the Course 1 and Course 2 students. He didn't let on that he found it amusing, of course.

"But if that's all it is, there doesn't seem to be a problem with leaving her alone," he said—not giving his impressions but rather what they should do now.

Kanon and Isori both looked at him askance.

"You know you're the one being targeted, right?" asked Kanon, less worried and more mildly astonished.

Tatsuya shook his head, apologetically for some reason. "Yeah… this harassment was meant for me, and I got you mixed up in it. But I won't make any trouble for you. It'll take more than a password breaker to get through our security."

"Well, we're having the robotics club help and keep an eye on all the equipment, not just the system security, so I don't think we have to worry, either…" said Isori, eyebrows knotted—and even that expression came off as troubling (seductive?), annoyingly enough. "But if she knows hacking won't work, she could always escalate things, right? If her sister is the cause of this, I think talking to her and having her change her mind is the best solution…"

Tatsuya still shook his head. "Let's not get Koharu Hirakawa involved in this," he said. "They may be sisters, but she's not related to the incident, nor is she responsible."

Hirakawa (the elder) was, at least, related in the sense that she was the cause of her sister's rash behavior. But Isori found himself in admiration at Tatsuya for declaring that she wasn't.

"Wow. I guess you can be kind sometimes," said Kanon, not teasing him but genuinely surprised.

Casually hiding the now-irritated Miyuki from his upperclassmen's sight, Tatsuya shook his head again, twice as firmly as before. "It's because I feel like it would get needlessly complicated. And besides, the younger Hirakawa sister isn't the only one to be running around nearby of late."

Kanon's, Isori's, and Mikihiko's faces suddenly tightened, and they glanced around.

They couldn't spot anyone suspicious, but Isori and Mikihiko picked up on a slight fluctuation in the fields—unintentional psionic ripples.

"...Do you want a bodyguard after all?" asked Kanon, realizing Tatsuya wasn't just being paranoid, and responding to the fluctuations spreading through the air and the fluctuation in Isori's expression.

"No. Without someone with Saegusa's level of perception, it would be too hard to catch them." Implicitly saying there was nobody they could give the role to, Tatsuya shook his head for the fourth time.

◇ ◇ ◇

Not an Ikebukuro multi-tenant building nor an upscale Yokohama Chinatown restaurant, but something in the middle: In a private room in a certain traditional Japanese restaurant in Shinagawa stood three men. Two formed a pair, consisting of a man in his forties and a younger one of twenty-five or twenty-six. Together, they faced another man in his twenties.

"I sincerely apologize. I hope you didn't have to wait long."

The singular man had just arrived. Along with his words, he struck an apologetic appearance. Nevertheless, there was almost no subservient impression, and his polite demeanor, coupled with his handsome features, gave off a noble air.

"Not at all. We only just arrived as well."

The older man's response included the appropriate platitudes, but his attitude was haughty and curt. He wasn't vulgar, but others might have characterized him as boorish. Of course, the man would surely brush off any claims that he was unrefined or thoughtless. And the final person, looking more virile than his age in his mid-twenties would imply, sat still, not motioning to speak.

"I'd like to get right to it, Mr. Zhou," said the older man to the newcomer. "The girl seems to have slipped up."

"I understand your concerns, Your Excellency Chen." The young man, Zhou, reacted mildly to the overbearing protest. "However, we have not told her anything about our identity. I don't believe there is any danger of an information leak."

"Really, now?" replied Chen upon hearing the confidence in Zhou's tone, directing a searching gaze at him. "You've set her up quite well as your helper."

"Children that age are genuinely passionate. They would rather speak than listen—to show their own worth, to have others look at them. It's a phase of wanting to be understood rather than wanting to understand." He smiled thinly. "Because of that, we had her tell us quite a few things."

Chen looked at him, slightly uncomfortable. But when he spoke, no unpleasant feelings were left in his voice of warning. "If you say so, Mr. Zhou, then it should be fine. Just take care of any 'one-in-a-thousand' chances."

"I understand. I plan to visit her in the near future to check on her."

After Zhou bowed politely, Chen looked at him with satisfaction, then shook the bell on the table.

Zhou noticed the young man next to him, Ganghu Lu, casting a sharp gaze in his direction, but it did nothing to change the indistinct smile on Zhou's face.

The student cafeteria during lunchtime. Though this was technically a magic high school, the cafeteria was the same as other high schools, and didn't differ very much from middle schools. (Perhaps, though, it would appear slightly different than a combined junior and high school aiming to educate children from society's upper echelons.)

Here, numerous strains of raucousness overlapped to create a singular tumult.

But one part of the chaotic space suddenly took on a singular order. For a moment, a spot next to the entrance fell perfectly quiet before changing into something more cacophonous.

Though it was just one area of the vast student cafeteria, it was Miyuki, whose beauty seemed to be growing more refined lately, who wielded enough influence—or perhaps better stated as *control*—to transform the mood in the air.

Drawing attention from every single person who passed her by (and not appearing to mind at all), Miyuki walked straight ahead and without hesitation to Tatsuya's table.

"Thank you for waiting for me," she said with a conscientious bow.

Tatsuya smiled and waved it away. Behind Miyuki, Honoka quickly bobbed her head while Shizuku bowed so slightly you'd have to be watching quite closely to notice.

It wasn't an intentional pattern that Tatsuya's group saved seats with Miyuki's group coming to meet them. The reverse occurred rather frequently as well, at about a 60:40 ratio. However, virtually all patterns saw Miyuki going wherever Tatsuya was.

"Oh, Miyuki, you were here?"

"I just got here, Mizuki."

Mizuki and Mikihiko had just returned from getting food.

"We'll get ours now," said Tatsuya, standing up as the two of them sat down, gesturing with his eyes to the newly arrived three.

With Miyuki, Honoka, and Shizuku in tow, Tatsuya headed to the serving rack, feeling a wholly different kind of stare piercing into him than the ones on Miyuki before.

When the four of them came back with their lunch trays, only Mizuki and Mikihiko were there to greet them.

"Are Erika and Saijou still registering for classes?" asked Honoka casually, not seeing the two of them anywhere. Still, it didn't bother him that much. In their case, not all of them were present every day—for example, the last few days Tatsuya had been busy making stage props (more accurately, programming them), so he hadn't been at the cafeteria for a while. (And Miyuki stayed with Tatsuya, as a matter of course.)

Given that modern class systems were in some ways flexible, each student commonly ended class at a slightly different time. Honoka's question was no more than a "Nice weather we're having today," just a way to start up a conversation—however…

"Oh, I think they took the day off."

Tatsuya's unexpected answer made Honoka's eyes light up. "Huh? The two of them?"

"Both of them at the same time, yes."

Tatsuya quickly realized a misunderstanding (?) when Honoka's eyes filled with anticipation. On top of that, he'd given a smirk, changed his phrasing a little, and nodded gravely as he'd said it.

"Surprising…or is it?" murmured Shizuku to herself, quirking her head to the side. Her tone was dispassionate, but her eyes were immensely curious.

"Wait, is it true?!" asked Mizuki, eyes widening.

"Mizuki, is there a point in asking us?" said Miyuki with a strained smile. Mizuki was their classmate, not Miyuki, so that only made sense.

"Oh, I guess so..." Mizuki's eyes wandered, disconcerted, looking for help.

"..."

"..."

"..."

All four of the girls' eyes gathered on Mikihiko, as though planned in advance, and he gave a somewhat flustered response. "Huh? No, I don't think they've been acting like *that*..."

And Tatsuya dropped some more fuel on the fire. "Come to think of it, they went home together yesterday, didn't they?"

As his friends started squealing, Miyuki directed an impassive stare at him. Her gaze was asking whether, by some chance, he was stressed out at the moment. He casually turned away from her.

"But really, I wonder why they're absent today," wondered Mizuki.

"You're right," replied Mikihiko. "Neither seems the type to suddenly fall ill..."

Once the contents of everyone's trays had changed from food to post-meal tea, the "both of them home from school together" doubts, which appeared to have been quelled for the moment, revived.

"I want to say you're exaggerating, but..." said Tatsuya, "I feel the same way. And it didn't look like either of them was unwell yesterday."

Mikihiko and Tatsuya both appeared to have come to the conclusion that they weren't out sick.

"Of course, it could just be a coincidence..." said Honoka to Tatsuya.

Shizuku was the one to answer her, though. "It could also *not* be a coincidence."

"Well, I guess so..." said Honoka, this time to Shizuku, possibility countered with possibility. "But were they good-enough friends for a *non-coincidental* event to happen between them?"

"I don't think it would be strange if it did..." replied Shizuku, looking over to Mizuki and asking what she thought.

"Oh, umm, I think so, too," she said, quickly agreeing.

"But if the two of them are together..." added Miyuki, tilting her head in confusion, "what on earth could they be doing?"

Mizuki's and Mikihiko's faces went bright red on a time delay.

"...What did you two just imagine?"

"N-nothing! Nothing at all."

"Th-that's right! Nothing!"

"...All right," sighed Miyuki. Their reactions had been far too easy to read. She glanced over at her brother.

"Yeah, well...this is nothing more than an opinion with no proof, a guess based on speculation, but...maybe Erika is actually working Leo pretty hard right now."

Tatsuya winked at her sardonically.

Miyuki giggled and smiled. "That does seem possible."

Clairvoyance wasn't a part of Tatsuya's skill set.

But he could do something similar.

Just as physical distance didn't directly affect magic, it didn't directly impede one's perception of the Idea, either. If a target in the information world could be singled out, then no matter how physically far away it was, there was a possibility to "see" it. For example, if someone could look at the moon through a high-magnification astronomical telescope and pick out a moon-landing vessel (or the remnants thereof), one could "see" the status of that moon-landing vessel. (No optical telescopes had high-enough resolution, though.)

But this time, he hadn't secretly taken a peek at what Erika and

Leo were doing—discovering what they were doing had been completely coincidental.

"Hey, it's wrinkling again!" scolded Erika as the one she scolded curled up at her feet, clutching his head.

"Agh, that hurt... How many times do I have to say this?! Say something instead of doing that! What do you even think words are for?!"

"But you wouldn't get it if I told you in words."

"Sure, and punching me will make me get it..."

Leo's protest tapered off and faded out.

One reason, of course, was that he was the student here and couldn't behave too forcibly. More importantly, though, he felt disappointed in himself. He wasn't getting the hang of this, no matter how many times he repeated it.

"Well...I guess so. Let's take a break."

Erika, though, didn't think Leo was disappointing at all. She probably knew better than him how difficult acquiring a new skill was.

"Here you go."

"Uh, thanks."

Erika, in a dojo uniform like Leo, who had sat cross-legged on the dojo's planked floor, offered him a drink, chilled but not too chilled, then assumed the traditional Japanese *seiza* position (politely kneeling while sitting on her heels) in front of him.

"You were great at it when you had the mantle on, too... I guess it feels different?"

There was no ill will within Erika or what she said, but Leo scowled. "...The one from the competition?"

Results aside, for Leo, that outfit was a memory he wished he could forget. It was clearly connected to the skill he was learning, though, so he couldn't pretend he had forgotten.

"It's not like it stretched out nice and flat like an ironing board. Maybe it had a few tiny wrinkles, but it was still a perfectly good shield. And the fabric had a spell to support extending and expanding it, too."

Erika, still sitting in *seiza*, put a finger to her chin and tilted her head. "Hmm… There should be a support spell in this one, too… Maybe it would be faster to ask Tatsuya after all."

"We can't." Leo shook his head. "If we bothered Tatsuya with this, we'd be putting the cart before the horse. If there *is* a spell applied to this, then I just have to figure out how to activate it."

"…You're such a boy," said Erika, giggling despite herself.

Her smile was oddly charming, and Leo looked away, unable to even snap back at her.

Today was Saturday, but school wasn't out. Magic high schools didn't have five-day school weeks. Students still had all their classes (including practical training sessions), and yet Tatsuya had come to visit Yakumo's temple this morning again. And this time, he had Miyuki with him.

As a matter of fact, Yakumo had been the one to invite them, asking if they wanted to test the modifications he'd made to the temple's distance target practice area.

Not many places offered magic shooting practice with live ammunition. Tatsuya, who couldn't use the school's practice grounds (he couldn't reveal his Mist Dispersion at school), was especially thankful for the chance to practice shooting somewhere close rather than having to go all the way to Tsuchiura.

Miyuki, unlike her brother, had no reason to conceal her abilities, but she couldn't use the practice grounds as much as the students in clubs. And besides, the magic she specialized in involved more spells that coated an entire area than ones that pinpointed targets. That made it hard for her to devote much time to shooting practice, so Tatsuya had brought her along, saying it was a good opportunity.

The temple's shooting grounds were spread out underneath the main building.

"…Eek! Take this!"

As expected, perhaps, the secret *ninjutsu* users' training grounds were somewhat different from their school's facilities.

Miyuki, her inherent competitiveness on display, was breathing heavily, sweat dripping from her brow. She'd tripped several times, and the hair that she'd put up earlier was becoming loose in places.

The floor was a spacious square. Of the four walls, three—plus the ceiling—had dozens of holes, out of which targets appeared, one after another. (Not all four, since apparently being isolated in the middle of the enemy was actually an unrealistic scenario, and in real combat you would want to flee before that happened.)

To add to that, ten or so targets would appear simultaneously, and all of them were set up to hide again after one second. Just that made aiming a handful, but to make the job even harder, any shots she missed would be fired back as mock bullets.

Miyuki wasn't letting the mock bullets hit her without resistance—she was blocking them all with magic—but juggling offense and defense had caused her to trip several times already.

"That's enough!"

At Yakumo's signal, the machines stopped, and Miyuki suddenly sank to the floor, an indication of how difficult this training facility's menu was.

"Nice job."

"Oh, Tatsuya… Thank you very much."

Tatsuya held out a towel to her, and Miyuki reached for it gratefully. Instead of giving her the towel, Tatsuya took his sister's hand with his free one and gently pulled her slender body off the floor.

"Ah…thank you."

"You look unharmed," said Tatsuya with a smile after giving his out-of-breath sister's body, clad in a thin training shirt and spats that ended above the knee, a quick once-over.

The blood rising to Miyuki's face wasn't entirely due to the extreme exercise, but did Tatsuya really notice that? The answer never came out. His sister said "I'm fine," and he just nodded curtly before proceeding to the center of the floor.

His attitude was curt, but no dissatisfaction could be seen in his sister. They hadn't come here to play; if Tatsuya had been overly concerned about her, she would have chided him herself.

That didn't happen, of course. Tatsuya briskly walked over, lifting his favorite CAD in front of his chest. A standby position, arms bent at the elbows.

The moment Miyuki left the floor, without any warning, the training course began.

Ball-shaped targets appeared on three walls. All of them, at the same time, turned to sand.

Tatsuya was in a shooting position now, right hand out in front. He had only pulled the trigger—pressed the CAD switch—once. Doing so had fired twelve targets with his dismantling spell.

Before there was time to breathe, more targets appeared, this time using the walls and ceiling.

There were twenty-four.

Not even bothering to aim at the one directly in front of him, he kept his CAD still and pulled the trigger.

Tatsuya twisted his body to avoid the fine plastic powder that fell on him. As he turned, he thrust his right hand overhead and squeezed the trigger.

As if to fill the gap caused by the crumbling spheres, more and more targets showed up. The frequency with which he pulled the trigger increased to two at a time, then three at a time.

Nevertheless, not one penalty bullet fired at him before the stock of targets ran out.

"Tatsuya, that was amazing!"

As the mechanisms stopped and Tatsuya lowered his CAD, Miyuki ran as if to jump onto him.

"Oh, dear. A perfect clear..." said Yakumo in mild astonishment, walking up from behind. "It's still not hard enough?"

"This is the kind of thing I do best," he replied. "I still only just barely made it, though. Who's the one who thought up that evil algorithm? It was like it was hitting every blind spot."

"I got the control program from Kazama, if that helps."

"Ah, so it was Sanada..." groaned Tatsuya, thinking of the engineering officer's face and how the Independent Magic Battalion's most black-hearted expression hid behind his sociable smiles.

As Yakumo saw his pupil groan, only to soften his expression into a grin, Miyuki stepped between them, in front of Tatsuya. "Tatsuya, when did you increase your simultaneous targeting to thirty-six?"

But it wasn't out of consideration for him; a significant portion of her action was out of the desire to express her own excitement.

"I believe three months ago, your upper limit was twenty-four."

Miyuki was referring to the number of targets Tatsuya could aim at and use a spell on simultaneously. His specialized CAD was shaped like a gun, but spells didn't fly out of the barrel. Multipurpose CADs didn't even have a barrel to begin with.

Categorized into four families and eight types, the essence of modern magic was to overwrite information possessed by events, not to shoot a magical bullet at a target. Therefore, it could exert the same effect on one event or many, depending on how the caster specified the targets.

To do that, however, the caster had to define multiple coordinates at once, and that required parallel thinking. He also had to identify all the subtle differences between the events—after all, to use magic against several targets of event alteration like he had, you had to perceive each individually rather than taking all those targets and perceiving them as a single thing to be altered.

Up through the single digits, mostly anyone could acquire the skill depending on their training. Any higher than that and things needed a different talent than magic. Even increasing your capacity beyond that by a single target was considered very difficult. Miyuki's sparkling eyes weren't *solely* due to the brother-complex filters she wore in them.

Tatsuya, though, smiled at her question and shook his head. "Well, they weren't firing back—that is, they were set up to wait for you before shooting. In real combat, where enemies don't wait, twenty-four is still all I can muster."

"Please, you don't need to be so modest. The training may be set up to wait for you to fire, but I can still only target sixteen at once. You're amazing, Tatsuya."

"All right, all right. Flattery won't get you anywhere. You can use magic over a wider area than me, *even when you're always attentive to me*, so you're probably better than me at controlling it, too."

"If we're going that far, then actually, you can apply interference far more strongly and deeply than I can—isn't that right?"

Yakumo grinned wryly at their enigmatic conversation and interrupted. "Come on, you two. The walls have ears, you know."

The siblings exchanged glances that said *oops* and then they both gave a similarly deceptive smile.

Tatsuya and Miyuki eventually left the underground practice arena to the veranda of Yakumo's private living quarters.

It went without saying that Yakumo was the one who had brought them here. He would frequently treat them to tea after training, but he didn't usually bring them to his quarters, instead favoring the main temple's veranda. *He must have something different from usual to talk to us about*, thought Tatsuya.

"I know you both have school, so I'll keep this short," began Yakumo, right after bringing three teacups in and sitting down next to Tatsuya. "I believe you've come into the possession of something quite curious."

Tatsuya didn't have to ask to know he was referring to the Ni no Magatama. It was a surprise attack but not a shock. If this level of *verbal* attack were enough to shake his composure, he couldn't keep up with the priest.

"It was left in my care." Though indirectly, Tatsuya plainly admitted to it. Feigning ignorance with this man was pointless; that had been made clear to him time and time again. Besides, Tatsuya knew perfectly well that Yakumo wasn't the type to rejoice over pointlessly exposing someone's secrets.

"You should return it as soon as you can. And if you can't, then you need to move it out of your house and somewhere more appropriate."

Tatsuya had expected Yakumo to give him a warning, but his tone of voice was tinged with an unexpected seriousness.

Tatsuya's surprise gave way to tension. Instead of continuing as he was, Tatsuya adjusted his sitting position to face Yakumo diagonally.

"I hadn't realized someone was targeting it."

His words included a desire for confirmation, not quite believing that was the case. Ever since he himself had run into that trouble—and been hurt—when Sayuri was attacked, he'd been paying more attention to his surroundings than usual. However, aside from one slight annoyance, he hadn't sensed any threat large enough for Yakumo to be concerned about.

"They're creeping around very carefully. And they're well trained."

Yakumo's answer, a warning about the enemy's extraordinary skills, also hinted that he'd learned their identity.

"I'd ask who they are, but you probably wouldn't tell me."

"Well, the question wouldn't be *completely* futile."

Yakumo's response was truly insinuating, but Tatsuya didn't hurry the man.

On the other hand, Yakumo, possibly surprised by Tatsuya not biting at the lure by this point, slowly continued. "Let's see… Here's another piece of advice. If you find the enemy, take care not to lose your sense of direction."

"Direction…?" asked Miyuki dubiously.

Tatsuya silently considered the priest, wondering what his answer would be.

"Any more, and you'll have to take out your wallet."

Unfortunately, the man didn't give him an answer.

With the priest's dark smile before him, Tatsuya decided not to inquire any further.

The Thesis Competition was in one week and one day.

"Presentation backup" was a system that—it would not be an exaggeration to say—involved the entire school.

Most of the experimental equipment they'd use during the presentation was finished. Still, for the sake of more effective production and more reliable operation, they ran through one rehearsal after another, constantly reviewing and making improvements and adjustments.

Some were involved with putting together the demo equipment, some planned the onstage production, some instructed others on how to effectively support the presenters from the audience seats, some provided means of transportation and handed out food… Even the "indoorsy" students who hadn't gotten a turn for the Nines were freely putting their talents on display.

Meanwhile, the more physically inclined students were also completely focused so they could reliably perform their own duties. A few of the heavyweights, for whom one wouldn't normally consider preparation necessary, were taking initiative and pouring their energy into training for unlikely trouble.

The hill next to the school had been remodeled into an outdoor training area. Magic high schools weren't prep schools for the military or police force, but since those were the things many students were after, there were a lot of shapes and sizes of such facilities, both indoors and outdoors.

In its artificial forest, for instance, Mikihiko currently lay hidden, watching his senior and training partner.

He was crouched under the shade of a tree while his partner was exposed in a spot unoccupied by trees. His imposing openness put pressure on Mikihiko, even though he wasn't looking his way.

He was practicing against the club committee chairman, Katsuto Juumonji.

For the upcoming Thesis Competition, Katsuto had been made the commanding officer of the venue's security team, which was composed of members from all nine schools. In addition to meeting the other schools' representatives, he took the lead of his own training routines, raising the morale of the other students selected as team members.

Mikihiko had been chosen as a practice opponent thanks to his display at the Nine School Competition. Of course, he wasn't the only one serving as Katsuto's opponent. When this started, it had been ten versus one.

Within three minutes, seven had retired.

Mikihiko had only fired a few ranged attacks from afar, and despite never having been attacked, he was drenched in sweat.

A cold sweat.

...Maybe I got ahead of myself.

When he'd first been told about this practice, he'd nearly jumped for joy. He was a freshman *and* a Course 2 student who wasn't in any magic competition clubs. Being the Juumonji's next leader's training partner would have been difficult even if Mikihiko had been the one to ask for it.

Mikihiko had agreed without hesitation to Sawaki, who had brought the idea to him, vigorously bowing in thanks.

He knew Katsuto was far beyond anyone he could compete with, but he'd still wanted to fight with all his might and gain valuable experience.

Unfortunately...

I need to calm down. This is just a mock battle.

...he'd been telling himself that for a while now.

Katsuto was holding back, as he should have. None of the seven who retired had severe wounds. But that didn't relieve the crushing pressure Mikihiko felt emanating from him.

Mikihiko was by no means weak-hearted. In fact, he was enduring Katsuto's pressure well. Moments ago—three minutes, to be exact—a freshman of the Hundred, Igarashi, had caved under the pressure and launched a reckless attack that ended in him being taken out.

Mikihiko's breath had become ragged before he realized it.

The volume of his inhalations and exhalations had, at some point, reached audible levels.

He immediately noticed it and quickly stopped.

Only two or three of those audible breaths would have made it out.

They should have been so soft you couldn't hear them from a yard away, even indoors.

And yet Katsuto's eyes locked straight on to the tree behind which Mikihiko was hiding.

A new layer of cold sweat broke out on his back. He forced himself to start breathing again and focused on his senses of hearing and touch.

He wasn't bold enough to investigate with magic. He knew Katsuto had found him, but he wasn't bold enough to expose himself. Peeking out from behind the tree was out of the question.

Instead, he listened carefully to the flow of air around him.

Through the cloth on his kneeling leg, he felt a slight vibration come through the ground.

That wasn't enough.

His eyes read the slight changes in refraction that the agitation in the airflow caused, and his nose and tongue sensed the ratio changes in the chemicals mixed into the air.

Mobilizing his five senses, he began to rebuild the vague information from his sixth sense into reliable data.

Katsuto steadily stepped toward him, neither hastily nor overcautiously.

...Three, two, one—now!

After counting down in his head, Mikihiko slammed his right hand into the ground.

His psions followed the fuses running through the ground, pouring through a spell circle.

He had set up this conditional-activation spell before hiding behind the tree, and now, with the caster's psi-waves as a trigger, it sprang into effect.

Four earth pillars erupted from the ground near Katsuto, surrounding him.

They were positioned in a square whose corners lay exactly southeast, southwest, northwest, and northeast; that is, earth, man, heaven, and demon.

A moment later, the ground on which Katsuto stood collapsed into the shape of a mortar.

Doton Kansei, an old-style spell whose name meant "earth-escape pitfall."

It was not a spell for escaping into earth as its name would imply, but for covering the enemy in earth and sand and dropping an opponent into a hole, then using the distraction and trap to secure time to escape.

Against low-level opponents, it could also prevent someone from moving and allow the caster to capture them. Against Katsuto Juumonji, he'd be lucky if it did anything more than buy him time, and Mikihiko wasn't arrogant enough about his own skill to think it would.

Not sparing any time to check if his spell worked, he bolted away from his spot.

His judgment was accurate.

Once the dust cleared, a circular hole in the ground was revealed, earth and sand piled up in a ring, and Katsuto himself without a speck of dirt on him.

His defensive spell had completely shut out Mikihiko's attack.

Still, the screen *had* forced him to let his prey escape from sight.

Katsuto grinned. Then, he stepped onto the ground—he'd been levitating slightly due to his wall's repellent force.

To prevent accidents, and to provide help in case of emergencies during these magical mock battles, many monitors stood watch both inside and outside.

"Wow..."

Mari let out a noise of admiration as she watched the screen.

Mikihiko was a freshman, and yet he'd survived this long. His skill was praiseworthy. They'd seen during the Nines that he had excellent abilities, unconcerned with the Course 1/Course 2 system. But seeing him fighting for real like this again, his practical use of magic, rather than his unique magic skills themselves, stood out.

"He's clever in a different way than Tatsuya," said Mayumi to Mari. "So many interesting freshmen this year."

Mari grinned wryly. "It honestly seems like there are more hopeful Course 2 kids than Course 1. That's ironic."

Mayumi smiled painfully as if to reprove her. "That's not it, Mari. Course 1 still has more kids who are altogether better. This year, the ones with unique abilities are standing out, and they're giving us the wrong impression, that's all."

Her remark struck Mari as likely. "I see." She nodded, looking back at the monitor. "He definitely still seems useful compared to the other freshmen, though. Birds of a feather flock together, I guess."

"The teachers were talking about how radically Yoshida has improved from his experience at the Nines, too. I hope we can continue to ride this wave..."

"Right, since he doesn't seem like the type to take a leadership role."

"Yes, he's more the type to make lots of enemies, isn't he?"

As Mari and Mayumi smiled drily at each other, the lookout

system monitor showed Mikihiko driven into a dead end and putting up a desperate last resistance.

Preparations against unlikely problems weren't only happening at school.

Leo had come here again today instead of school this morning, to the dojo of the Chiba family, one of the Hundred and known as the Sword Magicians.

For six hours, with lunch in the middle, Leo had been swinging a wooden sword and was dripping with sweat. The long, thick, metallic-core *bokuto* meant for practice swings would have even advanced practitioners groaning after three hours straight. Even Erika, who said mean things to him on a regular basis, couldn't help but be astonished at Leo's physical stamina and mental fortitude.

"All right, enough!"

At Erika's signal, Leo let down his arms and, as one might have expected, exhaled deeply.

In front of him, she was wiping the sweat from her brow with a towel.

"You're really tough, you know that? I mean, you've never had any *kenjutsu* experience before."

Her words couldn't exactly be called *polite*, but the usual teasing feeling in them was absent. She sounded honestly impressed.

Leo knew that, so he shrugged, somewhat embarrassed, then gave an intentionally brusque answer. "Even calling me a beginner would be too much compared to the others here. I'm normally swinging around ice picks and pickaxes, after all."

"Ice picks, sure, but pickaxes…? What on earth does that mountaineering club of yours even do?"

"I think the same thing sometimes… Anyway, if I'm tough, that makes you just as tough, doesn't it?"

As he said, Erika hadn't simply been watching Leo do his practice swings. She'd been standing in front of him doing her own as an example. He'd been watching how she swung and then imitating it.

"The one I was swinging around was a light one. I'd have given up a long time ago if I'd been using yours," she said, tossing the *bokuto* she'd been using to him.

He safely caught the sudden throw, then swung it with one hand to test its weight. Understanding and puzzlement appeared on his face. "You're right, it is…but it seems so light you'd have trouble swinging it with both hands."

"That's where the skill comes in," said Erika, without any modesty or affectation, putting the towel on her neck. As if feeling hot, she pulled off the front collar of her kendo uniform and fanned herself with it. He hadn't seen anything untoward, but he looked away anyway.

She was being attentive and purposely not showing anything, so even if he acted suspiciously, she wouldn't be embarrassed or alert. Having been his classmate for half a year, she knew that, despite his rough exterior, the boy was surprisingly pure-hearted and obstinate. Her impression was that he was the type, for example, to see the door to the girls' locker room slightly open, and even if he knew nobody was around, he'd stubbornly pretend not to see it, and leave.

Of course, him averting his eyes so blatantly still made Erika feel a little awkward.

"…What are you looking at?" she asked, giving him a sullen glare.

"Huh?!" Leo reacted with unnatural confusion. "No, I, uh, wasn't looking at anything!"

Seeing him so flustered made her feel embarrassed, even though she didn't need to. Even Erika had enough girlishness in her for that. "I know you're not looking at anything! I mean, don't go looking elsewhere!"

"R-right. Sorry."

An awkward air lurked between the two, but Erika wasn't the sort to keep on fidgeting forever. "…We're going to the next stage."

Erika stared sharply at him, but that made Leo feel relieved rather than perturbed. "The straw sheaves were next, right?"

"Yeah. Follow me."

Erika took the lead and brought him to a room with a wall of hard-packed straw stacks in a grid pattern. It was for training one's blade alignment—swinging the blade straight in and straight out. The idea was to cut through and leave perfectly level surfaces behind. If you couldn't do that, you couldn't perfectly bring out the blade's efficiency. This was an absolutely essential skill for Leo especially, since she was trying to teach him the *Usuba Kagerou*.

"Here. This is a real sword, so be careful, would you?"

This time, she obviously didn't toss it to him. Holding the middle of the grip, she held out the unsheathed katana to him.

Leo took it with both hands, his right just under the guard and his left on the bottom of the handle.

"You know the process, right?"

"Yeah. The sheaves laid across their sides—first I cut the top one of the stack. When I do, I have to stop the sword from touching the second one. After that, I cut the second one, and then the third one. After I cut all five of them, I move to the next stack. I'll do the stacks in order, from left to right."

"Very good. I'll be taking a rest in the back, so once you're done with the right end, come get me."

"What should I do with the katana?"

"There's a sheath next to the door, isn't there?" said Erika, pointing next to the entrance.

Leo had watched her take the sword out of it, so he didn't actually need to check, but he looked that way just to show he was paying attention.

"Just put it back in there. The sheath will do the cleaning."

The sheath cleaning the blade meant there was a feature inside the sheath that got the dirt off and spread oil on the blade. That was how Leo interpreted it, anyway. He responded with affirmation, to which Erika casually waved and left the room behind.

With a *kiai*, he swung the naked blade down.

At first, he'd been getting it stuck in the middle or using too much force and cutting into the next level. On the last stack, though, he'd cleaved all the sheaves in two with one swing. That swing was the last one. He was finished with the task Erika had given him. It probably hadn't even taken ten minutes. Leo shook his head.

It didn't feel right—it was too easy. Since Erika said to get her when he was finished, he left the room. She'd mentioned she was taking a break, which meant she would have enough time to relax before he was done. At least, that's what Erika must have thought. He'd taken no more time than it would to drink a cup of tea. He decided he must have done it wrong.

But he didn't know what he did wrong. Erika had certainly misinterpreted his physical abilities, so no matter how much he thought, he wouldn't figure it out. Fortunately, Leo didn't commit the foolish act of wasting time thinking about it. He didn't have the knowledge to come up with anything, so he figured that wouldn't mean anything. Erika had told him to come get her when he was done, and though he didn't feel like he was done, he decided to call her anyway.

He sheathed the katana as instructed and exited the practice room into a hallway, only to realize that he hadn't asked where Erika would be. *That was dumb even for me*, he thought, mocking himself a little and glancing around to see if there was a HAR terminal anywhere. Unfortunately, he couldn't find anything like it. Even if he had, who knows if it would have given him access privileges for private data? He quickly put an end to his search.

If he went back to the dojo, someone there would know where she was. He walked down the hall in the opposite direction from before, and conveniently enough ran into a young woman coming out of the central room. She looked like she was around twenty-five or twenty-six. She wore her calm-patterned kimono (Leo didn't know what kind it was) with a natural grace; she could have been married or unmarried. She had a plain sort of appearance, but her attitude clued him in to the fact that she wasn't a servant. And anyway, he was pretty sure there were no young, female servants in this estate in the first place.

"Oh, hello. You're an unfamiliar face."

Her relatively formal tone made Leo sure of it—she was part of the Chiba family. She didn't look anything like Erika, but maybe she took after their mother, and this woman after their father or something.

"Oh…could you be the classmate Erika mentioned?"

She put familiarity into her voice, but it sounded obligatory and insincere to Leo. The sisters—Leo had taken to believing they were sisters—didn't seem to be on very good terms.

"My name is Leonhard Saijou." Of course, he wasn't about to change his attitude just because they didn't like each other. He realized putting on airs would just betray him. "Actually…Eri—Miss Chiba—told me to go get her when I was done with a task she gave me."

He also had enough tact to be polite himself, but he almost flubbed it. The woman, thought to be Erika's older sister, didn't appear to mind it much.

"Where did she say she was waiting?"

She wasn't minding the leaves—her eyes were on the trunk. A super-serious type, maybe, but Leo thought there was something else there. Not that he had proof, of course.

"She only said she was taking a break."

"I see… Then she's probably in the lounge," said Erika's sister (unconfirmed) as she took a small terminal from her kimono sleeve. After fluidly operating its touch screen for a moment, she said, "You can borrow this," and offered it to Leo. "You just have to follow the path on here. This will open the door for you."

"...Is it all right for me to intrude?"

"Erika was the one who told you to come get her, right?"

"Well, yes."

He wasn't entirely convinced, but he was, in fact, looking for Erika, so this did help. Having persuaded himself, he took the terminal, and Erika's sister (unconfirmed) left him with the words *Take your time*—he didn't know what she meant by that—and started heading back to the dojo.

"Man, this place is huge..."

He'd felt no lack of vacillation when he'd borrowed it, but now he was genuinely glad he had taken the portable terminal from the "sister."

Still, the route to the lounge was incredibly difficult to grasp. It felt like—no, he was sure of it—he was being made to take the long way around, but he interpreted it as simply how the interior was arranged. In any case, after over five minutes of walking around, he finally made it to the door to the lounge.

He'd been given the okay to go on inside, but still, he held himself back. Erika wasn't a family member, nor was she his girlfriend. She was just a classmate he happened to know somewhat well (even in his mind, he didn't call her a "friend").

He decided to knock first.

He got no response, so this time he called out. "Hey, Erika, you in there?"

Still no response.

"I'm coming in."

Belatedly doubting she was actually there, he decided that if the room was empty, then he didn't need to hesitate. He held the terminal in his hand to the reader next to the door.

With a classic electronic noise, the door unlocked.

Suddenly, sound emanated from the room.

Oh, so you are *in there*, thought Leo, opening the *thick sliding door lacking a handle.*

A shout of "Hang on a second!" came a moment later.

"...Eh?" came a dumb noise from Leo's throat.

He didn't realize he'd made the sound. But right now, he had no time to worry about that. The idea of moving even a finger, let alone closing his eyes, never made it to his brain.

The same went for the person he was staring at.

Erika was standing there, half-turned toward him, frozen.

This was the scene in Leo's eyes:

Erika was in an unbecoming state, with only a bath towel wrapped around her. Because of her unnatural position, the knot at the top of her chest had loosened quite a bit.

At her hands was a massage chair that had fallen onto its back. She'd probably been lying on there until right before he'd opened the door.

Behind Erika, he could see a door with a proper doorknob. Leo finally realized the sliding door he'd opened had been an emergency exit.

The bath towel's knot fluttered undone.

Time slowed to a fraction of its normal speed. No, this must have been his mind accelerating several times.

Erika's hand quickly caught the slowly falling towel and held it against herself.

That finally broke the curse that kept Leo's body still.

"Sor—"

"Creeper, lecher, Peeping Tom—close the door already, stupid!"

Before Leo could say sorry, a storm of abuse rained down on him so fast that Erika's tongue could barely keep up with her thoughts.

He hastily shut the door, turned his back to it, and slid down to the floor.

"That spinster snake in the grass... I figured she was still my sister, I guess my thoughtfulness was misplaced..."

As Erika scattered curses and stomped on the floor, Leo, behind her, had a bright red autumn leaf stamped on his face. She'd demanded she get at least one punch at him, and he'd acquiesced, leaving him with that. She hadn't used her fist, though, but her palm—not out of consideration for Leo having been a deceived victim as well, but simply because she didn't want to hurt her fingers.

Leo didn't complain once about the treatment. He believed this was entirely his fault. She'd been relaxing in the massage chair because she'd mistaken how much time it would take Leo to finish the exercise, but Leo opening the emergency exit without thinking first was a different problem. He had just barely avoided seeing *anything important*, but that didn't seem to exempt him from responsibility. Deciding it would be best to go home for the day, he called out to her to apologize again.

"Erika?" "Leo."

His voice overlapped exactly with Erika saying his name.

"Leo," stated Erika again as Leo swallowed at her sharp gaze. "Forget everything that just happened."

A natural request but still an unreasonable one. Nothing would make this easier than if he could forget by simply trying to forget.

"...But I'm sure that's asking too much."

But the "understanding" words that followed didn't make Leo feel relieved; instead, he shuddered.

His premonition quickly became reality.

"I can't have you remembering anything you don't need to, so you have a lot more training in your future. Not just for the *Usuba Kagerou* but on the basics of *kenjutsu*. All of them," she repeated.

Maybe she thought that part was important. Erika filled him with such dread he couldn't even get a word in.

"You're staying here tonight."

"...I only brought one change of clothes." That response was all Leo could currently manage.

But even that Erika rejected.

"I can get you a change of underwear. Don't worry, the dojo will pay for it."

Even after the sun set, First High was filled with the energy of students rushing about. The school grounds were enveloped by tumult reminiscent of the last spurt before a campus festival. Magic high schools, crammed with normal high school education plus magic education curricula, had no school festival events. The yearly schedule had no room for them. Students participated normally in interschool sports and competitions, but school events where students overcame the barriers of clubs and grade levels to laterally create something did not exist, unfortunately. For magic high schools, unlike the Nine School Competition (the preparations for which were also done solely by those with superior practical skills), the Thesis Competition provided more opportunities for Course 2 students to be active as well, and during this time of year, everyone could fully enjoy excitement similar to a school festival.

The supply team, put together with female freshman volunteers from the cultural clubs as the main battle force, was going at full operation to match this last spurt. On normal days, they would have gone home a long time ago, but today, the girls were running all over delivering meals for dinner. Among their numbers was Mizuki, who belonged to the art club.

The sun set quickly in autumn, and this day in late October was no exception. The western sky, which had been dyed red until a little while ago, had been painted over in a gradient of lavender to dark blue. Looking at the outside scenery, for which the presence of night had grown completely strong, Mikihiko thought, *It's gotten pretty late*, and sighed.

He'd been called in today to serve as former club committee chairman Katsuto Juumonji's practice partner. Not one-on-one, of course. It was a ten-on-one mock battle, and he was one of the ten.

He hadn't thought it would be over in one match, and he hadn't wanted it to be, either. Ten Master Clans, Course 1 kids, it didn't matter—Katsuto's strength had burned itself into his eyes at the Nine School Competition. Mock battle though it may have been, he wouldn't be able to get many opportunities to have a contest with someone so powerful. He understood Katsuto's strength and his own weakness from experience—and that in itself made the time valuable. Mikihiko had used this chance to attend the mock battle with the enthusiasm of greedily gathering knowledge of how to fight with modern magical fighters.

And as he'd hoped, they'd fought in five mock battles, and he'd been crushed by Katsuto five times. As he lay on the ground (or being made to lay there), gasping for breath, his heart and mind were satisfied by the fulfilling time he'd expected. After Saturday's half day of classes ended, it was 4:30 in the afternoon when *he finished being Katsuto's training partner.* So that he wouldn't vomit during the training and embarrass himself, he'd only eaten a few simple supplements for lunch, and now he was understandably starving. Just as he'd been squinting at the radiance of the sun in the far west, he muttered, "Time to go home." When he got up, he heard the command that break time was over.

Katsuto was going to be the commanding officer of the venue's security team, made up of members from all nine schools, so it had been Sawaki, who had taken over command of First High's security team in his place, who had delivered the command. Mikihiko had stood reflexively, spurred by Sawaki's enthusiasm (washed away by it, actually) and had ended up participating in their later coordinated training as one of the criminals. It had been an hour since then. The security members were still training, but all the freshmen called as practice partners had been relieved. (The juniors still weren't allowed to leave.)

After changing out of his mud-stained training gear and into his school uniform, Mikihiko headed for the second gymnasium (nicknamed "the arena"), where the security team was doing hand-to-hand combat practice. On the surface, he had helped them, but Mikihiko was clearly the one to benefit most. He wanted to thank them for that. He was planning on just giving them a quick thank-you and leaving so he wouldn't get in their way, but…

"Yoshida, you too. Go have something to eat before you leave!"

Once again, Sawaki had caught him. They had clashed with the meal-delivery team. *Bad timing*, thought Mikihiko. It was mostly only juniors left in the arena right now. Not to say the freshmen selected for the security team were absent, but unfortunately, most of them were people Mikihiko had only just met today. He *was* hungry, though. In that sense, it was actually good timing. But eating in this group, he thought, would not only make the food hard to taste but also upset his stomach.

His mind raced as he looked for the words to decline. But as soon as he started thinking of a countermeasure, he felt an odd stare of anticipation mixed with relief on him. Normally, anticipation was paired with unease, but the emotion he could read from this gaze was clearly one of relief. Letting his curiosity get the better of him, he stole a glance back toward where it was coming from. But as soon as their eyes met, the girl he was close with (or thought he was close with) turned her face away in a fluster.

Then, Mizuki, who had immediately looked away from him, directed an awkward smile at him. He was quietly shocked.

Unable to work out an excuse to escape because he was preoccupied with Mizuki—though it looked like any excuse would have ended up the same way—Mikihiko was engulfed by the people sitting in a circle.

It seemed this was the last stop for their deliveries, and the girls on the delivery team were sitting politely and taking sandwiches out of lunchboxes on their laps (the boys had sandwiches plus rice balls with filling). Or maybe they had just sympathized with the hopeful eyes of the filthy, all-male security team. As evidence (?) of this, the girls, before sitting down on the tatami mats of the small gymnasium—now a judo hall—went around pouring tea for and handing out napkins to the boys sitting in the ring.

Mikihiko sat down when the delivery team's bonus service was about to end. Pulled into the circle by force, he sat down in *seiza* on the tatami, then obeyed the educational guidelines that immediately came to mind and sat in a more natural position. A moment later, a girl kneeled next to him and handed him a wrapped meal. He didn't need to look again to see who it was. He'd been following her out of the corner of his eye.

"Thanks, Shibata."

After Mikihiko's sincere thanks, Mizuki made an exaggeratedly bashful face. The lips of several upperclassmen (mostly girls) pulled up into a smile of amusement, but nobody made any remarks. They were students of the elite First High, and they knew how to be moderate. After all, careless banter would end the spectacle, wouldn't it?

Mikihiko and Mizuki, though, didn't notice the vortex of bad motives. Neither had the time. She'd sat next to him without thinking much of it, but she didn't have the bravery to speak up to a boy with all these upperclassmen around, even if he was a classmate. Mikihiko, for his part, wasn't bad at talking to girls, given the abundance of female students at home (a trend shared among any Shinto-type old magic families), but thanks to Mizuki getting spectacularly red in the face, he started to feel strangely conscious of her and was unable to find the right chance to say anything.

As a result—it bred a very "first-love couple" mood, extremely innocent and heartwarming to those who watched. And right now, girls weren't the only ones watching over them with warm (or lukewarm) gazes. Even the martial arts boys, who one would think disconnected from this sort of thing, noticed the subtle air floating about. The moment a cliché situation happened—like Mizuki pouring Mikihiko more tea, accidentally touching his hand, and getting flustered and drawing it back—silent murder and silent applause would fly about in equivalence from the entire circle of people.

Having come this far, though they didn't know others were having a good time at their expense, the pair began to realize something was going on; they were both sensitive enough to realize it. When they did, the eyes on them they'd disregarded began to feel uncomfortable. It was especially striking in Mizuki's case. Her restless, fidgety attitude slowly grew stronger until eventually, she said, "Umm, I, well, need to," which he didn't really understand, and stood up—or tried to, anyway.

Incidentally, in modern Japan, the practice of sitting on tatami mats had long since died out. The average lifestyle now involved sitting on chairs, and Japanese people accustomed to sitting *seiza* were limited to people in martial arts practices, certain other practices like tea ceremonies, or religious practices—those with special training. However, the generally accepted thought of girls having to sit *seiza* had survived to the modern day, and most of the girls on the delivery team were sitting that way as well.

The upperclassmen, though, were secretly using magic to make themselves lighter. Once you were a junior, even if you were in Course 2, spells like this that didn't especially need speed or precision were possible to trigger without a CAD. Of course, it would take anywhere from ten to thirty seconds for effects to appear, and sometimes the older girls would fall silent in order to reapply the weight-decreasing spell. The male students were aware as well, and wouldn't speak to a girl who suddenly grew quiet.

But for Mizuki, a freshman and a Course 2 student, doing such a thing was still impossible. In fact, she didn't even know a trick to make yourself lighter with magic when sitting *seiza* existed in the first place. In addition, she had no relation to any practices that would need her to sit on tatami…

"Whoa!"

…and her legs had gone utterly and completely numb.

A moment after rising, her legs got tangled, she yelped, and fell. Mikihiko instantly reached out but couldn't quite make it in time. Though he managed to get up to his knees and stop Mizuki's upper body, it was all he could do to brace himself so they didn't fall over together. He didn't have the time to read much into where he was grabbing or supporting.

In any case, after completely absorbing the momentum of the fall, he sighed in relief, opened his eyes, and saw the back of Mizuki's head in front of him. That meant he had his arms clasped around her from behind. And then he started to wonder—what was the soft, voluminous feeling in each hand coming from?

Mikihiko wanted to stop thinking right then and there. His thoughts, however, betrayed him, and he ascertained what his hands were grabbing. Mizuki's frozen mind rebooted at the same time he realized the situation he was in right now.

"…?!"

"I-I-I-I'm sorry!"

Mizuki gave a voiceless shriek and twisted her body away. Mikihiko hastily let go. Her hands went to the tatami, and she quickly realized that in her crawling position, her rear end was pointed right at him, and panicked even more. Forgetting her legs were numb, she rose, turned around, and then fell backward. Because of the string of forced movements, her skirt flapped pretty far up. Her legs, wrapped in leggings, became visible up to a fairly high part of her thighs. Then, with quicker motions one couldn't imagine from a regular girl, she sat back down on her knees, but with her legs apart and hands between them to hold down her skirt hem. Her face was already red, but it was

getting so much brighter it was like she was burning. Tears formed in her eyes, and when she rose again, without falling, she ran out of the gymnasium.

"What are you daydreaming for?! After her, Yoshida!"

As Mikihiko watched Mizuki leaving in a daze, an upperclassman girl he didn't know the name of scolded him.

He hastily stood up, went for the door, turned back to the shoe cubbies, put on his shoes, grabbed a pair of communal sandals for Mizuki—who had run out in just her leggings—and dashed outside, under the starry sky, searching for her in the distance.

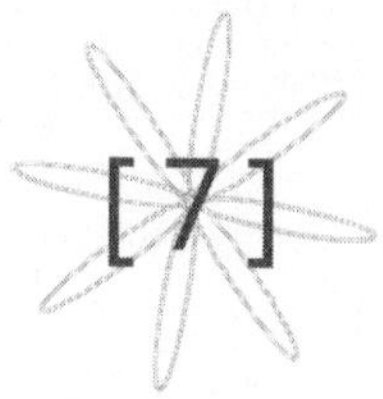

Today was Sunday, but Tatsuya still had to go to school. Not for remedial classes—but because the Thesis Competition was in a week, and naturally, he had to prepare for it.

But right now, he was on his jumbo electric bicycle, heading in an entirely different direction from the school. His sister, wearing a matching bike outfit, had her slender arms around his waist, and her soft chest pressed against his back.

They weren't on a date. Nor were they on a leisurely Sunday ride.

They were headed for the Four Leaves Technology lab to return the Relic sample at Yakumo's advice. Of course, they weren't returning it to the main office's lab but to R & D Section 3, where he worked under the moniker Taurus Silver. He'd planned to include them in the analysis work, but he'd gotten an agreement out of Sayuri when she gave him the Relic, so there was no problem (probably).

They didn't use public transportation because they were being cautious of another attack. It took about an hour at full speed to get to the lab. Using public transportation would send them on a significantly roundabout route, so this way was far shorter. It wasn't a long-enough ride for Tatsuya, who was physically trained, or Miyuki, who could always use inertial control, to need a break. Nevertheless, when they left the urban areas, Tatsuya stopped his bike at a café that was open early.

He gestured for the dubious Miyuki to enter, and they sat down at a window-side table and ordered only drinks (they'd just eaten breakfast at home) before Tatsuya finally answered his sister's unspoken question.

Tatsuya put his elbows on the table, folded his hands in front of his mouth, and quietly said, "We're being tailed."

"What?!" replied Miyuki, barely managing to keep her volume under control. "I didn't realize… A car? Or a motorcycle like ours?" she whispered, leaning forward.

The waitress blushed and looked away, her eyes still fixed on the siblings. She was pretending not to see, but Miyuki didn't have the time to be prying into her reasons. (In fact, she didn't even notice the suspicious behavior in the first place.)

"A raven."

Miyuki's eyes popped open at the simple answer, and it took a moment for her to understand. "…A familiar…?"

"Yeah. A compound one, too."

Of the surveillance systems that used disguised animals or birds were bird- or animal-shaped robots, machines implanted in birds or animals, old-style spells applied to birds or animals, and compound-form birds and animals.

A compound form was a temporary substantiation of spiritual energy.

That only applied to their appearance, though; their forms were constructed on a foundation of psionic particles underneath light reflection–controlling illusion magic. By using weighting, acceleration, and movement magic—or fields that granted the same effects—one could make them seem like physical creatures.

Creating a compound form sounded like more trouble than it was worth, but it had its advantages. Constructing a medium for the spell to act on, then making it visible and touchable, let the caster more easily visualize commands to alter the spell's operation.

"...Then the magician isn't from Japan. Where could they be from?"

Spells to create compound forms only appeared in old magic. The nickname "compound form" was something modern magic scientists had given it upon analyzing the old spells.

And, as Miyuki said, techniques using compound-form familiars were a thing of the past in Japan. And what familiars the old-style casters *did* use commonly lacked actual form—practically all of them, in fact.

The waitress brought them coffee and milk tea. Tatsuya didn't speak until she walked away. That waiting time ended up with him silently staring at Miyuki, further inflating the employee's misunderstanding, but he was neither aware enough to notice it nor sensitive enough to let it bother him.

"I don't know that much," he finally said. "Mikihiko might have been able to say."

Tatsuya moved their cups to the side and took his sister's hands in his.

That caused a quiet commotion around them, and he finally realized that others were looking at them. Still, pulling his hands back out of embarrassment felt like losing, and he had to hold them anyway. As his sister made a face that would cause a misunderstanding for anyone, Tatsuya endeavored to keep his own expression serious—though that had the exact opposite effect on the rubbernecks—and whispered to her.

"We can't lead it to the lab," he said.

"..."

"Miyuki?"

"Huh? I, umm, right, yes, you're right."

As her eyes glazed over even more, Tatsuya wanted to hold his head in his hands, but he forced the impulse away with willpower. "This is the compound form's position."

Tatsuya converted the position of the compound form he'd "seen" into psionic signals, and sent them through their touching palms and into Miyuki, deep into her mind, where her magic-calculation region resided in her unconsciousness.

When executing magic, a magician inputted the alteration target's coordinates into his or her magic-calculation region as a variable. This variable was an encoded image that each individual magician created in his or her own mind, so normally, magicians couldn't share them. As a result of the Yotsuba's unique magic technology, however, Tatsuya and Miyuki could exchange these psionically encoded images through physical contact.

"Miyuki, shoot it down."

A short command.

That, of course, was enough to tighten Miyuki's expression.

"...I understand," she nodded after a brief moment of hesitation.

She'd never had the option of disobeying an order from Tatsuya. Still, hesitation came anyway, since magical sniping was her brother's field of expertise, and she wasn't confident she could do it as well as he could.

"I don't want to expose my power in this situation. And with an emulator, it would escape while we set up the CAD. Miyuki, it's up to you."

"Roger!"

Excitement crept into her face. Her brother was relying on her, and she couldn't help but be in high spirits.

With the fingers of her right hand still entwined in Tatsuya's left, Miyuki gently sat back and looked down (the fact that it worked as camouflage, looking like a girl being embarrassed, was likely ironic for the siblings) as her left hand, out of sight of the waitress, secretly and quickly took out her CAD.

Her magic activation had no time lag.

Tatsuya's "sight" showed the familiar's body instantly freezing, while at the same time, the spell maintaining the temporary form froze, causing the psions making up the compound form to scatter in all directions and vanish.

It just seems like they're not trying..."

"Huh? What do you mean?" asked Miyuki from the tandem seat. Her posture was, as always, her arms around her brother's waist, with her chest and face pressed against his back.

Having brilliantly destroyed the familiar tailing them at the café and getting all the praise she wanted from her brother, she was effervescent, and her voice being decoded through the close-range wireless was just as bubbly.

Her attitude was objectively indiscreet given the situation, but nobody was around to criticize her anyway. The one listening to her didn't; he just answered her question. "Only one thing to tail us, and with a remote spell... They attacked Sayuri before, and today they were watching me. Somebody is obviously after the Ni no Magatama. Some of the ones who have been sniffing around recently are probably after the Relic, too. But I can't help feeling like they're not being very persistent about stealing it."

"Is it not just because your guard is so strong, Tatsuya? Making you an enemy over a second-rate Relic would be too risky."

Miyuki's usual brother-complex filter had automatically acted on her answer, which was reflexive and based on a strong self-conviction.

I see. Risk and return...

Nevertheless, her casual response made Tatsuya feel like he might have just gotten hold of a part of what was really going on here.

When Chen received the report that their shadow had been destroyed, he scowled. From the start, he hadn't thought highly of their conservative plan, watching from somewhere out of reach—not only from the one they were shadowing but from themselves—with a long-distance spell. He couldn't help a feeling of displeasure over the spell being spotted and broken within merely fifteen minutes.

Now all we've done is put him on his guard!

He knew angry yelling would only needlessly dispirit his subordinates, so he took the prudent option and didn't say it. Still, the charged air wasn't hidden.

"Did we figure out where Tatsuya Shiba was going?"

"He seems to be on his way to Four Leaves Technology's R & D Section 3 lab."

The subordinate who answered him also looked tenser than he needed to be. Chen got the impression he was only giving the bare minimum—and also not disagreeable—information so he wouldn't incur his superior's displeasure.

"ETA?"

"Approximately forty minutes."

That was why Chen needed to ask the important parts himself. "Forty minutes from now, I want the cyber team to attack that FLT lab," he ordered, giving up on his considerate responses.

That morning, the lab of R & D Section 3—called by engineers at FLT's main office "Captain Silver and his merry crew" in a way that was difficult to judge whether it was contemptuous or jealous—was filled with a different clamor than usual.

"Quit worrying and cut the damn line! Backups? We don't need newer ones!"

"Rack ten fully disconnected. Reconnecting now."

"Idiot! Why the hell would you reconnect when we're still being hacked?!"

"Great, I found how they got in!"

"I'll start up a counter-program!"

Listening to the yells flying back and forth in the operation room gave Tatsuya a good idea of what was happening.

"Ah, Prince Shiba!"

Tatsuya's good partner, Ushiyama, finally noticed the siblings after a solid minute of them standing there. (In terms of how good a partner he was—he'd built the flight device's hardware according to Tatsuya's specifications and in just two weeks, and he'd made the Mini-Communicator in half a day and sent it to him. To Tatsuya, the man was very *friendly*.)

Maybe it happened in other places, but this was the first time Tatsuya had to wait more than ten seconds for someone here. That went to show how urgent the emergency was.

"My apologies! Didn't notice you walking in… Hey! Which one of you dimwits didn't tell me the prince was here?!" shouted Ushiyama more loudly than before. Despite his slender frame, he had a voice like a cracked bell.

Half the people in the room battling with their terminals cowered.

When Tatsuya saw it, his face darkened. "Don't stop working! Keep monitoring!" he yelled, giving a dressing-down with at least as much punch as Ushiyama's.

"Y-yes, sir!" came the reply.

After being relieved at the staff going back to their desperate-looking battles, he turned back and saw Ushiyama now shrinking back for some reason.

"We're being hacked?" asked Tatsuya. He didn't understand exactly what went through Ushiyama's mind, but he felt—and Ushiyama more so—that bringing it up wouldn't be pleasant. He'd cut out any prefaces to avoid that.

"Well, yes…" Ushiyama hesitated in giving his response, but at least Tatsuya's intrusion didn't seem to have irritated him. Tatsuya wondered what the issue could possibly be, but it didn't take long for Ushiyama to explain.

"It is a hacking attempt, but…it's a strange one," he said. "The hacking techniques themselves are quite powerful, but we have no idea what it is the hackers want to know. They don't seem to be narrowing their search at all. It's like they're grabbing anything they can get their hands on."

"A real hacker, then—the curious type?"

"It doesn't seem like this is one person. The tricks they're using would need quite a few people working in concert to pull off. I wouldn't doubt you if you told me it was a government organization."

"And yet their goal isn't clear… Do you have a list of what data you expect to leak?"

Tatsuya's question implied a possible regularity hiding in the hackers' chaotic methods.

"No, there hasn't been any data leaked yet."

But Ushiyama's answer made him fall into thought. "…How long has the attempt been going on for?"

"About ten minutes."

In other words, it started right before Tatsuya got here—almost like it had been timed. In that time, all they'd done was break into the server. The situation appeared incredibly unnatural to him.

"Unauthorized access has stopped!"

"Don't let up! I want you monitoring this all day! …Right, excuse me. In any case, what did you come here for today?"

Tatsuya explained the events, the company's goals, and his own goals regarding the Relic, all the while organizing the string of attempted information thefts happening around him recently in a different area of his mind.

"Counterattack from FLT!"

"Cut the line *as planned*!"

At Chen's order, a man *physically* severed the line they used for hacking. As he watched the process, he spoke to his aide waiting next to him, Ganghu Lu.

"What do you think he'll do?"

"...I do not know."

It was difficult to call Lu's attitude toward his superior officer appropriate, but Chen continued anyway in a low voice. "They couldn't stop a hacking attempt for over ten minutes. Tatsuya Shiba must be having doubts about the lab's security."

"Indeed."

Chen wasn't looking for decorum or bootlicking from his aide but rather level-headed judgment and strength a match for thousands. He didn't need eloquence. "Even if Tatsuya Shiba is related to FLT, I find it hard to believe he would give the Relic orb to a laboratory with unreliable security."

"Logically speaking, that's correct."

"I know what you want to say. Tatsuya Shiba is still in high school. It's perfectly possible he'll avoid keeping something he knows we're after in his own hands. In that case, we just have to think about how we're going to get the data from the lab again."

Lu silently expressed his agreement.

"I'll probably need you to go out."

"Leave it to me."

Chen nodded deeply to his trustworthy aide's response. Then, his expression changed, as though he'd just thought of something. "Come to think of it, Zhou was going to check on that girl today."

His voice couldn't be called very friendly. He felt this vague sense that he wasn't being taken seriously. And this was with him restraining his emotions. It wasn't hard to guess how Chen really felt about Zhou.

Still, Lu didn't say anything to curry favor with him. His eyes moved as he waited for his next command.

"Get rid of her before he does."

That should have been an order Lu wasn't expecting. If he

completed the task, Zhou would lose all face, and Chen could lose a valuable collaborator.

"Shì."

But Ganghu Lu simply accepted the order, neither his face nor his mouth questioning it.

Despite it being a Sunday, they were going to school, so they couldn't stay in their personal clothes. Some "civilian" high schools allowed students to attend school in plain clothing, but they were a minority even among nonmagic schools. Regardless of whether you had classes, you had to come to school in your uniform.

The Shiba siblings stopped back at the house to change.

When they did, there was a message on their house phone—a message set not to transfer. Restricting a message from being sent to a portable terminal was a way of preventing others peeking at it. If it was packaged like that, it meant the sender was treating it as highly secret.

"Tatsuya, is something the matter?"

Miyuki, having finished changing a few moments after Tatsuya, walked over to him as he stood in front of the phone.

She peered at the display. "A message? Who is it...? Wait, Hirakawa?!"

Naturally, she was aware of the attempted sabotage incident. The part that stood out most when he told her was her utter lack of sympathy for the Hirakawa sisters.

The answer was already out, so Tatsuya decided to say what the message was. "Looks like she wants me to call her back," he explained, pushing the Reply button before Miyuki could say anything.

The call connected in one ring.

"Hello? Is this Shiba? I'm sorry for calling you like this..."

Of the members of First High's Nine School Competition team,

Koharu Hirakawa had been one of those friendly toward Tatsuya from the start. He'd never directly interacted with her, though. She didn't like confrontation, so she was always worrying about others—a standout timidity different from, say, Azusa's. From a different perspective, though, her hesitance could be taken as kindness and tolerance. In fact, maybe that viewpoint was the majority.

"No, I'm sorry for getting back to you so late. The house was empty for a short while this morning."

Considering when they usually left for school, it was a little late right now. It wasn't strange that she was at home, since it was a day off, but she'd probably been waiting for Tatsuya's call the entire time, evidenced by how she'd picked up in one ring.

The video feed was turned off. Videophones were commonplace now, but it was only a technological change. Human feelings hadn't changed—nobody was about to nonchalantly expose themselves in their houses to the eyes of others or unhesitatingly show their indoor clothes to anyone who called. Some houses had built-in phone rooms, but most homes with a phone in the living room would detect the incoming phone number and switch the feed on or off. Here, too, Koharu's face wasn't on the display; the screen remained blank.

"No, I'm the one who asked you to call, so..." Still, just listening to her voice brought a dark, downcast face to mind. *"About the other day, well...I'm sorry my sister caused you trouble."*

Or perhaps it wasn't a dark face but a pale one.

"It didn't come to anything, so please don't worry about it. I'm not."

He didn't say that out of consideration for her—that was exactly how he felt.

"But a lot still happened... They already caused you trouble by suddenly making you a representative, too. I've just been acting so cowardly that she got the wrong idea... Just the fact that she disturbed you during such an important time means it didn't come to nothing. All I can do is apologize, so...I'm really sorry."

Koharu was doubtlessly bowing deeply to him on the other side of the unconnected camera. Her voice easily brought the image to mind.

However, Tatsuya wasn't sure what to do about the apology. He hadn't wanted one, and listening to her worn-out words of self-torture actually just made him feel gloomy. From the bottom of his heart, he didn't care about what Chiaki had done—or, more accurately, tried to do.

Not one bit.

"I understand," he replied. "Out of consideration for you, Hirakawa, I'll wipe the slate clean."

Therefore, intent on ending the call quickly, he offered an insincere consolation (?).

"...Thanks. I knew you'd say that, Shiba."

If she'd actually seen his true intent, then that was extraordinary. But her words were probably built on a big, convenient misunderstanding.

"Don't mention it... Good-bye then."

"Oh, wait!"

Seeing that Hirakawa was satisfied, Tatsuya had tried to hang up, but it was a little premature. "What is it?"

In many ways, he wasn't free. Or maybe "had no free time" was more appropriate. He had to be careful not to let his displeasure seep into his voice.

"Umm, well, I don't think this is much of an apology, so..."

Seriously? thought Tatsuya. Going along with her in an endless loop was the last thing he wanted to do.

"I don't know if this will help you much, but..."

Fortunately, it was a groundless fear.

"I found the log of Chiaki contacting the thief group. Her private data is in there, too, but...I'll give it to you, Shiba. Please use it as you see fit. Umm, I'm really sorry, I know you're busy. Thanks for listening to what I had to say. Bye."

The call ended.

Without waiting for him to reply.

"You may be sisters, but hacking is a crime, you know..." he muttered, having meant to say that to Koharu, while looking at the log file icon assigned to his isolation box.

"Tatsuya, is something the matter?"

Miyuki must have heard him talking to himself. She had returned, a somewhat worried look on her face.

"What to do...?"

As he replied with an answer that didn't quite line up with the question, he mulled over what Koharu was after.

She said it was in place of an apology. Not directly, but there was no mistaking what she meant.

But her true intentions were almost certainly something else.

Koharu had probably hacked into her sister's communication log because she wanted to do something about the guys who had dragged her onto the path of evil. But it was more than she could handle. Tatsuya surmised that by leaking the information to Tatsuya, she wanted him to get revenge in her place.

Masterfully played, I suppose...

The term *feminine wiles* didn't come up for him due to lack of life experience, but he also wasn't innocent enough to avoid those "wiles."

"...Well, fine. I'll use anything I can."

With a vague expression, and leaving Miyuki be, Tatsuya punched in a different number. He wasn't confident that he could hunt down these network foxes going on only a log file of an access point they'd probably already abandoned.

But he knew someone who could.

As the siblings arrived at school, it began to rain. Neither had brought an umbrella, unfortunately, but thankfully, they only got a little wet. Besides, Miyuki was a student council member, which permitted her to carry a CAD in school. At once, she used magic to dry their damp clothing without leaving a trace behind.

However…

"We won't be able to do any fieldwork in this rain…" said Miyuki, her face clouding.

Tatsuya shrugged. "That's one thing we can't do anything about."

The preparations were going smoothly so far. It would feel a little cramped doing work indoors, but it didn't mean they wouldn't finish in time. Of course, in Tatsuya's case, he was planning on doing some debugging in the robot club's garage today, so the weather was irrelevant.

"I'll get going."

"Okay. Please do your best, Tatsuya," offered Miyuki, who had work waiting for her in the council room. In the end, she parted with him only reluctantly.

◇ ◇ ◇

Robot club was short for *robotics research club*. The club's garage was a small building used for creation and testing of robots of all sizes, as well as mechanical powered suits.

In order to control the robots, large computing machines were mounted in here as well, and the club had offered them for activation sequence debugging and spell simulations during the Thesis Competition's preparation stage.

Today's work was activation sequence debugging. Suzune and Isori would be doing operation tests on the already-completed stage props, so Tatsuya was on his own for this job today. The plasma nuclear fusion demo machine at the center of the presentation was already connected to the computer. After helping with the settings, the robot club members had all cleared out to assemble another machine. Right now, Tatsuya was the only person in the building.

Maybe I was a little late… He gave a dry smile—this was an off day with no set starting time, but perhaps he had played the "late executive role" too well.

"Welcome back, sir."

He was the only "person" in the garage, but a moment after he entered, a "figure" was there to greet him.

A black, balloon-sleeved dress four inches below the knee and a white, frilled apron. White stockings and black slip-ons. A maid headdress, also frilled, on the head.

Nice hobby… Grinning painfully, he introduced himself. "Tatsuya Shiba, Class 1-E."

The "girl" who greeted him stopped moving in an upright position for about half a second, after which she bowed deeply.

The pause was the time it took to authenticate his voiceprint. Eventually, through facial recognition and voiceprint recognition, Tatsuya was given a pass through this room's security.

"I shall prepare some coffee."

A slightly awkward voice with slightly awkward movements. But the differences between that and expected human behavior were minor enough that it wouldn't matter unless you observed closely.

Her name was 3H Type P-94 (3H Personal-use '94). The robot club had shortened her name to Pixie based on the words for *nine* and *four* in Japanese.

This Humanoid Home Helper, or 3H, belonged to the robotics research club, and was just that—a human-shaped robot that did domestic work. That was the robot's identity. One of the club's current seniors was apparently connected to a big HAR manufacturer, and it was on loan for monitoring so they could improve its AI.

A normal 3H was given the appearance of a woman in her late twenties, but this one was set to be in her teens so that it wouldn't stand out too much at school.

Indeed, if you put her in a First High uniform and mixed her into a classroom, as long as she was quiet and sitting, she'd probably pass for a deadpan female student. Perhaps one would even use the term *cool beauty*.

Of course, such fixations meant nothing the instant you put her in a maid outfit.

When he'd first come into this room for Thesis Competition preparation work, this robot maid welcoming him had been a surprise. Despite his initial astonishment, though, now he just felt a discomfort regarding her clothing.

Tatsuya sat in front of the console desk. As he booted up the terminal, he heard a quiet *clunk* of a coffee cup being set on the side table.

The software controlling the manipulators has room for improvement... he thought briefly before reaching for the cup. He took a sip, then nodded—acceptable.

Pixie, the latest model of 3H, had an automatic customization feature. She could learn up to fifty of her face recognition–distinguished users' tastes. That was how she'd brought out coffee to his preference without him saying anything.

"Pixie, stand by in suspend mode," ordered Tatsuya to the 3H waiting behind him, setting his coffee back on the side table. He knew it was a robot, but having something that looked so human standing behind him was unsettling.

"At once, sir."

Fixed phrases like that one had smooth pronunciation. P-94 bowed so smoothly she seemed biological, then headed toward a chair next to the entrance. She sat down and made her back perfectly straight. Then she stopped moving altogether.

A 3H's power source was a direct methanol fuel cell. She could supply herself with more methanol—in concrete terms, by drinking it with her mouth—so her users didn't have to worry about her running out of power.

Still, there was no reason whatsoever to waste fuel, and since just standing still consumed power (standing on two legs was a highly advanced act), he made sure to sit her down when he didn't need her. Incidentally, though her eyes were closed and movements stopped in this state, her sensors were on. This unit in particular that the robot club used for monitoring was a special version with upgraded home security features, and her eyelids, which appeared closed, were actually made of material that light could permeate. It didn't mean something that looked human was no longer watching him, but Tatsuya wasn't that high-strung.

He stretched out his neck (for no particular reason) then put his fingers on the keyboard. An orchestra of rhythmical keystrokes (actually the electronic sounds replacing them) began to play.

He took his left hand away from the keyboard and placed it on a pearl-gray panel. It was an interface for letting the caster communicate with the large CAD built into the demonstration machine. The caster would send the psions necessary for creating the activation sequence through this panel, and it in turn would be received by the built-in CAD.

With his right hand keying in the steps to operate the CAD one by one, and his left receiving the activation sequence formed one process at a time, he converted the activation sequence into a magic program and sent it back out (however, sending a magic program wasn't performed through physical contact).

He was currently performing a magic program operation simulation.

And on the surface, he was following the right process, but he was actually using his "eyes" to directly observe the program's operation as he did his checks.

His abnormally high magic-development performance was thanks to this trick, which used his Elemental Sight—his eyes that could see eidos. As a magic developer, this trick could be called cheating, but he wasn't enough of a straight shooter to worry about things like that.

With his naked eye he watched the display, and with his mind's eye he watched the dimension of information bodies.

About an hour passed since starting his work.

Until suddenly, he felt physically unwell.

A sudden sleepiness overcame him.

Did I overdo it…? he thought, but when he *took a deep breath, the drowsiness got stronger.*

Figuring he'd take a break outside, he moved to stand up…

…but his limbs felt heavy.

His body wasn't coming around.

With enough training, people could control their physical desire for sleep with willpower. Several all-nighters in a row was a different story, but he was pretty sure he didn't lead such a disorderly lifestyle.

Warning signals flared to life in his mind. His physical condition was clearly unnatural, abnormal.

```
Physical function abnormally decreased.
```

The state of "sleep" itself didn't hamper combat ability.

Forced slumber, on the other hand, from which he couldn't make himself wake up, was the main factor inhibiting combat.

```
Self-repair spell starting semiautomatically.
```

His self-repair ability saw the need for repair…

```
Loading magic programs.
Reloading core eidos data from backup.
```

…and sprang into action.

```
Beginning repair… Complete.
```

His body instantly returned to the state it was in before he was caught by the drowsiness.

The problem was still unsolved, though.

The coffee he'd drunk on his way from the house to the labs, the coffee Pixie had just made for him… He'd already checked them to make sure there was no poison in either. If there were substances involved…

Gas!

Someone had tampered with the air-conditioning system. He accessed the room's information and learned that though its virulence was low and had a short persistence, there was sleeping gas in the air and it was quick acting.

But that left him at an impasse. It would be easy to remove the poison from the gas with his Dismantle. However, magic-observation instruments were online all throughout the school. If he used Dismantle on the entire space—in this garage room, in this situation—his spell, which he needed to keep secret, was certain to be revealed.

Miyuki, Honoka, or Shizuku would have been able to select only the harmful gas and eject it from the room, but that skill was a bit too high a hurdle for him.

And he couldn't hold his breath forever.

The only thing he could do here was run away. The demo machine was fine as it was. He locked the computer and stood, then turned back toward the door.

But in front of him stood a slim figure to block his passage.

The figure reached a hand toward his mouth.

It wasn't a very quick act, which gave him the time to see who the figure was.

Her hand stopped right before reaching Tatsuya's face.

"An error has occurred in the air-conditioning system. Please wear this mask."

The Humanoid Home Helper Type P-94. The robot girl with the name Pixie was holding a simple gas mask out to him.

At a glance, it was a conventional reusable gas mask made of non-woven fabric, but it actually had a high-performance gelatinous filter inside that didn't let anything larger than carbon dioxide molecules through (which naturally meant oxygen could pass). If you stuck the side with the adhesive seal on it to your face, the filter would seal up, making it hard to breathe but blocking almost all of the toxic gas.

Didn't think she'd have something like this, Tatsuya thought, obediently putting on the mask. This time, she instructed him to close his eyes. "Your corneas could be contaminated. I will take your hand and lead you outside."

The speech software could have used some improvements, but he understood exactly enough of what she said. It would seem that P-94, top-of-the-line 3H, was also programmed for disaster response. Or maybe the robot club had "trained" her for it.

Tatsuya knew that sleeping gas wasn't the type to harm the eyes. Nevertheless, he did as he was told and closed them. But he didn't head outside.

"Pixie, turn on the forced ventilators. I'll stay here in case of any secondary disasters while I evacuate. Stand by in surveillance mode. You are not to switch out of that mode so that rescuers can enter."

P-94 accepted Tatsuya's string of commands. "Deeming secondary disaster avoidance as logical. Starting forced ventilators."

The disaster-response forced-ventilation system, constructed separately from the air-conditioning, began to work. An upright, two-legged frame using a small fuel cell as a power source wasn't meant for physical labor. The sensors she could have installed were limited by her human shape as well, so she couldn't do any highly precise work, either.

3Hs weren't made to act alone with superhuman strength or precision, but rather for people to have a stress-free interface to use with their home automation system. They were remote control terminals for HARs which could recognize voices, move like people, and look like people. They had standalone household functions added after the fact to support HARs in more delicate situations they couldn't handle, but those were nothing more than an extra.

Still, that extra piece tended to be so good that you could forget their original purpose as a HAR interface.

This wasn't just something he was idly thinking about—Tatsuya had forgotten about it until just now, too.

Being too convenient has its ups and downs... he thought, which had to be either him hating to lose or hiding his embarrassment, as he waited for the sleeping gas to be ejected from the room.

Considering a 3H's functions, P-94 would be restoring the air-conditioning system right now as well.

Tatsuya sat in front of the terminal again, took off the mask, then closed his eyes and sat back. This way, he wouldn't surprise the person who came to check on him *sleeping*.

As expected, a visitor came soon after.

Even after the gas was gone, Tatsuya sat perfectly still, eyes closed, senses keened. He immediately noticed footsteps sneaking in.

He'd ordered Pixie not to do any entrance checks beforehand to set the stage for someone to slip in unnoticed. If they *hadn't* come, he'd have been disappointed.

"Shiba?"

The voice of an upperclassman he knew.

It was spoken likely out of forethought as the person checked to see if he was asleep, and to have an excuse if he did wake up. But the timing with which the person entered the room was, in the first place, unnatural, and their attempt to create an alibi was poorly executed at best.

Tatsuya, of course, committed to his sham.

"Shiba, you asleep?"

After seeing Tatsuya not respond once again, the intruder gave the appearance of looking for something. But their eyes immediately went to the demonstration machine. Not to the terminal, since they'd either seen it locked and given up or they'd intended to get the data directly to begin with.

Despite Tatsuya's eyes being slightly open to watch them, despite Pixie in surveillance mode recording everything, the intruder used a hacking tool from a submonitor connector and began a desperate attempt to get the data out.

"Sekimoto, what are you doing?"

Then, suddenly, a voice came from the entrance. The intruder's shoulders jerked, and he turned around.

The jig is up… he muttered silently. His fun little challenge ending prematurely frustrated him, but the related parties—the one who was stopped, and the one who stopped him—probably didn't care one bit about his mean-spirited entertainment.

"Chiyoda, why are you here?!"

"Why? I got an alert from the safety system that something was wrong with the air-conditioning. But why did you come here, Sekimoto? What do you have in your hand?"

"No…I thought I cut the alarms…"

Sekimoto was either very disturbed or extremely weak to unexpected things happening, because that line was very ill spoken.

Chiyoda glared sharply at him. "I see. The alarm didn't come automatically. It came manually."

It wasn't Tatsuya who'd sent it—it was Pixie. She'd done it on her own judgment, which made it sort of automatic, but Chiyoda had no way to figure that out. More importantly…

"You just said something I can't let slide."

…was what Sekimoto had accidentally confessed to.

"What do you mean, you cut the alarms?"

Criminals never acted rationally and logically 100 percent of the time. In fact, given the excessive tension while committing the crime, they frequently made stupid mistakes they never would have otherwise.

That was how law enforcement, who could only move hours or days after the fact, found clues to identify perpetrators. And now, Sekimoto had fallen right into the trap, the psychological pitfall that other criminals succumbed to.

"Sekimoto, I see you're staying quiet. You're basically confessing you're the culprit."

Kanon controlled her tone of voice well, but that only made her seem all the more serious. She raised her right hand in front of her so he could see. A powered-on CAD. It was already charged with the psions it needed to instantly expand an activation sequence.

This wasn't a game, or training, or a prank—this was a direct descendant of one of the Hundred, the Chiyoda, prepared for battle...

"Ha-ha, Chiyoda, that's a harsh joke. I'm the culprit? Of what, exactly?"

Sekimoto tried to throw off pursuit with an empty, theatrical laugh. But he didn't have a bunch of sympathizers ready to help. It wasn't going to work in a one-on-one situation.

"You're the one who tampered with the air-conditioning and sent sleeping gas in here. Plus, I caught you in the act of being an industry-university spy."

"That was rude! I was afraid of the accident destroying the data, so I was just backing it up."

"With a hacking tool? That won't work. Right, Shiba?"

When Sekimoto turned around—aghast—he saw Tatsuya standing there with a forced smile. Kanon seemed to have seen right through his sleeping act.

"Impossible! The gas didn't work...?"

"He's not your average cute high school kid. It would take more than a little sleeping gas to knock him out." Kanon's tone was too unfriendly to sound like an overestimation.

Tatsuya's pained grin deepened. "I won't argue I'm not a 'cute little high school kid,' but..." he said. "Well, the rest of what the chairwoman said is correct. You can't take a direct backup from the demo machine. And you don't need to."

All that the CAD built into the machine did was record activation sequences and expand them. You couldn't use it to edit the programs within. Program modifications were done with the electronic computer always connected to it, and that had a stock of backups stored.

"Sekimoto, don't make fun of us too much," said Kanon, staring at him with displeasure. "I may not know much about technology, but I at least know that."

Sekimoto clenched his teeth and growled. It was proof he'd run out of arguments (and excuses); it was the cornered rat baring its fangs.

Kanon's tone changed. "Isao Sekimoto. Put the CAD on the floor."

A demand for the criminal to surrender.

And Sekimoto's answer—

"Chiyoda!"

—was to expand an activation sequence.

Sekimoto was only in his second half of junior year, but he was strong enough to be selected for the disciplinary committee.

His spell activation process was fluid, and the speed at which he read in the activation sequence and constructed the magic program was comparable even to Nine School Competition representatives.

However…

"…You always did try to act too cool, Sekimoto."

Sekimoto's spell didn't go off, and Kanon's oscillation spell traveling through the floor knocked him unconscious.

You didn't need to say the spell name to trigger it. You didn't need to shout the target's name, either.

Modern magic battles were instantaneous.

Kanon had already prepared her CAD for this. If he shouted her name for no reason, he'd never get the best of her.

At Kanon's call, support from the disciplinary and club committees came running, then hauled Sekimoto away to the student guidance room (also known as the "interrogation chamber").

During that time, Tatsuya didn't interfere whatsoever, be it verbally or physically.

After he saw everyone else off, he spoke to the waiting P-94.

"Pixie, release surveillance mode. Record all video and audio from when I first ordered you to monitor the room until this moment, save it on a memory cube, and delete the master file."

Pixie belonged to the robot club, and Tatsuya didn't have administrator privileges. But she had recorded what had happened as evidence at his request, so he was the recording file's owner.

"Of course, sir. Copying data to memory cube… Copy complete. Completely erasing master file."

In accordance with his rights to the file, Pixie copied the recorded video and audio to a memory cube and deleted the original file from her own memory.

After sticking the cube containing the evidence recording—which he hadn't even told Kanon about—into his jacket pocket, he ordered the feminine robot to stand by again.

Visiting hours at the NMU-affiliated Tachikawa Hospital went from noon to seven in the evening. Right now, it was just past four, so it wouldn't seem strange for a young man in a suit carrying a bouquet of flowers to be walking down the hall. Even if it were a man with features like a young aristocrat.

But despite his prominent appearance and prominent behavior, it did seem strange that the other visiting guests and nurses passing by from time to time didn't concern themselves with him at all.

He must have come here several times already, or else was familiar with the layout of the hospital for a different reason. The young man walked along *silently* with an unhesitating stride, without even looking at the maps on the wall. He used the stairs, rather than the elevator, to ascend to the fourth floor, then abruptly stopped as he entered the hallway.

Ahead of him was the back of a large-statured man. He

recognized the person's appearance. The man was slightly younger than him, but not by much, and he was standing in front of a certain hospital room.

The young man, Zhou, had informed Chen, his well-built superior, of today's visitation. Chen hadn't said anything at the time, so he shouldn't have had any qualms with Zhou coming here to visit the girl.

Regardless of Chen's intentions. That was how Zhou had interpreted it. Therefore, there wouldn't be an issue between him and Chen if he intruded on the man about to intrude on his hospital visit.

With a look of nonchalance, with no hesitation whatsoever, Zhou pushed the emergency alarm button.

While the young man was still going from the third floor to the fourth, a couple entered the hospital lobby. The man's name was Naotsugu Chiba, and the woman's was Mari Watanabe. One was the second son of the Chiba, who fully exploited his title as "genius swordsman," and the other was the former disciplinary committee chairwoman at the National Magic University Affiliated First High School.

"Shuu."

Normally, Mari's trademark was a dashing figure that all the younger girls would admire, but in front of her boyfriend now, a softer, more feminine air surrounded her. Not only was she naturally exuding coyness with him, but also she was making an apologetic face.

"I'm...well, sorry," she said. "You're busy, and yet I made you come with me for something like this."

Mari had arrived under the pretense of a hospital visit so she could question Chiaki Hirakawa, currently staying within. She personally felt that this was First High's problem, which was why she was apologizing.

But Naotsugu looked down at her with an expression that said he hadn't expected this. "Don't be so formal. You don't need to worry about these things."

"But you're shipping out early tomorrow morning, aren't you? You need to get ready..."

"It may be a training voyage, but it's mainly for the guys in command and gunnery. We're focusing on overseas training after that. Lots of physical labor, but I'm used to the exercise," replied Naotsugu in a somewhat joking, silly tone.

Mari's worried look softened a bit. "Combined amphibious landing training in Guam this time, right?"

"Yeah. Unlike Thailand, it'll be short—just ten days. I don't need to bring much, so you don't need to worry."

Naotsugu smiled at her, but when she smiled back, her face still showed she had reservations about it. "...Is something still bothering you?"

"...It's, well, Erika," she stammered, sounding unsure of whether to explain.

"Erika?" On the other hand, Naotsugu's voice was colored with confusion—he hadn't expected her name to come up.

"...You always practice with Erika the day before you leave the house for a while. What about today?"

A complex mixture of disappointment and mild disgust came into Naotsugu's expression. "Erika's practicing with a classmate. He looked pretty hopeful, so I'm sure she's having a good time."

"Classmate? A boy?" asked Mari casually.

An unexpectedly firm answer came back. "They're just *friends*, I'm sure."

"..."

Mari said nothing and stared at Naotsugu. He answered her look by clearing his throat.

"Shuu?"

"Anyway, you don't need to worry about Erika. And besides, I wanted to be with you, Mari. Don't let it bother you, okay?"

"Y-you don't need to be so embarrassing about it."

Their roles swapped. The person used to making the quips was surprisingly weak when they had a deadpan remark turned on them. Mari had incessantly teased Tatsuya to somehow get under his collar before retiring as disciplinary committee chairwoman, but it only took a few blunt, loving words to tragically sink her ship.

Naotsugu exhaled, relieved to have controlled his girlfriend's reactions, but his relaxed nerves were quickly attacked by an even stronger tension:

The emergency alarm went off.

"Shuu?!"

Mari, who, until that moment, had been busy feeling enamored with her lover, looked up at Naotsugu like the television channel had suddenly changed.

"It's not the fire alarm. It's the violence one."

The anti-violence alarm. It was at once an alarm to prevent third parties from getting involved in violent or criminal acts as well as a signal to summon help to restore the peace.

"Fourth floor," said Naotsugu, skillfully picking out the alarm's details from the message board on the wall.

"Fourth floor?!"

"Is the underclassman you were visiting on the fourth floor?"

He saw the gravity in the expression on Mari's face and realized this had something to do with them.

"Let's go!"

Without giving the nodding Mari time to hesitate at getting him involved, he ran up the stairs, practically pulling her.

Utterly unperturbed by the sudden alarm, Ganghu Lu placed a hand on the hospital room doorknob. He'd already found out his target was in this room, and he was confident he could take care of a single girl before police arrived with, quite literally, a flick of his wrist.

After tugging on the knob, he gave a puzzled look. The door was locked. He'd assumed all the doors would be unlocked when the fire alarm went off so that people could escape. Was the system malfunctioning? Unfortunately for him, he had not been informed about the anti-violence alarm.

The slight cultural difference created a time lag. Lu had been planning on breaking the lock anyway. He'd thought the alarm would unlock the door, but it was still locked, which had puzzled him. It barely took any time for Lu to set himself back on his goal of busting the door open, but it was enough for unexpected interference.

A moment after he pulled the doorknob out of the frame with a loud noise…

"Who are you?!"

…somebody challenged him.

After Naotsugu used the Chiba's special self-acceleration spell to dash up the stairs in one breath, he came face-to-face with a well-built man several years older than him breaking a door lock.

He'd shouted his question reflexively, but by that time, he'd already dragged the answer from his memory. This man, emanating so much danger that all his hairs stood on end…

"The Man-Eating Tiger…Lu Ganghu! Why are you here?!"

As a member of the Chiba family, renowned for their authority in close-combat magic technique, Naotsugu knew this man's face and name well. He was a hand-to-hand magician from the Great Asian Alliance, usually counted among the top ten duelists in the world. Given his age proximity, the topic of which one of them was stronger came up often—and most concluded that in terms of violence, Lu Ganghu, whose name struck awe and dread into opponents, had him beat.

"Huàndāoguǐ…Naotsugu Chiba."

From Lu Ganghu's mouth as well came a soft voice, saying what was surely Naotsugu's nickname, the Illusion Blade, and his real name.

A moment after their eyes met, the battle between the two behemoths began.

Naotsugu removed an eight-inch-long rod from his inside pocket. With a press of the button near its tip, it made a nice *click* and extended into a sword with a six-inch blade.

Ganghu Lu, meanwhile, assumed an unarmed stance. Without showing any fear of the knife in Naotsugu's hand, he charged ahead.

Once the distance had closed to the length of a long sword, Naotsugu swung his right hand downward.

A dagger couldn't reach at this distance. Nevertheless, Lu held his left hand over his head.

A *thump* rang out at the intersection of a line drawn from the blade to his hand.

The weighting magic Pressure Cut. A close-range spell that created an incredibly fine repulsive field along a thin rod or wire to sever objects touching it.

Naotsugu had created that field in the middle of nowhere, with himself as the origin, using nothing but his dagger to go on.

If that skill was surprising, the fact that Lu stopped the repulsive blade with his bare hands was astonishing.

Gang Qigong. An expansion of "hard qigong," this was called "steel qigong" by its users in North China. Qigong was not magic but a type of classical martial art; Gang Qigong used qigong techniques as a base to magically create a layer of armor harder than steel of one's skin. Ganghu Lu was the best user of Gang Qigong in the world.

His repulsion blade blocked by the wall of biowaves, Naotsugu brought his right hand the rest of the way down. Canceling his own spell *returned* the Pressure Cut into an empty swing. With no resistance, he slashed the blade without resistance down to his waist, then quickly cut upward at an angle.

Wanting to stop the invisible slash, Ganghu Lu slammed his Gang Qiqong–enhanced right hand into his right side. It met with no resistance, though. Naotsugu had canceled the repulsive blade as it materialized.

Ending a triggered but incomplete spell midway—that wasn't a special skill. When conflicts occurred between magicians, the act of amputating the interfering force and thereby canceling a magic program about to overwrite eidos was actually an essential skill when using magic in teams.

But doing it instantly while activating the spell was a whole different beast. If you only output a magic program with the intention of not actually causing event alteration, the instant it passed into the gate—the door connecting a person's mind to the Idea, located at the bottom of one's conscious mind and the top of the unconscious mind—the magic program would fizzle. It wouldn't show any signs of activating, so it wouldn't deceive an opponent. To deliberately cancel a spell midway through, you had to project the magic program with the true intent of activating it, and then hold back before it finished activating. You needed the ability to immediately switch gears mentally.

Since Lu had prepared himself for a slash from the repulsive blade that didn't come, his body swayed to the right. Without a moment's delay, Naotsugu slashed diagonally from the shoulder and released a Pressure Cut. The invisible blade drove toward the right side of Lu's neck.

Another *thump* sounded. No blood splattered. Lu's body fell *backward*. He had twisted and stopped Naotsugu's slash from the front. As Lu fell, he used his back as a pivot to rotate and kick out at his attacker, who jumped back to avoid it. With distance between them now, Lu rapidly stood up.

Their duel, however, didn't restart. When it came to judging distance, the previous clash made it clear the odds were in Naotsugu's favor. Ganghu Lu was no fool; he wouldn't fight an enemy on their own turf if he could help it. No sooner had he stood up than he took a large step forward and thrust out with his arm.

Naotsugu swung his dagger down at Lu's outstretched right arm. However, the six-inch blade bounced off a spiraling force field around the man's arm. This was another traditional Chinese martial art skill—working all your muscles and bones together and transferring the

force of that twist into the strike area, thus creating a weapon both offensive and defensive; it was a skill developed magically out of Chansijin.

Naotsugu's body swayed like a leaf floating in a flowing river. Still in his position of having dodged Lu's straight, he retreated to the windows.

He slid his entire body away from Lu's immediate finger strike, placing wide distance between them. However, Lu gave him no time to regroup. A fist, a palm, a rake—he made his hand into many forms, mixing in elbows, shoulders, and tackles, an onslaught like a raging wave. Naotsugu didn't have time to use Pressure Cut as he dragged himself back. Still, despite the continuous attacks, Lu hadn't landed one clean hit on him. Only the will to fight could be read in Lu's expression, but nobody could say for sure he felt no unease. His attack rhythm gradually sped up, and each blow's power decreased to match.

Eventually, Naotsugu used the length of the hallway before finding his back pressed against the wall. There, Lu came in with a windmill-like punch. But as he brought his right arm down, Naotsugu matched the punch with the edge of his right hand.

He wasn't holding a weapon. For the first time, confusion passed through Lu's face.

A downward blow.

The edge of Naotsugu's hand diverted the trajectory of Lu's strike. The man's body lurched forward; Naotsugu switched the dagger to his left hand.

Instead of the back of his head, which was exposed and defenseless, Naotsugu drove the blade into Lu's side. His body was about to swing around vertically, and his abdomen, the axis of rotation, couldn't avoid the blade. Nevertheless, he somehow twisted to avoid getting stabbed deep within his internal organs. The dagger broke through his skin, slicing deeply.

Hands now bracing on the floor, Lu sent a kick at Naotsugu's head. The teen dodged it, then took a step back. Turning his forward roll into a cartwheel, Lu's feet met the wall—there wasn't enough space to stand up.

A moment later, he launched himself off the wall and at Naotsugu.

He brought his wrists together, and his hands formed the jaws of a tiger. The strike's power was comparable to a beast's fangs, too. If the strike caught someone, it would tear away entire chunks of flesh. It had the potential to even rip out bones.

Sensing danger, Naotsugu twisted far to the side to dodge the strike, not worrying about the risk of losing his posture. Even after Lu's leap went past his prey, its force remained, and he landed two yards from Naotsugu. Then, with both hands on the floor, Lu changed direction. Once again, he shot toward his opponent. Now that he was wounded, the energy and force in his attacks had increased beyond even when he wasn't.

This time, Naotsugu was the one to show unease.

As Lu was about to launch a fourth charge, he abruptly stopped in the middle and turned around, likely a reflexive evasive action.

Two mirage-like blades flew at Lu. They were made of superthin compressed air, heated to a high temperature with insulated compression. Lu's large frame pushed itself between them. A moment later, though, the release of air turned into a shockwave that shot at him from either side.

With an agonized groan, Lu threw himself to the end of the hallway, right next to the stairwell. Naotsugu chased the man's dive, but he had vanished in a split second.

"Mari…thanks for the help."

It had been Mari's spell that saved him from peril, but she hadn't purposely timed it that way. She'd entered the battle as soon as she saw Lu and Naotsugu fighting. That was just how fast and dense their skirmish had been.

"Shuu, are you hurt?!"

Mari ran over, not replying to his words of thanks—she probably hadn't heard them—and her face darkened. Naotsugu's right hand had swollen into a dark red lump.

Naotsugu and Lu's fight had actually been a draw after sacrifices on both sides. When he'd diverted Lu's windmill strike, it had greatly damaged his right hand. Between that and Lu's side, Naotsugu had the advantage if it went for longer, but in a short brawl, not being able to use his dominant hand would have been a major handicap.

"No worries. I'll need an expert healing magician at first, but I can handle the rest of it. Fortunately, we're in a hospital."

"But you ship out tomorrow…"

"That's fine, too, considering who I was up against. I can get them to make it an occupational injury."

Naotsugu's words—or, more accurately, the way he spoke the same as he always did—seemed to give Mari back her calm. As her anxiety faded, a different concern rose to the front of her mind.

"Who…who was that? I can't believe he was your equal in close combat."

Hesitation flashed across Naotsugu's face, but only for a moment. "His name is Ganghu Lu. A magician in the GA3's Special Covert Forces."

"Ganghu Lu… That was him…?" The man was mentioned in the same sentence as Naotsugu Chiba quite often, so Mari at least knew his name.

"Mari," said Naotsugu, suddenly grabbing Mari's shoulders and turning her to face him.

"Wait, what's wrong?" She looked away, embarrassed.

"Mari," he said again. This time, his unusual tone caused her to look at him seriously. "I need to leave tomorrow. I'm extremely concerned that I can't be at your side at a time like this, but…"

"Shuu, I understand. What did you want to say?"

"Right before Ganghu Lu disappeared, he saw your face. He knows you're an enemy now."

Mari nodded firmly. There was no fear in her eyes. That only made Naotsugu's fears worse.

"That violent magician is known as the Man-Eating Tiger. You saw how powerful he is. So, for a while, I want you to make sure you're never alone."

She was about to say *You're exaggerating*, but his serious stare made her swallow her words.

Ganghu Lu, forced to retreat after Naotsugu and Mari's intervention, was now in the passenger seat of the luxury car Zhou drove.

"Was I too forward?" he asked from the driver's seat as they left the hospital gate.

Lu said nothing, just stared out the front windshield.

Without showing whether Lu's attitude offended him, Zhou continued, voice carefree, "Still, that was a surprise. To see Mr. Lu injured, that is."

Even that, which could have been taken as criticism for his failure, didn't get a blink out of Lu. Instead, he asked about the trick Zhou had used to help his escape. "You use Dun Jia?"

"Well, this is embarrassing. Compared to His Excellency Chen's godlike works, this is simply a somewhat advanced sleight of hand. I could never show it to the others."

And Lu's words, which could have been taken as criticism for hiding his hand, only received a calm, completely ordered smile out of Zhou.

◇ ◇ ◇

Tatsuya headed for the videophone as soon as he got home from school. He called a number for the second time today.

"Hello?" responded the voice of a young woman (not a girl) with the fixed greeting from two centuries ago. The increase in not just video but also audio quality was remarkable, but he could tell from

the slight cloudiness that she had picked up on a mobile telecommunication terminal.

"It's Shiba."

"Oh. It's unusual for you to call me twice in one day."

Along with her cheerful response appeared the mask of a young corporate secretary, softly smiling but without an ounce of vulnerability. Normally, she purposely wore plain clothes to remain inconspicuous, but seeing her with normal makeup and accessories accentuated her flowering, above-average looks.

"I'm sorry. Are you on a date?"

Fujibayashi, dressed up for a night on the town, chuckled just as flirtatiously. *"I'm afraid I'm* on the job. *I do wonder why men only flock to me during work, though. None of them were any good, so I suppose it doesn't matter, but still..."*

Her manner of speaking felt somehow different—doubtlessly thanks to alcohol. Of course, Tatsuya wasn't enough of a daredevil to say *I see you've been drinking* to her face, through a camera or not.

Even for cities that had installed collective self-driving car control systems, drunk driving private vehicles was grounds for severe punishment. In particular, drinking and then getting into the driver's seat was the crime. Society's consensus was that because one *could* still drive the car manually, one needed to maintain proper judgment and driving ability.

By the same token, it was unthinkable that Fujibayashi would be using a normal car on the job. She'd have been riding her own, with all its massively improved intelligence capabilities. She'd used her own car, and she was drunk. That had to mean somebody else was sitting in the driver's seat.

"Ahhh..." she sighed. *"If only there were a boy out there as cool as you, Tatsuya."*

Whether or not she knew about Tatsuya's suspicions, Fujibayashi let an even more amorous color into her expression, even winking at him at the end.

"I see. I had something to discuss with you—should I call back tomorrow?" he asked, completely ignoring what he was convinced was a joke.

On her end, Fujibayashi grinned musingly, forgetting to play the coquette. *"So collected… I suppose that's why they call you the 'freest of them all.'"*

"Calling me the 'freest' sounds incredibly sarcastic…" he said. "By the way…"

"No need to worry. I'm alone, for now," answered Fujibayashi, anticipating Tatsuya's doubts regarding information leakage. Then she urged him on. *"You can get as involved as you want."*

"Thank you very much." Even Tatsuya, who could penetrate the easygoing way people like Haruka did things, always found himself drawn in to Fujibayashi's rhythm. He decided to put up a white flag with his expression and get to the point. "The school had a robbery today."

"A robbery? This is about what you mentioned this morning, isn't it? They finally used force?"

"Yes. They used sleeping gas."

Fujibayashi's eyes widened on the display as if to say, *Oh, my.*

"Fortunately, the attempt failed."

"I'm sorry. This is because we make you do so much…"

"No, the army isn't the only one under obligation here."

Fujibayashi bowed apologetically because, since his magic was a classified military secret, they were forcing him to go through more trouble than he needed to.

That was the plain truth, and what Tatsuya had said was a pretext—the Yotsuba didn't have the decency to be particular about how they did it. Still, this exchange was ceremonial, and they repeated it at every opportunity to let the conversation proceed smoothly.

Neither the one apologizing nor the one being apologized to actually felt that way.

"I took the opportunity to record a video of the attempted robbery."

"Really...? How?"

If you wanted to steal information, the most basic, fundamental thing to do was disable the surveillance cameras. And if you couldn't do that, you wouldn't try to commit a crime indoors in the first place.

"I had an independently operating security terminal take it."

"Oh, a 3H? Didn't know you were into those."

"I'm not. I was in the robotics research club room; the 3H is their equipment."

3Hs were designed with such elaboration that people tended to think of them as catering to certain people with specific tastes. Tatsuya knew that, so he'd evasively described it as an "independently operating security terminal," but that didn't work on Fujibayashi.

"About the video..." he said, feeling her suspect him for being evasive in the first place, and thus forcing the conversation back to its point, "I'll give it to you, so could you investigate it?"

"What does it show?"

She replied honestly anyway, a testament to her good-natured personality. Though it was an incredibly natural response, good and bad were relative. Having to call this a "good-natured personality" was, in turn, a testament to the relationships Tatsuya found himself having.

"The unsuccessful thief and the tool he used. I attached a log of the CAD he was breaking into as well."

"I see. Basically, you're telling me to catch the sly foxes already, right?"

"I would never put it so arrogantly, but in essence, yes."

"You don't need to worry about it," said Fujibayashi with intentional vigor, despite Tatsuya not showing any sign whatsoever of worrying about it anyway.

She really did have a good-natured personality.

"The C.O. has been talking about taking care of things soon, too. We already narrowed it down from the log you gave us earlier, so we should be able to nab them within the next couple of days. Hold tight for some good news."

She gave advance notice of her success, without showing any enthusiasm.

Tatsuya briefly thanked her, without saying anything unnecessary, and sent the data to her terminal.

After finishing her conversation with Tatsuya, Fujibayashi beckoned Chief Toshikazu Chiba, whom she'd driven out, to the passenger seat. Despite her blood alcohol level, she had taken up a position at the helm; Tatsuya had been mistaken on that point. After all, she belonged to an unofficial group: the Independent Magic Battalion.

From Toshikazu's point of view, everything that had happened was really quite odd. He'd only been planning on getting a few tips from the Roter Wald bartender, known by those in the underworld, so he could break the deadlock in their investigation.

And now, for some reason, he was with a beautiful eligible woman he'd met at the café. She'd said she wanted him to help, but it seemed to him that *he* was the one being helped. In his mind, he kept asking himself how things came to this, but he still didn't have an answer. He certainly hadn't lost himself to her attractiveness, he kept reminding himself, but he was starting to lose confidence in that statement.

"I'm sorry, Mr. Chiba. It was a private call."

"No, I don't mind."

Toshikazu wore a casual suit with a sense of extravagance to it, like Fujibayashi's own outfit. It was a sad truth, even now, that police officers were underpaid, but in his case, he had a second stream of public, police-recognized income related to his family, so his pockets were lined.

"What sort of tips did your private information source give you?" he asked, maintaining his vaguely irresponsible, frivolous mood, as though he were holding a cocktail glass in one hand.

Fujibayashi turned the same amused smile she'd given to Tatsuya on him. She loved people quick on the uptake. On the other hand, she got irritated when they were too slow to catch on, so she was pleased with Toshikazu's attentive wit. "A sketch of the poor rat being used by the foxes, and a sketch of the little tail they lent him."

"...A video of the collaborator and the hacking, tool?" Even Toshikazu was perplexed as he asked the question.

Fujibayashi nodded with the kind of smile a teacher would give to a student who'd correctly answered a question. "Chief, do you know what the first step in foxhunting is?" she asked, eyes a bit too serious.

"No... Unfortunately, I know nothing about guns...and I've never had the chance to go hunting."

The young chief couldn't keep up with the change in topic and was unable to give a smooth reply. The elite second lieutenant hiding her identity, still looking serious, answered her own question. "The first step in hunting foxes is to find their den. Destroy the nests they would escape to, and once they hide in the bushes, drive them out with a rifle."

"...You want us to search for their hideout?"

"I'll give you the video from the high school student helping me. Look into where he was with the roadside cameras. You don't get that kind of hardware anywhere; he must have met someone directly."

Obviously, it was illegal to use the roadside camera videos for that without a search warrant. And if the target was a minor, you wouldn't get the warrant very easily. Toshikazu, however, pointed out a different problem.

"Where he was—how big a time span should we search? A single person's sphere of activity over just one or two months is basically infinite. Picking out someone suspicious like that, well…"

"There are thirty-two points to search within the city. Grab the places he's been to in the past month."

Toshikazu's jaw dropped. "Thirty-two places…? You've narrowed it down that far already?"

"I have another source of data you don't know about, Chief. I was just thinking that this would be the hard part, but conveniently enough, I just got a new clue."

A tinge of criticism made it into Toshikazu's eyes. "…Another source? Why wouldn't you…?"

"Because the person is a woman, of course."

Her unconcerned answer struck him dumb.

"I couldn't put a girl with a future on a police blacklist, could I?"

"…But you could if it were a man?"

"It's a matter of responsibility," she explained.

Toshikazu had no idea what to say to that.

"I believe in paternal rights. It's only natural gentlemen grow to be more distinguished than women. Therefore, gentlemen must firmly control themselves and take responsibility for all their actions."

With all the sudden old-fashioned expressions—particularly convenient ones at the moment, too—Toshikazu stared at her for a good while, wondering if she was actually serious.

The wounded tiger within the skulk of foxes didn't return until a little after the date had changed. (Though, of course, the foxes doubtlessly considered themselves to be the hunters.)

Chen was taken aback at seeing Lu injured, but he didn't ask how he'd gotten that way; he'd already received a full report on the mission. Lu had insisted on a second attack before returning, but Chen had denied it and called him back. He had no intention of blaming Lu for the failure to assassinate Chiaki Hirakawa, but the way it failed, especially in how Zhou conducted himself, smelled fishy to him. He felt like criticizing Lu now would be playing right into Zhou's hands. And more importantly…

"The situation's changed."

…a higher-priority problem had occurred, and he needed Lu to deal with it.

"*Our* collaborator at First High, Isao Sekimoto, failed his mission and fell into the authorities' hands. He's being kept at the Hachiouji Special Detention Home."

A hospital would have been one thing. But if they'd placed him in a special detention home, a facility for holding minors with magic abilities under protective custody, they'd need more than an average amount of skill to do anything about it. Plus, Sekimoto had been in direct contact with Chen's group. The priority on *dealing with* him was entirely different than Chiaki, who had only an indirect connection to Zhou.

"Chiaki Hirakawa comes later. Get rid of Isao Sekimoto."

"Shì."

Despite the jump in their mission's difficulty level, Lu answered with his usual composed expression. Not even a hint of pain showed through.

The next day, Monday.

As he waited for Miyuki to exit the cabinet, Tatsuya found his classmates riding together in the cabinet two behind them. They must have noticed he was looking; the boy and the girl sitting next to each other both made an openmouthed, surprised expression at the same time.

"Tatsuya, do you see something funny?"

As Miyuki alighted the car's interior, manner refined, she followed her brother's gaze—only to put a hand to her mouth in surprise.

Beyond the front windshield of the cabinet two behind theirs were Erika and Leo, giving awkward, stiff smiles.

Today, there were four members in their group heading from the station to school. It was rarer for all eight of them to be together at once during this time, but still, only having four was fewer than usual.

And that, really, was only natural.

"...Hey, why are you here so early this morning, anyway?" asked Leo unhappily.

But it was entirely Leo's fault that his mood had soured; him venting anger didn't scare Tatsuya. "We're down to one week left. There's a lot to do in the morning."

It was over an hour earlier than they usually arrived.

"What about you, Leo?"

Tatsuya had a reason—the Thesis Competition was this upcoming Sunday. Viewed objectively, it was less strange for him to be here now than Leo.

"You're up quite early this morning as well, Erika."

Before Tatsuya could press the unsure Leo, Miyuki loosed her verbal arrow at Erika. Miyuki gave an invigorating smile, assuring her classmate that she had no ulterior motives.

"...Well, I usually get up early," answered Erika shortly, expression annoyed, before walking faster toward campus.

"Really? Then maybe Saijou got up early this morning," said Miyuki, almost a mumble.

Erika's feet stopped abruptly. *That* was too much for her to endure and walk away. "Wait, Miyuki! You're making it sound like I go wake him up every morning. Would you stop?!"

"That's right! I mean, I was the one up earlier anyway!"

Erika's counterattack, however, came to nothing thanks to the hornet's nest that had just come out of Leo's mouth.

"..."

"..."

"..."

Erika, Tatsuya, and Miyuki glared silently at one another. (Specifically, Erika was the only one glaring; Tatsuya and Miyuki both wore poker faces.)

"...Huh? What's going on?"

Only Leo didn't understand the situation (that he'd caused).

"...Why aren't you saying anything?" Erika's tone was cocksure, but her face was red and she almost had tears in her eyes.

"Well...the early bird gets the worm," said Tatsuya.

Even he wasn't savage enough to attack again. Or maybe he just didn't have the tact to do anything but divert the conversation. Next to him, Miyuki smiled with discomfiture and Leo was still tilting his head, wondering what was going on; in a way, it was a beautiful contrast.

With the start of classes approaching, Tatsuya returned to the classroom to see Mizuki in the middle of carefully pacifying the angered Erika.

"Oh, Tatsuya!"

Mikihiko was the one to call to him, sounding like he was glad Tatsuya was here. Leo was sitting backward in his seat as usual, a glum look on his face.

Tatsuya saw, quite clearly, that Mizuki had stepped on a landmine and Mikihiko had fanned the flames.

"Come on, Erika, cheer up already," said Tatsuya, lightly touching the can in his hand to Erika's turned cheek.

"Ow!" She jumped up like a duck in a thunderstorm. "That's hot! What'd you do that for?!"

"Here." Tatsuya slipped his can of hot chocolate into Erika's hands. She was 50 percent more aggressive than usual.

"Ow," she said again in a different voice this time, juggling the drink and casting a confused stare at Tatsuya.

"Drinking something sweet will calm you down," he explained.

"…Hmph. You can't fool me," she said, opening the drink and putting it to her lips.

Tatsuya saw her cheeks soften a little. He narrowed his eyes into a strange smile at her.

"…What do you want?" demanded Erika, finding fault with his smile. Still, while glumness remained in her tone, it was significantly more relaxed.

"The whole Chiba dojo was drilling a new spell into Leo, right? Nobody has any strange suspicions about this, so lighten up."

Tatsuya only meant that as a way to soothe her, but it had a bigger effect than he'd realized. Erika's eyes filled with unadulterated surprise. "…Are you clairvoyant, Tatsuya?"

"No, that's not a skill I have. It just seems like Leo's willpower is worn down, but on the other hand, his magic power looks energized."

When Tatsuya said *magic power*, he meant a combination of the psion energization that came with using magic and his event-altering interference power. Psions' level of energization depended on magic program construction speed, construction accuracy, and construction scope, but these weren't enough to alter events by themselves. Magic only came into being when combined with the power to overwrite the information attached to those events, which was based in a sentient being.

"Willpower, magic power… You say it like it's all so obvious, but…well, I guess it's a little late for that."

Though magicians could sense psions, it took experience and skill to distinguish the interference's energy. At this point, Erika was starting to tire of being surprised at how irrational Tatsuya was—or maybe she already had, in her own way.

"By the way, Tatsuya, I heard there was some trouble yesterday," Mikihiko said, showing relief that the storm was finally past them.

"Yesterday? Oh…news travels fast."

Tatsuya had paused not out of an attempt to feign ignorance or put on airs. Both Chiaki Hirakawa and Isao Sekimoto were incidents already resolved for him, so he hadn't associated the word *trouble* with it right away.

Fujibayashi had taken it over, promising to resolve it within a day or two, so to him, it was an already-established fact that they'd catch the entire information theft organization today or tomorrow.

The Electron Sorceress.

This nickname given to Kyouko Fujibayashi marked her as both a magician excelling in electron- and EM wave–interference magic and as a demonic hacker who could bend information networks to her will.

Some said she was actually better at tampering with information networks than altering events in the real world.

Just as Tatsuya could read the data attached to past events that the flow of time had overwritten, she had a unique skill where she could reconstruct overwritten and deleted data on magnetic and optical storage. And unlike Tatsuya, she could go back as far as she wanted. The flipside of that was if the physical storage media was destroyed, she couldn't trace anything. It was improbable, though, that all the media recording specific information of the equipment making up the global network would be eradicated.

In other words, if there were any traces in an electronic information network, she could follow the network virtually anywhere.

Fujibayashi had taught Tatsuya his network-chasing know-how, but he didn't think he'd ever compare to her in this field. In Tatsuya's estimation, you could count the world's "foxhunters" rivaling her on a single hand and still have fingers left over.

"Well, they caught the criminal, so I don't think we need to worry."

Hence, Tatsuya answered Mikihiko thusly.

However, Erika and Mikihiko didn't know about Fujibayashi's actions, so they weren't convinced.

"I don't think it's over just because they caught the criminal."

Once Erika voiced her complaint (?)...

"It didn't seem like a solo crime, either. I wonder what organization was backing him..."

...Mikihiko also expressed his concern.

"Why not ask the man himself?"

Once Mikihiko spoke, Leo, who had been listening to the conversation quietly, blurted this out in his usual easygoing manner.

It was easier said than done to ask the person in question. Chiaki would have been one thing, but Sekimoto was in a special discrimination office. Even so, the usual retort for anything Leo said didn't come.

"Yeah...maybe we should go put the heat on him," said Erika, normally the straight woman in their little comedy routine. Her agreement was unusually positive.

"Huh? But, Erika, Sekimoto got..."

"Thrown into a special detention home. We can't just walk in and talk to him."

Erika, the one argued against, finished Mizuki's stammered, paused sentence. That, of course, was not because Mizuki had stopped her and she'd changed her mind.

"But it's not like it's impossible. If it comes to it, we could just sneak in."

"Wait, wait," Tatsuya interrupted, naturally unable to let any more of this go. "You don't need to be rash. All you need to meet him is a letter of proxy from the school. He's still a First High student, you know."

Magic training came with accidents. More than a few magic high school students lost their magic during training and dropped out. But that was all the more reason students didn't easily drop out, barring any atrocious crimes. What Sekimoto had tried to do had been incredibly malignant, but it hadn't worked. They would check to see if there was room for him to improve before dealing with him. A proxy, even a student one, to determine that would be allowed a meeting with him, exactly *because* special detention homes placed holders of *rare* talent in their custody.

"Really?" Erika had to have known that. "But the disciplinary committee basically controls those proxy letters, right?"

Erika had proposed her near-criminal method because she had a reason she didn't want to go through the proper process.

"It would be easier than sneaking into a special discrimination office."

However, Tatsuya firmly turned down Erika's selfishness.

But then, after school, in the disciplinary committee HQ:

"No."

Kanon's answer to Tatsuya's request for a meeting with Sekimoto was very simple.

"...Won't you tell me your reason?"

It was so simple that Tatsuya was very nearly speechless.

"No means no."

Kanon obstinately repeated the word. It was less that she was getting emotional and more that she was worried that, if this came down to an argument, she'd give in.

"But why?" pressed Tatsuya. "Meeting applications for detention homes go through the disciplinary chairwoman or the student council president. But the final authority lies with the school. I just can't comprehend why you would turn me away at the door without a reason."

Kanon scowled, not trying to hide her reluctance. With her being so clearly hard-hearted toward him, he started to wonder if he'd done something to offend her.

Still, Tatsuya wasn't possessed of the admirable quality of backing down quietly, so it was hard to call Kanon's tactic a success.

Eventually, deciding that refusing him any longer was pointless, she reluctantly answered, "...Because it'll cause problems."

"What proof do you have…? And what do you mean by 'problems,' anyway?"

Of course, that kind of reason would never persuade Tatsuya. His return question was only natural.

"Are you saying nothing would happen?! With all of you running around?!"

But for some reason, Kanon came back with a stream of questions. Sharp, angry ones, too.

"You don't seem to realize this, so I'll spell it out! Shiba, trouble loves you! You may not mean to, you might not make any mistakes, but the trouble is going to come to you on its own. We're already busy, so don't give us more work to do!"

That was a truly unfair way of saying it, but Kanon spoke with such force that it didn't allow defense—and Tatsuya thought to himself that, upon reflection, he couldn't completely dismiss the claim.

"Kanon, that wasn't right to say to Tatsuya."

The timely help he got was from Mari, who showed up at HQ frequently despite her retirement.

"He's involved in this," she said. "It's only natural he'd want to hear the details personally."

"But, Mari—"

"Now, wait, Kanon. I understand how you feel, too."

You do?! thought Tatsuya, but he kept his statement of protest to himself—Mari did seem to be defending him, after all.

"Tomorrow, Mayumi and I were planning to check up on Sekimoto. Can't he just come with us?"

"Well…I guess if he's with you…"

Even Kanon couldn't carry through with her stubbornness in front of Mari. Half-hearted though it was, she agreed to Mari's proposal.

"That's fine with you, right, Tatsuya? Not that you'll be able to bring everyone, but still."

Honestly speaking, he wasn't satisfied. Still, with how Kanon was acting toward him, he decided he needed to compromise, too, and submitted to the proposal.

In her bed in a hospital room with no windows, Chiaki sighed.

She was so bored she didn't know what to do with herself.

She wasn't sick, and she wasn't injured. Well, technically she *was* injured, but not enough to be hospitalized. As far as she was aware, there was nothing wrong with her body that required them to keep her in this bed.

Neither sickness nor injury was the reason she was *locked away* in this room.

Yes: This was just a luxurious prison cell.

She knew she'd done something that deserved being sent to jail. She had no intention of complaining about having her freedom taken like this, regardless of her true feelings. She just wanted them to do something about this boredom. Nothing crazy like a television, video games, an Internet terminal, or model building; a cheap, off-network reading device would be enough. It didn't even have to be entertainment—forced labor was fine with her. All she wanted was to stop sitting here and doing nothing.

Not long ago—well, it was more than two hours ago—a nurse had come in to check on her and said she couldn't meet anyone today. An agitator had just broken in yesterday, and it was just to be safe. That was only natural; the emergency alarm connected to the police had even gone off instead of the fire alarm.

And nobody would want to come visit her anyway—she was certain her sister had run out of patience this time—so the lack of visitors didn't affect her. They didn't need to be safe or anything. She'd caught on; the "agitator" had been after her. They'd tried to tear this room's door off. It wasn't as though she'd been deep asleep. She couldn't have missed that if she'd tried. She figured "they" had come to get rid of her. That was inevitable, and she'd even given up on that. They'd only been helping each other temporarily. They weren't friends. That was her impression, and they would think the same. It only made sense that they'd plot to kill her so she wouldn't spill any of their information.

Right now, she didn't care about her life. Nothing mattered anymore. She didn't even know why she'd had such enmity toward *that man*. She scorned herself; maybe rotting away in this empty white room was a fitting end for her.

Just then, there was a knock on the door. Chiaki was steadily lapsing into lethargy, but enough intellect remained to think the knock was strange. The nurses were done with their afternoon rounds. She hadn't called one, either. She was pretty sure nobody would come visit her, and besides, nobody was allowed to.

Another knock at the door interrupted her doubts. Quickly—without thinking much of it—she unlocked the door with her remote.

"How are you feeling today, Miss Chiaki?"

An unexpected person opened the door and entered. Deep down, she knew that if anyone was going to visit her, it was going to be this young man.

"Mr. Zhou..."

The one who had given her those kind words as she'd run away through streets by night, her sister's cornered emaciation too hard for her to watch. The one who had agreed with her dark thoughts, that there was no reason the two sisters had to be the only ones suffering. The one who had told her a little revenge was all right, because revenge didn't have to mean killing. The one who had shown her where to aim her emotions, which had nowhere to go. The one who had given her the means of exacting that "revenge."

This person had saved her mind, and he stood before her now, holding a large bouquet.

"But...how? They said no visitors today..."

There was so much she wanted to thank him for, to apologize

to him for, but that was what she was fixed on? Chiaki felt pathetic. Right after saying it, she wanted to go back ten seconds and deck herself.

"I used a little trick," said Zhou, closing one eye. It was a wink, but he was one of the rare men for whom it didn't come off as sarcastic.

"A trick? ...Magic?"

"No, it's a little different from magic."

In line with her own common sense, Chiaki had interpreted *trick* as *magic.*

But Zhou smiled and shook his head.

"People can cause all kinds of miracles without needing magic. Well, this technique is too minor to be called a miracle."

He smiled at her again, and Chiaki finally regained the ability to think straight, or at least felt like she did.

"Umm, Mr. Zhou, I... You let me borrow so much, but I couldn't do it, so I'm..."

Right before the word *sorry* left her mouth, he held the flowers out to her.

They were strange and beautiful, and she found herself taken by the mysterious sense of captivation they granted her.

"You don't need to worry about any of that."

Zhou's voice sounded a little bit distant to her.

"You don't need to worry about something I did. But if..."

As Chiaki looked at the flowers, dazed, she listened to Zhou.

"If that will cause you regret..."

Chiaki's eyes lost their focus.

"If that will be a burden on you..."

Her mind was filled with his voice.

"...then you can forget about me."

"Forget...?" she mumbled unconsciously. She listened to the sound of her own voice, unaware of what she was saying.

"Yes, forget all about me."

"Forget...? Is that okay...?"

Guided by Zhou, Chiaki gave herself permission to forget.

"Yes, it's okay."

"All right... Then I'll forget..."

Chiaki gave herself the *order* to forget.

After school on Tuesday, October 25. Tatsuya, along with Mari and Mayumi, had gone to the Hachiouji Special Detention Home where Sekimoto was being held. With the Thesis Competition in five days, they were in the final stretch of their preparations, but Tatsuya's share of the work was going well. He had more than enough time to take a few hours off.

Erika, Leo, and Mikihiko had actually wanted to go with him, but their upperclassmen being there seemed to scare them off. Erika was the only one with something against Mari, but for pure-hearted (?!) boys in high school, female seniors they weren't really close to appeared to be a pretty high hurdle.

Of course, the letter of proxy had only included three people on it in the first place. Incidentally, Miyuki, who couldn't leave her student council work, saw him off with a beautiful, not-the-least-bit-smiling expression.

Getting into the building was a process in a few ways, but once they did, they had enough freedom to make the effort seem like a letdown. No employees escorted them; they'd only been handed guide terminals. Still, Mayumi had dropped the name *Saegusa*. They hadn't informed Tatsuya of that particular part of the plan, but the special treatment they were afforded from it didn't even bear questioning.

The room Sekimoto was being held in wasn't a jail cell. He wasn't behind bars such that anyone could see straight in; it was more like a small private room in a business hotel. However, a hidden room sat next to it from which one could look inside.

Mayumi and Tatsuya entered that hidden room. Mari would be

the only one talking to Sekimoto. It was on Mari's insistence, but neither of the other two argued. If Sekimoto went crazy, Mayumi was confident she could deal with him even from the next room over. Besides, Tatsuya knew his skills in that arena couldn't beat Mari's even on a bad day.

From what they could see, Sekimoto wasn't being restrained by anything. He couldn't leave the room, of course. He sat still on the bed, wearing simple clothing that resembled a hospital examination robe. Obviously, they'd been doing thorough physical checks. There was zero chance of him hiding weapons or CADs anywhere.

Beyond the observation window disguised as a wall, Tatsuya and Mayumi saw the door open. It went without saying that Mari was the one to enter. Sekimoto, who had been watching the door open with disinterest, gave a look of shock. A moment later, his eyes filled with suspicion and caution instead. Mari appearing alone had caused him to feel danger.

"Watanabe...? What are you here for?" Still sitting, Sekimoto rubbed his left wrist, probably unconsciously looking for his confiscated CAD. His voice didn't shake, which was a wonder because he looked incredibly tense.

"To hear what's going on, of course."

As another (former) disciplinary committee member, Sekimoto probably knew Mari's methods pretty well. They were merciless. He couldn't suppress the fear roiling within him. "E-even you can't use magic in here!"

Sekimoto's remark was *technically* true. This facility was for detaining law-breaking magicians (up-and-comers and hopefuls) who weren't of age. Unmanned Cast Jamming oscillators, for example, had yet to be invented, but every corner of this building could detect when magic was being used. And if it was, those on watch could introduce neutralizing gases, turn on rubber-bullet gun emplacements, or have police officers armed with antinite storm in.

"You think?"

—If the surveillance systems were working properly, that is. Sekimoto correctly understood the smirk on Mari's face.

"I don't have much time, so let's get to the important bits."

Seeing her sneer (or so it registered with Sekimoto) made him quickly hold his breath—though it was already too late, and he didn't have any spells to escape by holding his breath.

Suddenly, his mind began to haze over. Without realizing he had fallen victim to Mari's spell, he started answering her questions.

"Mind control using scent?" pondered Tatsuya, seeing at a glance from the hidden room what Mari had done.

Smells directly stimulated a person's emotional memories. Doctors had discovered this last century, and the folk remedy of aromatherapy was used for its strength in affecting emotions. Mari was manipulating the air to send several scents into the olfactory cells in his nasal cavity and forcing him to perceive smells that lowered his mental resistance, achieving the same effect as a truth serum.

"Tatsuya, is this your first time seeing it?" Mayumi wasn't surprised he'd figured out the spell. She knew this much was only natural given his intelligence and insight in magic. She was actually surprised he'd never seen Mari do this during the half year they were together on the disciplinary committee.

"It is. I assume it would cause trouble if she used it in the open."

"I suppose you're right," agreed Mayumi. Magic usage was strictly controlled by law. Plus, this technique could be used for brainwashing. If used lightly, others would be torn between their sense of fellowship and their duty as upright citizens.

Even as he spoke to Mayumi, Tatsuya didn't let Sekimoto's confession slip by him. He picked up on the admission that he'd "planned to look through Shiba's belongings after extracting the data from the demonstration machine." When asked about his goal, he answered, "a jewel Relic."

"...Tatsuya, you had something like that all this time?" asked Mayumi, eyes wide.

"No, I don't, actually." He perfectly understood her impulse to ask, but responding truthfully was a different story.

"But..."

"A little while back, I was doing research into Relics related to the philosopher's stone. Maybe he got the wrong idea."

He'd used this excuse days before, too, during the student council elections. Mayumi remembered that; she didn't ask again. Mostly because she didn't completely believe the explanation but also because now wasn't the time for that.

A moment after Tatsuya's plausible lie, the Hachiouji Special Detention Home's emergency alarm went off.

All three of them reacted quickly to it. Mari pushed Sekimoto, his mind still foggy, onto the bed (rather than put him to sleep), left into the hallway, and locked the door. By that time, Mayumi and Tatsuya had already exited the hidden room.

"There's an intruder," said Tatsuya, looking at a message board on the ceiling. Mayumi and Mari looked up at the same time, confirming his statement.

"Who would be so reckless...?" muttered Mari with a shiver. After the incident two days ago when the NMU affiliated hospital was attacked, the entirety of western Tokyo had been placed on alert by the Metropolitan Police Department. It still hadn't culminated in the Ministry of Police mobilizing its peacekeeping riot police (a domestic peacekeeping force) to the local police level (its essence aside, organizationally speaking the MPD was the police for the city of Tokyo), but there were five times as many police officers on patrol today. The Hachiouji Special Detention Home was on 200 percent alert. To charge in any way, you'd need either a great amount of skill or a great degree of stupidity—and Mari's gut told her it was the former.

"Tatsuya, can you tell where they're coming from?"

Tatsuya hit his LPS terminal. Its clamshell-shaped permeable display lost its transparency and showed a three-dimensional map of evacuation routes. Going backward from those courses would let him infer the intruders' present location.

"It looks like they came in from the roof. They likely jumped from an airplane or used a catapult. I think they're near the third floor's eastern stairwell."

Mayumi turned and looked into empty air, eyes unfocused, using her innate skill, the perception spell Multiscope, at full power in the direction Tatsuya said. "...Spot on. Good job as usual, Tatsuya. Four intruders, and they're armed with high-powered rifles."

A high-powered rifle was a portable anti-magician weapon. To gain the bullet speed needed to shoot through anti-physical defensive magic, it used enough gunpowder to get three to four times the explosiveness of a normal assault rifle. Its power meant it needed advanced manufacturing technology. Random terrorists couldn't get their hands on something like those.

"The police set up a barricade on the landing, and they're fighting now."

"It looks like the entrances and exits to the hallways are blocked by walls." After Mayumi relayed the situation, Tatsuya read the three-dimensional building diagram. They were on the second floor right now, near the middle stairwell. This wasn't all that anxiety-inducing, but... "Here's their real attack."

Tatsuya looked sharply at that middle stairwell, and a moment later, Mari glared at the doorway as well.

"Huh? What?" Mayumi didn't seem to understand what they were wary of, but her confusion didn't last long.

A young, well-built man appeared before them. He stood a head taller than Tatsuya, which placed him at just under six three. His toned muscles had no sense of dullness, and Tatsuya could feel the flexibility of a large, carnivorous animal from them. Oddly, the man felt like he lacked presence, perhaps as the result of some technique.

He almost felt invisible, like Tatsuya might lose sight of him even though he was right there, but at this close range, his lack of presence didn't matter. Mari knew who he was.

"Ganghu Lu..."

Despite Mari's mumble, Mayumi looked on blankly, having no idea. Tatsuya's expression was still severe, but that was because he knew the man without Mari telling him—and, of course, his true strength.

As Lu began to approach, he set his eyes on the three. In particular, on Mari.

"We should have fled, but it seems we were too late," said Tatsuya dispassionately, stepping in front of the other two. As he walked toward Lu, Mari grabbed him by the shoulder.

"I'll take point. You guard Mayumi."

Don't be absurd, thought Tatsuya. Sure, Mari was already skilled enough at magical combat to be called top tier, even as a high school senior. But when it came to close-quarters fighting, Ganghu Lu was super top tier. Her odds of winning in a straight contest were terrible. An "irregular" like Tatsuya had better chances.

"Mari, be careful."

Surprisingly, however, Mayumi agreed to the formation. This was no time for infighting, so Tatsuya had to back down as well.

"I know—he's not normal," said Mari, not turning around.

Her right hand came up slowly before sweeping down and swinging back up as if to dust off her skirt. With a rustle, the triangular pleats on its side, made with superthin material normally hidden by its form-retaining function, spread apart and turned up. It exposed her shapely thigh in brown leggings—and a holster. She drew immediately. Her weapon: a short, rectangular stick eight inches long.

As her fluttering skirt calmed, it hid her leg lines. After seeing her draw her weapon in her left hand, though by no means taken in by the view, Lu finally assumed what looked like a combat posture.

He leaned forward slightly, letting his arms dangle in front of him, loosely curling his fingers. An energy filled his body, as though he could pounce at any moment.

But it was neither Mari nor Lu to start the fight—it was Mayumi.

The moment they saw a haziness collect on the wall and ceiling, a deluge of white bullets flew at the foreigner. He immediately dashed forward, but half the bullets caught him.

They didn't leave any damage, though. He'd reflected the bullets of dry ice with the Gang Qigong armor covering his body.

The berserker continued to charge at Mari. She met him with a sixteen-inch-long blade.

A dull, metallic noise rang out as Lu blocked her smash with his right hand. But a moment later, his face reeled backward. The sharpened edge of a strip of paper eight inches long flew across his vision. Mari's weapons were an eight-inch hilt connected to two eight-inch rectangular paper strips by thin wires—a small, three-part sword.

Mayumi's second wave came. Lu jumped a good distance away. His gut had been right: Countless scratches appeared in the floor and walls. These bullets she'd made were finer, harder, and faster than her first wave, giving them double the penetration power.

For the first time, a human expression crossed Lu's face—confusion. He knew he wasn't in peak physical condition, thanks to the wound in his side. But he found it hard to believe mere students, and female ones at that, were giving him difficulty. Nevertheless, the indecision in his mind vanished in an instant. He removed his invisibility, deciding to throw everything into this battle.

Layer upon layer of psion information bodies manifested across his entire body. Tatsuya knew they were information bodies with the same properties as anti-physical defensive spells. Until now, Lu had been reinforcing his skin's structural information by circulating a high density of psions over top of it. He'd switched it into a defensive spell.

Mayumi fired her third wave. Ganghu Lu blocked it with his matter-blocking wall. Then, with speed that could be called godlike, he closed in on Mari. She fixed her two blades in a straight line and prepared to intercept, but given the strength of his defensive spell, a *simple* counterattack wouldn't work.

The instant he made contact with her, he disappeared. Mari quickly looked right. It was entirely instinctual, but thankfully, her intuition had been correct.

But she wasn't in time.

Ganghu Lu's body had slipped past the outside of the short sword's range. In her mind, she yelled her classmate's name, but she didn't have time to say it out loud.

Lu faced straight at Tatsuya, who stood in front of Mayumi—and was swallowed up by a maelstrom of psions.

Program Demolition.

When Tatsuya had seen him switch his Gang Qigong from information boosting to an anti-physical wall, he'd been increasing the pressure with a mass of psionic particles. The cluster tore away Lu's armor.

There was undeniable shock in Lu's eyes.

Mayumi wasted no time initiating a ranged spell.

Lu's reaction to it certainly matched his "super top-tier" rating. In a split second he quelled his confusion at his Gang Qigong breaking and reconstructed the information-boosting version.

However, while she'd decreased the number of bullets, each individual one was more powerful, and he couldn't pull through the barrage completely undamaged.

Lu stopped as his senses were battered by bullet impacts and swarms of psions.

Mari came up behind and attacked. From out of the short sword in her raised left hand fell the two blades. The thin, rectangular edges spun through the air and reached Lu's crown. Then her right hand thrust out, and black powder scattered from it toward Lu's head.

As soon as Lu turned, he covered his eyes and nose. The black powder spread around his neck and over his head, glinted with a dim light, and vanished.

Lu staggered. The carbon powder had burned rapidly thanks to Mari's absorption spell, which she limited to just oxidization, suppressing the heat and light. It had devoured the oxygen in the air, turned into carbon dioxide, and created a momentary state of low oxygen around Ganghu Lu.

Her left hand swung down her weapon, now only a thin wire. She'd applied the repulsive blade, Pressure Cut, along it. But there wasn't only one repulsive blade. The two strips of paper falling toward him—their edges were bordered by Pressure Cut, too. They descended as Mari struck, faster than gravity pulled them. Three attacks all slicing at the same time from different directions. No matter how much expertise you had, it was impossible to dodge, and the Man-Eating Tiger, Ganghu Lu, was no exception. He tried to avoid the incoming wire, but the two strips of paper struck him in the shoulder and back. The Gang Qigong was still active, but after being hit by Mayumi's projectiles and cast into a state of oxygen deprivation, he couldn't harden his armor enough, and the papers dug into him. Though they didn't manage to split bones, the shock of deeply gouged skin gave him the last push he needed to finally crumple to the floor.

More often than not, the cavalry didn't arrive on time. Therefore, in the cases where they did, it was dramatic.

Police support made it to them not a moment after Lu went down. The four officers were astonished to see blades sticking out of a collapsed young man's back, but after seeing the students' uniforms, they went to constrain Lu. They'd probably been informed about Mayumi.

Tatsuya was prepared for questioning, but contrary to his expectations, it didn't happen. That, too, was probably the power of the Saegusa name at work. Still, he wasn't unhappy with it. He was glad he wouldn't have to waste time. The same likely went for Mayumi and Mari, too. He traded glances with them, and then they left.

When they left the special detention home's gate, Mari hesitantly spoke to Tatsuya.

"Tatsuya, well, I'm sure you know this, but not a word of this to anyone."

That wasn't enough for Tatsuya to completely understand what she wanted to say, of course. "Not a word—about your weapon? Or about your *Douji-Giri*?" he asked, just to make sure.

Not only Mari, but Mayumi as well, sighed. "So you knew about it..." said Mari.

"Tatsuya, you really do know everything..." added Mayumi.

By that reaction, he figured Mari had meant the *Douji-Giri*, but it seemed a little oversensitive to him. "It isn't that I know *everything*, but... Genji's secret move, *Douji-Giri*, is a pretty well-known spell, isn't it?"

The simultaneous slashing attack from three directions Mari had used to deal the finishing blow was called *Douji-Giri*, meaning "simultaneous cut." As with *ninjutsu*, this secret technique's identity as magic had been hidden. It had been passed down among a small handful of swordsmen of the Genji school, its name of "simultaneous cut" hidden by the alternate name "child cut," both being pronounced the same in Japanese. But once magic's secret had gotten out, the term *Douji-Giri* had made its rounds among scientists.

"I would never say anything about what the spell is, of course," he answered.

Mari made a face that was a mixture of hesitation and embarrassment. "I mean, I believe you, but...I don't want you to tell anyone I can use it."

Tatsuya didn't happen to have interest in gossip. If she wanted him to stay quiet...

"That's fine, I won't."

…he would accept, of course. He didn't particularly care about why. But for some reason, she started explaining anyway. "Thanks a lot. The spell wasn't actually passed down to me officially. I got Shuu to help me modify a skill written in my family's old manuscripts, and after some trial and error, we somehow got it to work."

"Shuu" must mean Naotsugu Chiba, thought Tatsuya as he listened. Come to think of it, when she'd used *Douji-Giri* before, it had been alongside one of the "Magic Melee Genius's" favored spells. "I see," he said. "Which is why the Pressure Cut spell was mixed into it."

"Yeah, basically. And…my family is supposedly descended from the Watanabe no Tsuna. It was technically a school of Genji, but one with pretty low status. If people start talking about how one of them can use Genji's secret technique, well…I can imagine the trouble that would follow."

Tatsuya understood that. Thinking about it just made him think of the mess it could make. Still… "But if you're going to be a successful combat magician, you wouldn't be able to keep it secret forever, right?" *The trouble's going to come whether you like it or not, isn't it?*

Mari made a sour face. "Yeah, I know. I just want to get through school without that happening."

Mayumi giggled at her.

"All right. I won't say a word to anyone."

Anyway, Tatsuya didn't feel like getting involved with low-level harassment, and he didn't honestly care. A little lip service came easily.

The call from Fujibayashi came two days before the All-High Magic Thesis Competition, on Friday while he was relaxing, after night had fallen and he'd eaten dinner and bathed.

"*…To sum up, we arrested pretty much the entire active spy force in these last three days,*" said Fujibayashi, finishing her well-organized explanation in a businesslike tone. On the display, her expression softened. *"That information you gave helped us a ton. Unfortunately, their leader, Xiangshan Chen, got away, but you and your classmates got Ganghu Lu for us, so we can be happy with the results. Thank you."*

"No, I was the one who asked you to do this."

"Technically, yes, but your magic high school and FLT weren't the only ones to suffer damage. Other special manufacturers like S.S. Electronics and Tsukumo Magic, and even nonspecialist ones like Touhou Tech were getting bothered by these industry and university spies. Intelligence and counterintelligence aren't our responsibility, but given how our unit works, we can't turn a blind eye to spies after magic technology. Even if you hadn't contacted me, we would have mobilized in the near future. We just had to push the schedule up a bit, so you honestly did help me out."

"Well, all right, then. By the way, how did info about the Relic leak?"

"I'm embarrassed to say, but the military's accounting data got leaked. The army ended up going after every single place paying consignment costs for magic research."

I see. So that's why it all seemed half-baked. Tatsuya nodded. It really was haphazard. It seemed like it had pretty low-cost performance, but information was always a jumble of dirt and diamonds. If you got one useful piece of data in a thousand IP database searches, you were lucky. *Maybe spies are the same way,* thought Tatsuya.

"The members come from all over Asia, but we might even be able to get something on that town, too."

"You seem happy about it."

"There's no point hiding it. I can't stand thinking how there might be bad guys in my own backyard. I'm a coward like that. When the time comes, we might need your help again."

"If it's a mission, there's no saying yes or no for me. Thank you for taking the time to contact me."

"You're welcome. Good luck on Sunday. I'll be rooting for you."

Leaving him with friendly encouragement, Fujibayashi ended the call. She clearly didn't see this incident as very serious, just yet another incident with spies after magic technology. Tatsuya, too, was only thinking "there was a pretty big-name bad guy this time."

Unfortunately, this would turn out to be a little premature.

When Tatsuya returned to the living room, he sat heavily on the sofa. His unusually crude behavior must have been his fatigue. In terms of physical stamina, he could go for a week with almost no sleep and not have a problem. His fatigue was emotional. Grappling with *a different approach than his own* to the gravity-controlled thermonuclear reactor, one of the Three Great Practical Problems of Weighting Magic, for the Thesis Competition; receiving a Relic said to be impossible to analyze, much less duplicate, with modern *technology* and then being asked to *meaningfully* analyze it with his personal skill and *translate* it into a chemical formula; and being watchful for industry-academic spies. Even Tatsuya was mentally exhausted.

Deciding to empty his mind for now, he closed his eyes from within his armchair, then tilted his head back and rested it on the back of the couch. The position had no special meaning, of course; it was just a matter of his mood.

Miyuki, who was always sitting next to him, wasn't unhappy that her brother had suddenly shut himself in his own world. She was the only one he would show vulnerability to. Miyuki was actually happy he was letting his guard down this much.

She didn't want her brother to always be thinking about her. Just being next to him satisfied her, and if he cared for her once in a while, she was perfectly happy. The term *convenient woman*, when it came to Tatsuya, was only a compliment for her. Still, almost nobody would ever say such a thing aloud.

Rather than being unhappy right now, Miyuki was worried about him. She couldn't recall very many times Tatsuya had shown himself to be this *candidly* exhausted.

She rose from the sofa carefully so as not to make a sound. Coming around in front of him, she quietly peered at his face, his closed eyes. She held the left side of her long hair back with her left hand so it wouldn't fall on his face and alert him. Lest she touch his arm, she supported her body weight with her right hand on the sofa's armrest. Her pleated skirt hem nearly touched his leg, causing her heart to start pounding, but Tatsuya stayed still. Wearing the shortest skirt she could tolerate had borne unexpected fruit, she thought.

From what she could see, his face wasn't pale enough for concern. Relieved, she searched for any other signs of irregularity in his face. As she watched her brother's face from close-up, her mind steadily misted over. Dreamily, she forgot why she was doing this in the first place, and without realizing what she was doing now, brought her face closer to his.

Her heart beat faster, blood rose to her head, she couldn't think. She stared at her brother's face mindlessly. She forgot to soften her breath, and he would feel that this close. Tatsuya had to notice that, and he did—his eyes burst open.

Their eyes met.

Time stopped. Not just for Tatsuya, but Miyuki as well, the one normally freezing others finding her own motor functions frozen.

Facing each other with naught but astonishment on their faces, one gazing at the other.

Suddenly, unable to maintain her unnatural position any longer, Miyuki tilted forward.

Her face approached his face, her lips approached his lips.

As they were about to cross a line that should never be crossed…

…Tatsuya recovered his physical functions.

By the time he quietly said, "Watch out!" his hands had already stopped his sister at her shoulders.

"Kyah!"

Whether having let up on the arm supporting her or running out

of energy, Miyuki staggered and put a knee on the sofa. More accurately, on the thigh of Tatsuya as he sat on the sofa.

The two froze again.

Almost close enough to kiss, they stared at each other, eyes wide.

Tatsuya's hands were around both of Miyuki's shoulders…

…and Miyuki was up on one knee on top of Tatsuya.

This time, though, the ice melted quickly.

They carefully pulled their faces apart so that this mistake wouldn't become reality, and Tatsuya returned his head to its original position, with his neck leaning back.

His gaze naturally dropped from Miyuki's face to her neck, to her chest, and then below that.

Following her brother's eyes, Miyuki looked down at herself with much trepidation, for she could tell without looking.

And as expected, not only was she embarrassing herself by having her knee on her brother, but her short, pleated skirt had spread far beyond tolerable limits, now only just barely hiding her underwear.

"I'm terribly sorry!"

Miyuki moved her leg off her brother with great force, bowed fast enough to cut through wind, then turned into a gale as she ran out of the living room and rushed up to the second floor (without doing anything unsightly like stubbing her toe on furniture).

She dived into her room in a mad rush and locked her door before leaning back against it and sliding down to the floor. Try as she might, Miyuki couldn't make her legs stand. Perhaps unconsciously, as a result of the ladylike education instilled in her, she tried to at least get her legs under her to sit in *seiza*, but she'd used up all her energy fleeing into her bedroom. Her body couldn't even do that, and her hips sank between her legs.

Her skirt had spread out as she flopped down, and in her slovenly posture—but her back still straight as a needle—she stayed awhile, dazed. Her head was delirious with heat, denying her the ability to think.

But as time passed, her thoughts, which had emergency evacuated, slowly returned to their duties.

Where was she?

What was she doing?

Why was she alone like this in her room—?

Suddenly, she covered her face with her hands and looked down. Her palms were hot. She knew without looking in a mirror that her face was red as a beet.

What on earth was I doing to my brother…?!

She couldn't understand what she'd been thinking at the time. She must have been possessed; that was the only explanation.

Just a little more and I would have k…ki…

Once again, her mind began to overheat and her thoughts froze.

If left alone, she probably would have been in this state until morning. Or else in an infinite loop of rebooting and freezing.

But Tatsuya couldn't leave her like that.

"Miyuki?"

"Yes?!"

Miyuki nearly jumped out of her skin responding to his considerate voice calling her from the other side of the door.

She brought her hands away from her boiling face and made them into fists on her lap. Her eyes were wet, like she was a moment away from crying. Putting too much energy into her back, her shoulders, and her arms stretched straight down, her body was trembling slightly. As though she were scared.

"May I come in?"

"Please wait a moment!"

Nevertheless, the option of going against her brother's words never existed in her thoughts. With swift motions to make her previous lack of energy in her legs seem like a lie, she stood up, then, with her still-trembling hand, slowly unlocked the door.

"Please come in."

Miyuki opened the door, then slid to the side to give her brother room to enter. Tatsuya didn't step inside.

He's watching me…

Unable to meet his eyes, she looked away as casually as she could, but still felt his gaze on her.

Her body immediately heated up.

This wasn't the heat flushing her out of embarrassment like before, but a heat that felt like it would melt the very core of her body. Her temperature—not her body temperature but how hot she felt—continued to rise without limit, and eventually, she could stand it no longer; she turned her averted face and averted eyes back to Tatsuya.

Her head tilted up to cover the height difference, over five inches. Just as she did, a tear welled in her eye, fell. Flustered, she tried to lift a hand to wipe it. But Tatsuya's hands were on her cheeks now—when did that happen?—and blocking hers. He used his thumb to softly wipe his sister's tear.

"Well, I, hmm…" began Tatsuya abruptly, while Miyuki had lost her voice and widened her eyes. "I'm sorry. I guess I worried you. I'm fine, so *don't worry about it anymore.*"

He spoke with a clumsy smile, then took his hands from the girl's face.

"I'll clean up downstairs. You should get some rest."

After giving Miyuki the command, his tone subtly embarrassed, he turned his back without waiting for an answer.

Miyuki watched him as he disappeared down the stairs, then clapped the door shut.

She wobbled over to her bed, shakily removed her clothes, and buried herself in her blanket in her underwear.

Then, finally snapping out of it, she started rolling from side to side.

Her whole body writhed, but unlike before, she seemed genuinely happy.

The short hand on the clock had passed its peak. Tomorrow, in terms of the calendar date, the All-High Magic Thesis Competition would begin here in Yokohama. Of course, there was no special air enveloping the city or anything like that. The competition was a special event for magic high school students, important enough to affect the futures of students chosen as representatives, but for everyone else unrelated to magic, it was just another of the dozens of events held throughout the year.

Even in this age, Yokohama's Chinatown was a central district for entertainment. The usual guests were entering the usual stores that still had billboards out at this hour, which was most of them.

One of the many shops, an eatery with a particularly large frontage, already had its outside lights off. A room inside, illuminated with a calm light, was a private, sequestered living room not visible from outside.

Two men sat in this room facing each other. Two glasses, resting on a table. One could describe the aged Chinese wine filling them as of the highest grade, but neither man made an effort to drink. The young man who took out the wine thought it was a bit wasteful, actually, but the man in his prime sitting across from him wasn't picking up his glass, so he left his alone as well.

"Mr. Zhou, you've been an enormous help."

"It was my pleasure, Your Excellency."

Chen's tone was condescending, despite his words. Zhou reverently lowered his head to the man, without letting his eyes, smiling modestly, leave him.

"Our nation has contacted me—they're dispatching a fleet. It will allow us to carry out the next operation safely."

"I am honored to have been helpful."

Chen and Zhou's expressions were the same as always. They'd remained that way since sitting down at the table.

"There is, however, one unsolved problem."

"Oh, and what might that be, Your Excellency?"

Each knew the other's usual expression was a mask, and each was sounding out the other's true thoughts.

"As you may be aware, my aide has, unfortunately, fallen into enemy hands."

Both of their faces changed. Chen's expression filled with regret.

"I am aware. I can only call it a stroke of terribly poor luck," answered Zhou, face melancholic, voice sounding truly sad at the event. "To think Mr. Lu would..."

"Despite his blunder landing him with the enemy, he is an essential warrior, one that our country needs."

Zhou nodded silently, indicating his agreement—and so that he wouldn't make any needless commitments.

Because he wasn't saying anything, Chen gave up and made his request himself. "Would you lend us your aid, one last time?" he asked, without bowing.

Zhou's eyes widened slightly in surprise, but then he broke into a smile. "Yes, of course, Your Excellency. I would never ignore the plight of a comrade."

He leaned over the table, still smiling. "To tell you the truth, the day after tomorrow—oh, tomorrow, technically—Mr. Lu's custody is to be transferred to an alien penitentiary in Yokosuka."

Chen showed *real* surprise at the information Zhou offered. "Is this true?"

"Yes. It is truly fortunate timing. In fact, I've already investigated the transport route."

Leaving out how he'd made preparations in secret to delay the transportation until early tomorrow morning, Zhou explained the details to Chen.

"I hesitate to speak of this as a suitable exchange, but for tomorrow's operation..."

"Yes, of course," nodded Chen to Zhou's reserved request.

"The operation's primary goal is the Magic Association of Japan's Kanto branch, after all. Some combat is unavoidable, but I will remind the mission's commanders to keep damage to this Chinatown to a minimum."

"I thank you very much for your consideration."

Zhou bowed respectfully to the promise Chen made *that he couldn't necessarily back up, a fact Zhou knew well.*

—One day left until the Thesis Competition. Tatsuya still didn't know that the storm had already edged so close to them.

(To be continued)

Afterword

The Irregular at Magic High School series has reached its sixth volume. Time flies, doesn't it? It's thanks to everyone who has given me support. Thank you all so much.

I've never tried completing an episode in one volume, and this Yokohama Disturbance Arc will be split into two books as well. Not three, though, so rest easy—though that brag isn't much of an excuse.

As some of you may already know, this series is an improvement of a Web-published series of the same name. In other words, a complete version. Furthermore, there are currently no plans for a "new complete version," "true complete version," "final complete version," or "ultimate complete version" after this.

...All jokes aside, there were more than a few episodes that had to be cut when I put it on the Web, mainly due to time constraints. Filling those stories in has turned into one of the main jobs of publishing the story in paperback. This book, volume 6, and the next, volume 7, have particularly numerous episodes to compensate. Things like what *that person*, who hasn't appeared yet, has been up to, and what *that person*, who has appeared only in name is doing... I actually added episodes for things like that in part two, about how *that person* and *the other person* got into *that kind of* relationship. I also added some scenes that hadn't been in my mind at all at the time, like that particular school festival scene, or that unfortunate (?) accident during training, but I hope you enjoy them all the same.

Volume 7 is slated to come out not next month, but the month after that, in September. When it does, I believe I'll be able to give news of a mixed-media project.

Please look forward to Yokohama Disturbance Arc ②, which will be filled with exciting battles.

Tsutomu Sato